THE Q DOCUMENT

JAMES HALL ROBERTS

The
Q Document

WILLIAM MORROW AND COMPANY
New York

To Paul R. Reynolds,
with appreciation, affection and respect

One

1

THERE was a letter from Stevenson in the morning post and he recognized it the moment the Japanese maid brought the stack of mail through the door. It stuck out from the rest of the letters, the envelope oversized, blunt-shaped. It was appropriate, he thought, that Stevenson's stationery should so accurately reflect the man himself. Stevenson was straightforward, persevering; the fact that he had written another letter despite Cooper's long silence was proof of that.

Cooper told the maid to put the letters on his writing table and then he proceeded with his shaving, running the blade over the underside of his jaw and the taut skin of his cheeks, watching the diminutive woman in the mirror as she rolled up the thick quilts of his bed and stowed them away in a wall compartment. Kneeling by the charcoal burner, she sparked a flame into life and blew it into the coals before she began to prepare his morning tea. With the kettle in place she pushed back the shojis to open the room to the day. There was no sunlight, only a gray haze heavy over the city, a sure sign it would drizzle by midday.

Once her work was done, she looked to him for further instructions as she had every morning for the past six months, and as usual there were none. He thanked her in polite but halting Japanese and she bowed and left the room as he washed the shaving cream off his face into the shallow basin. Once he had finished his ablutions he sat down cross-legged on the reed floor next to the writing table and looked through the mail. Besides the letter from Stevenson and an official-looking communication from Adwan, Smith and Renster, Attorneys, Boston, there was nothing in the stack except advertisements and subscription renewals which had been carefully forwarded to him from the States and which he now weeded out and discarded.

He opened the letter from the attorneys first. Adwan, Smith and Renster had nothing new to communicate, they were merely forwarding two carbons concerning the probate of Nan's estate for which they had had no further use. He glanced at the carbons; they were nothing he wanted to keep. He tore them into small pieces and dropped them into the wastebasket.

He drank his morning tea before he opened the letter from Stevenson, delaying it as long as possible. But when he finally brought himself to it, he found it far more placid than Stevenson's previous letters. There was a good bit of scholarly gossip—Jergens had finally found a publisher for his monograph on Charlemagne; old Steadly was drinking again—but there was no rebuking advice until the last paragraph and even this was remarkably mild.

"I've lectured you enough on what I think is your folly," Stevenson wrote in his cramped script, "and other men have suffered terrible losses before without going off the deep end for such a prolonged period, but I won't try to reason with you. However, there is something I think you should know. Since your six months' leave of absence has expired and you show no interest in coming back, Adams is in favor of filling your chair immediately and I am having trouble talking him out of it. In any case, he will wait only until the spring semester. So unless he receives word from you that you intend to return by February—and I emphasize this point, a declaration of intention is all he needs—then he will most certainly fill the vacancy. And I must remind you, even at the risk of seeming the querulous adviser, which I am, of the great harm which you will do your career if you let your chair pass to another man. Think about this," he urged. "Escape has been necessary, I realize that, but your voluntary exile has served its purpose and gone on long enough. Come home." Below the signature was a postscript. "Let me know what you're doing."

Cooper looked at his watch. He had an hour before he was supposed to meet Hawkins and it would be more than enough time to write to Stevenson, to delineate the facts at least, but he found as he began to write that a simple outline of his life here was impossible. He could not write, "I am doing translations for a bogus Englishman who has a most unusual traffic in documents and human beings." Everything in his life now was dependent on something else and he could not mention any one thing without going into a great deal more explanation than he cared to make. Finally he wrote a brief note to Stevenson. "I am reasonably content here, as much so as I could be anywhere else, I suppose, and from the looks of things, my work here will continue another year at least. So, with regret, I must leave Adams to his own devices."

Sealing the envelope, he left it on the writing table for the maid to post, then he put on his overcoat and gathered the latest batch of photostats and accompanying translations into his attaché case. As he went out into the corridor the door to the room adjoining his opened and Willa Cummings looked out, holding the door closed just enough to preserve the illusion of modesty.

"I thought it was you," she said, smiling. "You in a hurry?"

"I have to meet Hawkins."

"Have time for coffee?"

"I'm afraid I don't. Aren't you working today?"

"I'm supposed to go over to the Diet Building at noon and if a man who knows another man has any influence at all, then maybe something very good is going to happen to me."

"Good luck."

"Thank you. Do you want steak tonight? I think I can arrange it."

"That would be fine," he said. It was Friday of course. He lost track of time here; one day was remarkably like the next until she reminded him another week had passed and it was Friday again, another mark on the sexual calendar.

He had forgotten her by the time he reached the narrow street. His presentiment concerning the weather had been correct. He had gone less than a block before the chill October drizzle began to fall, driven by a slight wind off Tokyo Bay. He pulled the collar of his coat up around his neck against the cold, waiting for a break in the heavy traffic moving into the Shimbashi warehouse district before he crossed the street.

It was nearly ten o'clock by the time he turned off the arterial street into a landscaped entryway which led through a miniature garden to the stone building, a very late hour in the morning for Victor Hawkins' clientele, and yet when Cooper reached the gate he was forced to wait as two small Japanese businessmen in Western suits came out, giving him obligatory and peremptory nods for his courtesy in letting them pass. They were still slightly drunk; their faces had the deep flush which always came to a Japanese when he was intemperate; they walked down the street with a shuffling, uneven gait.

The façade of the building was deceptive, with sculpted indentations and setbacks and a concealing fringe of plantings to soften the harsh rectangular lines and make it seem less like the fortress it actually was. Victor himself had designed the building, erecting it on the ruins of a temple which

12

had been destroyed in the bombings, and he was defensive about the security measures he had been forced to take. "They would rob me blind, my dear boy. They would steal the carpets, the furniture, the girls, everything. And of course the manuscripts. They would steal those first because they are light and easily transportable and immensely valuable. So, much as I would prefer a more traditional sort of building, something on the lines of the Higashi Honganji—now there is a magnificent structure—I really have no choice."

Cooper nodded to the uniformed doorman and let himself into the building, glancing up the wide and carpeted stairway which ascended to his right off the foyer—it was always silent, not a shred of sound was allowed to escape from that second floor, never a wisp of scent, as if the walls were absorbent and could soak up the evidential remnants of the sexual events which took place in those locked rooms. He went down the hallway on the left, tapping lightly on the door of Victor's office before he went in.

Victor was occupied in a negotiation and did not turn around to see who it was. It was exactly ten o'clock and Cooper was always punctual, therefore there was no need to shift the corporeal bulk, to pivot the head on the neck, just to confirm what he already knew. But the two women in the room looked at Cooper and he glanced at them briefly before he retired to the table near the window to deposit his attaché case and to wait.

One of the women was middle-aged, dressed in the baggy *mompei* of the working class, sitting passively on a bench, smoking a cigarette and occasionally reaching out with a bony finger to jab the girl who stood in front of her in an effort, Cooper supposed, to get her to straighten up. The girl was no more than ten or eleven years old, frightened, ill at ease, fidgeting in her brightly flowered kimono, her almond eyes blinking out of a round moonface at the man who stood in front of her.

13

Victor had put them both on the defensive, or at least he was trying to—Cooper doubted that this natively shrewd little woman could be intimidated by the wrath of an army, much less a single individual, no matter how convincing he happened to be. Victor stood on the balls of his feet, rocking back and forth slightly as he regarded the girl with sad and rheumy eyes as if she had in some way offended him, implying that he would somehow bear the weight of this affront and forgive only if he saw some concession on the part of the girl and her mother—he could not be expected to go all the way. He fingered the white silk scarf around his heavy neck and then turned to his translator, Itsugi, a small bespectacled Japanese who sat to one side of Victor's dramatic grouping, a human machine to facilitate the transmission of Victor's thoughts.

"Tell the mother I am chagrined," Victor said in his cultivated bass, and immediately Itsugi began his running translation in a low voice to the mother, who blinked against the cigarette smoke and nodded warily as Victor continued to speak without pause. "I am chagrined because I asked her here in good faith, all good faith, remind her, because I know these are hard times and I have the strongest desire to help her in this hour of trouble. But there is such a thing as abusing a beneficent gesture and trying to take advantage of a charitable nature, and even in my desire to help her I cannot, as a gentleman and a Christian, tolerate this." He took the girl's arm and urged her into a turn, looking her over with a dispassionate skepticism without missing a beat in the monotonous rhythm of his commentary. "And in a purely practical light, the price is much too high because the girl is unformed and not of the highest physical type and far too young. And although I lowered my standards once—in order to accommodate her, remind her of that—and out of the goodness of my heart took the responsibility of her oldest daughter when she was not yet of a practical age, I lost a considerable amount of money. And even the most ever flowing well eventually runs dry. Yes, tell her that, it runs dry. Therefore, as my last offer, and even this I make with misgivings, I will give her seventy-five thousand yen, not because I think the price is an equitable one but because I think haggling is in the worst of taste."

Cooper turned his attention from the bargaining. Opening his attaché case, he began to lay out the photostats side by side with the translations on top of them, making a few final notes as the conversation in the room reached a terminal phase. The mother insisted on a hundred and twenty-five thousand at the very least; this girl would mature more beautifully than the last and in the time of transition she could work very hard and would thereby more than pay the cost of the meager food and clothing needed to sustain her. She was a superior girl, free from blemishes, scars, and birthmarks. Her flesh was even-textured, her legs properly straight and long.

Finally Victor offered a hundred thousand and she accepted this compromise, counting the oversized bills which he handed her from the drawer of his desk. She nodded curtly when she was certain the full amount was there, then she placed the money in the exact center of a white cloth square and tied up the corners. She made a brief and formal bow to her daughter before she left the room. Once the mother was gone, the girl began to cry, covering her face with her hands. "Tell her this is a happy occasion," Victor said to Itsugi. "Tell her she is entering a bright and joyous world in which tears are out of place. Then take her to the second floor." Itsugi did as he was told.

"The mother was quite right," Victor said when Itsugi had taken the girl from the room. "She will be quite a beauty by the time she is twelve or thirteen—not by our standards of course, but a perfect moonface draws a premium in this part of the world. That's the secret of my success, I think, the ability to get beyond my conditioning, to identify with the oriental viewpoint and see what is beautiful and desirable in their eyes." He opened a teakwood box on his desk and removed a cigarette which he inserted in an intricately carved ivory holder. A jade lighter clicked; a flame shot up to be sucked into the tobacco. He glanced toward the documents. "Do you have anything worth while today?"

"Not much," Cooper said, picking up the first document. "This is obviously a forgery—nineteenth-century, I'd say from the lettering. It's supposed to be an open letter from Marcion denouncing his heresies. There are some collectors in the States who buy forgeries for their novelty value, but this one is badly done, not worth more than a hundred dollars."

"Scarcely worth the trouble," Victor said.

"The second is a copy of Irenaeus' *Against Heresies*, made about A.D. 900, I'd guess, not complete, probably a section copied by a scribe to send from the Vatican to an official in the provinces. You'd do better to sell this in Great Britain. It should bring about fifteen hundred dollars."

"You'll give me some sort of paper attesting to its authenticity?"

"Yes, of course. There's no doubt about what it is."

"That's better," Victor said. "Considerably better."

"The third," Cooper continued, "has no meaning at all. It's a training exercise for a scribe or copyist, fourteenth century. But the illumination is nice. I would divide the codex into leaves and sell them separately as art objects. A hundred dollars apiece. And the last manuscript is doubtful. It appears to be a corrected section of the *Diatessaron* with the author's notations in the margin for changes he wishes to make. It's a remote possibility that Tatian himself wrote out the main text and the corrections. The penwork is the same. Or it could have been done by somebody working directly under Tatian, a kind of dictation from the master. Or it could be a very good forgery, working backward from the known text to develop an earlier one. Its value, of course, depends on which it is."

16

"Suppose it were the original?"

"Then you could sell it at auction. It should bring fifteen thousand dollars, maybe more. There's been considerable interest in Tatian since the Greek fragment of the *Diatessaron* was turned up at Dura."

The ash from the cigarette fell against the edge of the desk and showered onto the carpet. "Your certification would be all I'd need, my dear boy."

"No, I won't certify it," Cooper said.

"Well, it shouldn't be too difficult," Victor sighed. "I should be able to find somebody to certify it, if it's that close."

"No doubt you will," Cooper said without rancor. "Anyway, that's the crop."

"It's not so bad," Victor said. "And as a matter of fact I have an even better one coming up, one with an absolutely phenomenal potential, so to speak. The documents are being processed and photostated right now and the first part of them should be ready sometime this evening. I really feel as if I have pulled quite a coup, dear boy. You've heard of Martin Baum-Brenner?"

"Yes. I read quite a few of his articles in the journals, in the late thirties; not all of them but most."

"Good," Victor said, trembling slightly with palpable excitement. "Then you should be interested in this. I have all his papers, not just his memorabilia, understand, but his private manuscript collection as well, and I have been led to believe that much of this material was collected by the German Ministry of Education from old monasteries that were sacked by the German armies, that sort of thing. It's entirely possible he would have such manuscripts, dear boy. After all, he did work with them as an appraiser."

"It's possible," Cooper said. "Where did you get them?"

"You would never guess," Victor said, crushing out his cigarette. "It was a most unlikely source. The collection came from an old priest in Hong Kong."

"What kind of priest?"

"Roman Catholic, of course." Victor laid one finger across his gelatinous cheek, visibly pleased by his own cleverness and good fortune. "It is really quite dramatic, my dear boy, and a little mysterious in that I don't have all the details. Nevertheless, it seems that this priest—his name was Father Stafford—was fleeing from the authorities in Red China. There was some dispute over the ownership of the Baum-Brenner papers—the Red Chinese government claimed them—and Father Stafford was determined not to let them fall into Communist hands, so he escaped to Hong Kong. There was quite a row, I tell you. The Red Chinese complained most bitterly to the governor about what they considered a theft of property belonging to the state, but of course the governor could do nothing. He didn't know anything about the Baum-Brenner papers. And even the Red Chinese, despite all their very alert intelligence resources, had no tangible idea what had become of them."

"Tell me something," Cooper said thoughtfully. "If this priest was so anxious to keep these documents out of Chinese hands, why should he sell them to you?"

Victor assumed a rueful attitude which Cooper supposed was meant to imply remorse. "As a matter of fact, the unfortunate man was quite ill and in no shape to determine the disposition of his property one way or the other. His Chinese Christian friends simply could not find a way to get him across the frontier into Hong Kong so I agreed to help and in recompense for my time and trouble I agreed to take the manuscript collection in lieu of the customary fee. They were quite anxious but, as it turned out, it was a fruitless bargain for them. The old priest died soon after he crossed over into Hong Kong. And my representative looked over the collection and informed me it had all of Baum-Brenner's papers and documents in it. So I had it flown here—not shipped, mind you, but flown—at considerable expense. As soon as you have

18

had a chance to look it over, dear boy, to see what we have, I shall contact the Red Chinese and invite them to make a bid."

"You're going to sell it to them?"

"If the bid is adequate. But I feel hopeful that it will be. After all, they would scarcely have gone to all that trouble if the collection didn't hold a certain interest for them."

"So the priest brings it out and you send it back," Cooper said quietly.

Victor looked at him brightly. "Does that bother you, dear boy?"

"No," Cooper said.

"I'm pleased you should accept it for what it is. One of the ironies of life. I look on this as a stimulating intellectual adventure myself. There is simply no way of knowing what treasures we may find. When I was in Europe I heard such engagingly provocative rumors about Baum-Brenner and what he did for the Nazis." He lowered his voice. "It was said that he had, with the help of the Germans, uncovered the Q document. Do you think that's possible, dear boy?"

"No," Cooper said. "I don't."

"Not even remotely possible?"

"Not even remotely."

Victor sighed lugubriously. "Well, the collection should be interesting nonetheless. He was a magnificent scholar."

"At least before he joined the Nazi party, he was," Cooper said. "As far as I know, he never published a thing after that. Do you know how his papers reached China?"

"It's just a guess," Victor said, "but the members of the Japanese Embassy were notorious for their thievery in Berlin. And there was a lot of confusion there in the last days. So I suppose one of them stole the material, brought it to Japan, and sold it after the war. How it got to Red China I have no idea."

"But you're sure the collection is Baum-Brenner's?"

"There's no doubt of it. There's too much trash in it, personal letters to his daughter, bills from printers for supplies, things that are not worth forging. But you'll see for yourself. I'm having everything photostated. Everything. And as the items are finished I will have them delivered to you. Which reminds me, your money." He opened the desk drawer and removed a sheaf of bills, then after a moment's deliberation he doubled the stack. "A bonus," he said. "Because our relationship has been so worth while."

"Thank you," Cooper said, putting the bills into his attaché case.

"You're not interested in how much is there?" Victor asked curiously.

"No."

"But I might be cheating you. It's an unhappy thought and untrue, of course. But the possibility does exist. And yet you don't even count the money."

"I really don't care. It's not important."

"You are an unusual man. Not to want to be rich. You could be, you know, if you were willing to give some of these documents the benefit of the doubt. For instance, this Tatian thing. It *could* be authentic, you yourself admitted that, and what would be the harm if you *presumed* it was? No one would question you. No one would doubt you, and it would, after all, mean the difference between fifteen hundred dollars and fifteen thousand dollars, thirteen thousand five hundred right there. And I'm not a greedy man. I would be more than willing to share the results of that difference with you, say, sixty-five hundred dollars for yourself. And that's only a single document. You could use the money, couldn't you?"

"No."

"Not use sixty-five hundred dollars?"

"I have what I need."

"Well, there you are," Victor said, sucking in his cheeks.

20

He walked over to the narrow casement window and peered out. "It's still raining. I'll have my car run you back to your place."

"I have to go over on the Ginza," Cooper said. "I'm having lunch with O'Connor."

"Father O'Connor?"

"Yes."

"I'll have my car take you over there then."

"Don't bother. I'll walk."

"Why wont you take my car?" Victor asked unhappily.

"Because it would get me there too soon. And I would have time left over."

Cooper closed his attaché case and tucked it under his arm. Victor had been wounded because he liked to think of himself as a magnanimous man and he was about to insist when he was interrupted by the telephone. He picked it up. "Yes?" He listened, nodding his head toward Cooper as if to tell him to wait a minute, that this would interest him. "Thank him but tell him no," Victor said into the telephone before he put it down. "I told you," he said to Cooper, pleased with himself. "I have an eye for beauty. The girl who was here— when Itsugi took her upstairs she caught the attention of an elderly and very rich Korean gentleman who offered two hundred thousand yen for her on the spot. Much as I enjoy the thought of profit, I turned it down, of course, but it proves my point."

"Yes," Cooper said. "I suppose it does."

"So I ask you to consider the benefits of money," Victor said cryptically. "Not just the accumulation of it or the pleasures connected with its dispersal, but the pleasure that the gaining of it brings. It's all a game, my dear boy, and a large amount of money is merely something which shows that you have played it well. And you might find it enjoyable to participate."

21

"I have what I need," Cooper said again. "I'll talk to you after I see the Baum-Brenner papers."

"Yes, my dear boy, you do that. I'll be on tenterhooks."

2

Occasionally, when Father O'Connor felt the need for a self-imposed penance, he deprived himself of the one physical pleasure he held above all others, the enjoyment of tea. It was a harmless enough gratification, he supposed. After all, one could not be rebuked for compiling a mental catalogue of remembered tastes and it was such an eminently portable collection. He could bring to mind, if he truly concentrated, practically every cup of tea he had ever drunk, the amber Darjeelings, the clear and subtle Formosa oolongs, and the smoky and pungent Lapsang souchongs, all the way back to the flowery orange pekoe tea his mother had given him when he was six years old and demanding coffee at the breakfast table with the rest of the family. He had been placated with tea only because his father, a weak man, regarded it as the lesser of two evils and was sure that coffee stunted physical growth and overstimulated the brain cells in a child.

It was Father O'Connor's interest in tea which had led him to the small restaurant on the Ginza, and whenever he had visitors from the States he brought them here despite the long and hazardous drive from the university. Compared to the shiny new cafés which had been erected along the Ginza to cater to tourists and affluent Japanese, this small place was shoddy indeed, just one step above the rickety food stalls which lined the curbs. It catered to the working-class Japanese but through some small miracle the tea here was always perfect, a special blend of young hyson imported from China, the tender, curling young leaves delicately handled and brewed by the old man in the kitchen with a care that approached dedication. The tea was always served in its individual pot just a degree below the boiling point to allow Father O'Connor to determine for himself the precise temperature at which the tea reached perfection. Personally, he preferred it very hot, not hot enough to scald the mouth but just hot enough to steam the piquant aroma through his nasal passages. It was, in its own way, a harmless intoxication, more mental than physical.

Today, however, the tea did nothing for him. It was flat against his palate, but he knew that the fault lay not in the tea but in himself. He was agitated, afraid that Cooper wasn't coming. He glanced at his watch. It was already ten past twelve and the rain was pouring down outside, heavier all the time. It was possible Cooper had forgotten about the appointment altogether; more likely he had remembered it and simply decided not to come.

From the beginning, six months ago, the arrangements for these Friday lunches together had never been more than tenuous. When Father O'Connor first heard that Cooper was in Japan, he had decided to invite him out to the campus to lecture on medieval manuscripts. He had written him a couple of notes which Cooper did not answer, but Father O'Connor, being distrustful of the Japanese postal system, could not be sure they had been delivered at all. So one Friday, when he found himself in Shimbashi on other business, he called at Cooper's hotel to deliver the invitation personally. It was just as well, Father O'Connor decided later, that Cooper had declined the invitation to lecture—considering Cooper's spiritual bankruptcy, it would not have worked at all—but their conversation had been an interesting one and they had come here for lunch, and before they separated they had agreed to meet here the following week and so it had grown, informally, into custom. But from week to week the agreement to meet was seldom made explicit; it was assumed. Father O'Connor was not pleased with this arrangement but he could not run the risk of driving Cooper away by making demands on him, by trying to pin him down. And if Cooper did not come to-day, well, Father O'Connor would have to go to him.

At twelve-twenty he was about to leave when Cooper came through the door, shaking the water off his overcoat and handing it to the Japanese waitress, who took it to the kitchen to dry. As he approached the table Father O'Connor stood up to shake his hand, irritated and relieved at the same time. "You're late," he said.

"I walked," Cooper explained without the slightest trace of apology. He sat down, unfolding the hot towel which the waitress had brought him, using it to wash his hands. They ordered a luncheon of tempura and when the waitress had gone Cooper poured himself a cup of tea, absently. "Do you know of any contemporary German reference collection in Tokyo?" he said.

"German?"

"I need material on the Ministry of Church Affairs under the Third Reich. From about 1940 to 1945."

"You'll have trouble with that one," Father O'Connor said. "I don't think there's a specialized collection like that anywhere in Tokyo. Why do you need it?"

"Hawkins has just bought the Baum-Brenner manuscript collection."

"Martin Baum-Brenner? The Jewish scholar?"

"Yes."

"And where did Hawkins get them?"

Cooper told him briefly.

"And you're going to translate these papers for Hawkins?"

"Yes."

As the Japanese waitress brought the food, Father O'Connor lapsed into an uneasy silence. He thought about protesting the speed with which the meal had been served. It meant the tempura had been prepared in advance and was bound to be soggy. But he said nothing; it did not make that much difference. Cooper never complained about what he ate. He

24

consumed his food mechanically, with neither relish nor displeasure.

Watching Cooper as he ate, Father O'Connor felt a sharp pang of frustration. It was as if Cooper had so completely disengaged himself from the world that he was absolutely unaffected by anything around him. But there was little physical evidence of the spiritual disease which had afflicted him. He was a tall, spare man, too pale perhaps from lack of sunshine, but his pallor was a mark of his occupation. Actually, Father O'Connor thought, Cooper had the kind of face which had been depicted in so many medieval illustrations of the saints: there was absolutely no expression at all.

Father O'Connor cleared his throat. "I feel it is my duty to advise you," he said tentatively, "that what you are doing is morally wrong."

"Morally wrong?"

"The Chinese Christians had no right to sell manuscripts belonging to a priest," Father O'Connor said, "and Victor Hawkins had no right to buy them."

"The priest was dying," Cooper said. "The manuscripts were used to finance his escape from Red China."

"The circumstances make no difference," Father O'Connor said. "It's the principle that is important."

"If there's a principle involved here, then it's none of my concern," Cooper said. "I work as a translator for Hawkins and I give him some idea of the value of the manuscripts he collects. That's all I do."

Father O'Connor tested the teapot with the back of his hand. It was cold. He signaled the waitress and ordered a fresh pot. "You are committing a grave moral wrong by even associating yourself with Victor Hawkins. I asked a student who lives in Shimbashi about Victor Hawkins and he was reluctant even to discuss the man. Boys of seventeen are always so afraid they are going to shock a priest. They forget we are men and have seen practically everything in the devil's repertoire. But

I must admit, when he finally did talk about Hawkins, I found it hard to believe. Do you know what he has on the second floor of that building of his?"

"Yes," Cooper said.

"And still you work for him?"

"His office is on the first floor."

"Do you consider that an excuse?"

"The second floor existed before I came. It will exist after I go. What kind of man he is, what he does, has absolutely nothing at all to do with me."

"It has everything to do with you," Father O'Connor said adamantly. "You help enable him to do what he does."

"My talents as a translator aren't unique."

"That's beside the point. Just consider for a moment how he gets those documents you translate for him. Perhaps he doesn't steal them himself but he lets it be known that he is in the market for old documents with no questions asked and that's the same thing. And by helping him, you put yourself in danger of perdition. If one co-operates with corruption, then one becomes corrupt. There is simply no way to avoid the logic of that conclusion." He was getting nowhere with Cooper, he knew that, and he had to be so everlastingly careful to avoid the pat phrases which he had learned and practiced throughout his life as a priest. It was as if he had to develop a new language to discuss the truly important things of life, unlearning the old at the same time.

He looked around impatiently for the little Japanese waitress and saw her serving an elderly workman at the front of the room. Through the rain-smeared window he saw the movement of a vertical shape preceded by a boxlike shadow, a visual impression which needed translation into the reality of the chestnut vender and his cart on the street outside. Talking to Cooper was much like that. Cooper could only see the shapes, not the realities behind them.

"You know," Father O'Connor said, "I think I've diagnosed

26

your trouble. Now don't dismiss it even before I say it, just because it sounds so simple. But I think you blame God for what happened to you, so you've turned against Him."

"I don't blame anybody for anything," Cooper said with a half-smile. "And why is it you always try to turn religion into a science? Diagnosis, disease, cure."

"You have a disease," Father O'Connor said. "And there is a cure."

"I doubt that. Both parts. And why does it make any difference to you? Do I represent a professional challenge to your skills as a priest?"

"I suppose there's some of that in it," Father O'Connor said candidly. "But not much. I know you don't like me to bring up metaphysics, so I won't. I'll just say that I intend to bring you back to faith."

"As a Catholic," Cooper said, smiling.

"As an anything," the priest said. "As long as it's positive. I think you are wasting yourself and your God-given talents. I'm saying that you have obligations above and beyond your personal welfare. And once you've assumed them you'll find that there are rewards to responsibility."

"Perhaps for you," Cooper said, "but not for me." He stood up now. "I'm afraid I'm going to have to leave. I have some research to do before I can get started on the Baum-Brenner papers."

"The hot tea should be here any minute," Father O'Connor said, not wanting him to leave, not yet.

The little Japanese woman brought Cooper his coat from the kitchen. He thanked her and put it on. "Next week?" he said to the priest.

"Next week."

Father O'Connor watched him pass into the flurry of rain as the door opened and closed and then Cooper was a blurred shape passing by the window. Father O'Connor felt depressed. It always ended like this, with Cooper leaving a

27

residual gloom behind him. And, as usual, Father O'Connor felt the temptation to make this meeting the last, confining himself to the problems at the university, which were more familiar and therefore more easily resolved.

But he knew, even as he despaired of Cooper, that he could not abandon him. The interviews would stretch out into the future like beads on an endless rosary and they would not end unless Cooper himself terminated them. It was more than Cooper's soul at stake, it was the broadening influence of the man himself. Spiritual sickness was highly infectious. In Cooper's present state he could do a great deal of harm in the world.

The waitress brought the fresh pot of tea. He touched the back of his hand to it and waited for it to cool.

3

Cooper spent all afternoon wandering from one crowded bookstall to the next along the Jimbô-Chô, a street in the Kanda section near Meiji University, knowing that the odds were very much against his finding anything at all. There had been a number of books written on the work of Dr. Martin Baum before he changed his name but Cooper was not particularly interested in these. He found one of Baum's early works, a commentary published in Hebrew on Leviticus, and bought it in lieu of anything better, but he knew he would find little of interest in it because it was one of those treatises Baum had written in the early thirties when he was still exploring the established Jewish literature and before he had begun his creative scholarship.

There was one book Cooper especially wanted, a small polemic volume which had been written by a Jewish scholar named Hollenstein, shortly after the war if he remembered correctly. In it Hollenstein had tried to discredit everything Baum-Brenner had ever written, but Cooper could not remember the exact title and after trying in his halting Japanese to make a dozen willing but baffled clerks understand what he was looking for, he gave up trying to find it. He did find one pertinent volume in a bookstall which specialized in old German books, a volume published in Berlin in 1943 which contained a brief biography of Martin Brenner along with the other leaders of the new German church. He had the volume heavily wrapped to protect it against the rain, then he found a stationer's store which carried writing paper meant to be used with a pen instead of a brush and bought a ream of it along with a dozen pen nibs and a box of pencils.

By the time he finished his shopping the day had darkened into night and the rain was still drumming down. It was scarcely past six and yet the streets were still crowded and he realized the trains and subways would be packed, so he took a taxi to the Ginza and decided to walk the rest of the way. Once he was off the main thoroughfare of the Ginza and into the weblike pattern of connecting streets and alleys, the noise and the traffic dropped off sharply and in the parts of the warehouse district which had closed down for the day he felt very much alone, isolated by the opaque curtain of the rain.

It was almost seven by the time he reached the hotel. At one time, he supposed, the structure had been used for something else, a small office building perhaps, but shortly after the war it had been converted into a makeshift hotel to accommodate the crowds of people swarming into the city. It was a drafty building and his room on the second floor was small, but it was close in and he had no desire to better himself.

He went up to his room to find that the maid had anticipated his arrival and kindled a charcoal fire in the hibachi to take the chill off the room. Clicking on the lamp, he saw the box from Hawkins on the writing table, but he was in no hurry to open it. He unpacked the paper and the pens, put-

29

ting the former in a cramped wall compartment and the latter in a small lacquer box on his desk, emptying the money from his briefcase into a drawer. Removing his coat, he put on a quilted robe and sat down cross-legged on the mat floor within the bright circle of light from the lamp and unwrapped the biographical volume.

It was a physically impressive book, printed on glossy, expensive paper, bound in black leather with a red swastika emblazoned on the front of it. He opened it at random and found himself looking into the face of Dr. Hans Kerrl, Minister of Church Affairs; he skimmed through the brief biography to acquaint himself with the ponderous German in which it was written. No language could be quite so pompous as German. "The Party stands on the basis of Positive Christianity and Positive Christianity is National Socialism. . . . God's will reveals itself in German blood." He thumbed past Bishop Marahrens of Hanover, Borman and Rosenberg and Dr. Reinhardt Krause, and in the final pages of the book found a small portrait of Dr. Martin Brenner and a brief biography.

He held the picture to the light to examine it more closely, canting the book at an angle to reduce the glare from the glossy surface of the page. Obviously the photograph had been taken about 1943, after Baum-Brenner had capitulated to the Party, and it seemed a little ridiculous to picture the old scholar in a uniform with the vague outline of a draped swastika in the background. However, it was easy to see, from this portrait, how the old man had managed to make the transition so easily, because his features were definitely Aryan and non-Semitic and he had shaved off his patriarchal beard and allowed only the faintest suggestion of iron-gray hair to show on his scalp. But Cooper was as much interested in the expression on that face as he was in the shape of the features. The eyes were grave, sober, almost bitter; the mouth was set in a suggestion of a scowl. The tone of the portrait was almost militaristic.

Cooper was surprised to find that Baum-Brenner was such a large, square-jawed person. Somehow he had always pictured him as a frail skeleton of a man existing in a self-imposed imprisonment with his books and his manuscripts, so surrounded by the ancient past that he was no longer a part of the present. Of course it was always possible this was not a true picture of Baum-Brenner at all, that the authorities had merely substituted a more acceptable face to influence the public to believe what they were supposed to believe.

He uncapped his ink bottle and was preparing to take notes from the biographical data when he heard the rapping on the wall from the room next to his; he remembered he was supposed to go to Willa's room for dinner. Evidently she had heard him come home and had given him a chance to remember on his own before she reminded him. Dutifully, he went next door to join her.

Willa's room differed from his in that it was considerably larger and had a small kitchen attached to it, with a hot plate and a cabinet pantry and an inadequate sink with a single faucet which occasionally spewed forth a slight stream of water but more often than not refused to work at all. Her sleeping room contained an odd assortment of Pompeian chairs and carved mandarin chests and even a canvas folding chair with her name lettered across the back strip, a souvenir of the Hollywood period when the Pulitzer prize had catapulted her into sudden national prominence and a movie had been made of her life.

The one thing characteristic of all her possessions was their look of impermanence. He had the feeling she did not really live here, that she had merely set up camp, and eventually the chairs would fold up or break down, the extraneous gear would be stowed away in the chests, and she would be off to make camp somewhere else. There was the same ephemeral quality about the gallery of photographs on the wall, portraits of generals and statesmen and foreign dignitaries, all autographed to her. She had arranged them in a whimsical manner according to skin color with a black African chief occupying the far right position and a fair-skinned Scandinavian ambassador on the extreme left. None of them were first rank and most of them had had only a brief moment of qualified fame before they had been deposed by death or politics.

Apparently she was neither angry nor hurt that he had forgotten their date. She kissed him warmly and then left him to his own devices, waving him to a chair while she put the steaks in the skillet and finished mixing the salad, chatting about her day and what she had been doing. His mind was only partially with her. It was difficult for him to disassociate his thoughts from Baum-Brenner and the book in his room and he was suddenly brought up short when she seemed to be reading his mind.

"Victor Hawkins has the Baum-Brenner papers, doesn't he?" she said.

"Yes," he said, puzzled. "How did you know?"

She laughed sharply. "You haven't been listening to me, have you?"

"No," he said. "Where did you hear about the Baum-Brenner papers?"

"At the main bar of the Press Club," she said, amused, "sandwiched in between the latest Asian shaggy-dog stories and a few alcoholic propositions. One of the boys from *Time* came in from Hong Kong this afternoon. He was covering a protest made by the Red Chinese over the Baum-Brenner papers but he didn't file a story because he couldn't find out what happened to them. But he did learn they had been bought by somebody in Japan, spirited out of Hong Kong, and flown to Tokyo. So I dredged my memory and my intuition and came up with Victor Hawkins."

32

"Your intuition is right."

"What's in the Baum-Brenner papers?"

"I don't know."

"You haven't seen them?"

"Not yet."

She was prying now, fishing, and Cooper could feel the strength of her rising curiosity. "There was a lot of talk today about the Q document. Have you heard of it?"

"Yes."

"Do you know what it is?"

"A theory," he said.

"And that's no answer at all."

"All right," he said, "the Q document is a hypothetical document invented by German biblical historians in the 1800s to explain a gap in our knowledge of the early Christian Era. The four gospels in the New Testament are repetitious and there was obviously a good bit of conscious duplication. For instance, both Matthew and Luke undoubtedly made use of the book written by Mark. Luke, as a matter of fact, lifted out large sections from Mark's work and inserted them into his own gospel. But some historians think there was another source common to both Luke and Matthew, a manuscript which contained most of the sayings of Jesus. In reconstructing this hypothetical source, the Germans theorized that it must have been an account which was set down by somebody who had traveled with Jesus. For want of a better name, they called this document the *quelle* or 'source' document. Later this was shortened to 'Q.'"

"And you don't think Baum-Brenner found it?"

"No," he said. "I don't think such a document ever existed."

"The consensus along the bar was that, if it did exist, it would be the most valuable literary property of the century," she said brightly. "And worth a hell of a lot of money."

"I suppose it would," he said. The discussion of his work

33

made him uncomfortable and he decided to change the subject. "How did your meeting at the Diet Building turn out?"

"It didn't," she said with a rueful smile. "At the last minute this courteous little son of Nippon decided he didn't want to see me after all. Of course, his secretary phrased it with a lot more oriental finesse than that, but that was the gist of it. He had an emergency appointment, something like that. But as my unlamented father used to say, there's more than one way to climb a tree." As she continued to talk about her plans, he could see that the main theme of her cheerful monologue was hope, with one action predicating the next and the next supporting an extending one, until she had built a flimsy, if logical, structure of success.

Tomorrow she would see another Diet member who was a close friend of somebody she had met at the Press Club and the Diet member would introduce her to a very influential industrialist who could arrange for her to have an interview with the Emperor himself. The Emperor was not her real target—he had been done to death by the press; what she really wanted was an interview with the Emperor's wife, a shy and lovely little woman who stayed in the background and who undoubtedly had a terrific story to tell if Willa could get her to talk. Willa was sure *Life* would pay twenty thousand for a story like that. But this would not be the end of it. No, she would write the Empress' personal story in a book which would sell a hundred thousand copies in Japan alone.

There was only one flaw in this beautiful plan, Cooper realized; the fanciful sequence of events would never get any further than tomorrow's introduction to the Diet member, if indeed it went that far. Her reputation had spread in front of her like a beaching wave. There would be no interview with the Empress, no story to make her fortune and renew her fame. Anybody could have told her this; in the last six months she had created a dozen such fantasies, all of which had exploded, but there was no one of her acquaintance who would

34

reduce the myth to truth. Cooper doubted if this was even possible. Her power to rationalize was too strong.

"What do you really think of this Empress thing?" she said. "You have a detached, analytical mind. Do you think it's as big as I think it is?"

"You're a better judge of that than I am."

"Someday I'm going to get you to commit yourself on something," she said with a tolerant smile, "and there's going to be one hell of an earthquake. All right, I'll tell you how important it's going to be. It's the big one, probably the most important story I'll ever do, and if things go right it'll put me right back up there."

"And that's important to you, being right back up there?"

"Don't scoff," she said, "just because you've given up. It's a hell of a good place to be. And I didn't win the Pulitzer just for being a novelty. No, I have a talent for bringing out the significance in a story." She examined the steaks, turned them over, and then began to open cabinets and drawers until she found what she was looking for. She held the bottle up to the light. "Would you like a drink before dinner?"

"No, thanks."

"You don't mind if I have one?"

"No."

"For your information, that's the usual answer," she said indulgently, "but it's the wrong one. When a woman asks that question she wants somebody to say no." She poured gin into a pitcher and added a dash of vermouth. "If I'd had any self-discipline I would have stayed on top when I was up there. Because it's a hell of a lot easier to stay there once you've made it than it is to climb back." She transferred the mixture to a glass and grimaced as she tasted it. "That's one thing the Orient has taught me—to survive without ice." She drank it down an inch now. "Maybe I'll have to learn to be like you and not care about anything. I thought when I first met you that it was all a pose, you know that? I thought you

35

really did care but you didn't want to show it. But then I realized it was true, you really don't give a damn about anything. That's true, isn't it?"

"Yes," he said. "Approximately."

She shrugged slightly, finished the drink, and poured herself another one. For a moment she had been close to making claims on him in that baiting way she used to establish her point of view, but in an instant all criticism of him was swept away as her thoughts returned to herself and the urgency of the story waiting to be written. "I think *Life* will pay me at least twenty thousand. Did I tell you that?"

"Yes," he said. "What will you do with the money?"

"Clothes first," she said. "And some debts—I have a lot of debts—and then I may take another lecture tour. I did pretty well on the one after the prize. Only this time I'm going to conserve my resources, and when I find the right man I may get married again. But not for a long time." She ran her fingers through her long, straight blonde hair, self-critically. "I need to have something done with *this* in the morning. When I was in Korea I had it all cut off, all of it except a boyish bob. It looked all right under a helmet liner, but I was younger then."

"You're not an old woman."

"Old enough. I haven't lost my shape but it's harder to keep at forty. God, how I wish I was twenty again, knowing what I know now." She examined the steaks again. "They look ready to me," she said.

The talk at dinner was colored by what lay beyond it and the conversation became strained and a trifle hollow. He had come here to go to bed with her and she had prepared herself for it, dressing in a frilly red peignoir with a matching gown, discarding for the evening the rather mannish trappings which had become her trade mark over the years. He found it hard to equate this Willa with the one he had known only in the

36

newspapers, the blonde in fatigues who stayed on the front line in Korea and produced a kind of horror writing no man could possibly have matched.

But the change between the correspondent and the woman was more than physical. It was deeper than that. For the moment her sardonic attitude toward life was suspended and replaced by a feminine and sexual mystique. Paradoxically, she was helpless and aggressive at the same time. She became kittenish, aware of her own body, and she catered to him, filling his wineglass and leaning over to brush against him as she did so, forcing his awareness of her as a female, as if for these few moments she had created roles for both of them to play and was determined that they should be filled despite the incongruities involved.

The strange thing about this ritual of hers, contrived and artificial as it was, was that it affected him. From week to week he was always without passion as he entered this room; he neither anticipated their weekly union, nor did he carry any mental images away from here. Yet once he was in this room, caught up in the whir of her need, listening to her purring nonsense, assailed by her perfume and the dramatic and obvious provocation of flesh and silk, he found himself irritated at first, offended, suffering an obscure inner pain which made him want to leave, and then, quite without knowing how it happened (there was no distinct line of demarcation to mark the change), his nerves tightened involuntarily and he was full of a quick, insistent desire.

He finished half the steak and drank another glass of wine before he pushed back from the table. She had eaten practically nothing, picking over her food to give him time to finish his meal, and now she stood up, feigning a soft languor, actually taut as a bowstring, talking only to give her passage to the bed no great importance (he heard her voice but he had no idea what she said), crushing out her cigarette in the convex abdomen of a brass fish, placing one hand on the carved post of the antique bed, turning to him with a quizzical smile which under any other circumstances would have been ridiculous. She kicked off her slippers before she sank to the bed and extended herself, arms held out on either side of her, palms up in supplication, fingers half curled. He arose from the chair very slowly, so short of breath he felt that he would smother, and crossed to the bed to look down at her. Her eyes were closed, the eyelids fluttering, and on her face was the vacuous defense of a half-smile.

He lay down beside her. When he seized her he felt himself engulfed. Their love-making was brief and violently searching, as if both were seeking something they could not find, moving toward the final frantic moment when she uttered a sharp cry and fell back on the bed, exhausted.

For one fleeting moment as she lay there, her defenses disarranged, he saw her in a different light. She was pale, frightened, insecure, and there was a glint of pain in her eyes, as if she were too weak to disguise her desperation. But this lasted only for an instant and then she sat up and smiled at him and her guard was up again as she went to the kitchen, a trifle unsteady on her feet.

He allowed his mind to drift, caught in the enervating backwash of passion. For a moment his body had been drained into lassitude and his mind had been quickened so that the unwelcome flow of memories started again. Curious, but there had been a moment in the tumult of that sexual congress when suddenly, unbidden, Nan's face had come into sharp focus in his mind, not the face of the woman of this year but the Nan he had married at nineteen, the face of girlish innocence. Peculiar, that counterpoint of thought, the paradox of that face springing into his mind even as he lay across a woman he scarcely knew and yet knew too well.

He stayed with Willa long enough to have a cigarette and

re-establish normalcy, then he excused himself and went back to his room to work.

"Martin Brenner, philosopher, was born in Bremerhaven on the twenty-third day of July 1897. He was the sole son of Heinz and Gretchen Brenner, German farmers. . . ." How foolish it was, he thought, that the Nazis should rewrite history so flagrantly to convince themselves of the validity of a lie, twisting the world into a form which was more to their liking. But when he thought about it he knew it was not so rare; even the people around him did it as a matter of course. Willa's interview with the Empress, Victor's delusion of the reservoir of art within him just waiting to be realized, and a vision of conversion and demonstrable faith on the part of a little priest who lived in a glow of miracles and the supernatural. So perhaps it was not so illogical that a nation should do what all individuals did to some extent, wiping out the real for the more acceptable, converting Martin Baum, Jewish rabbi, into Martin Brenner, Nazi scholar, giving him a totally new set of antecedents.

But in a way it seemed unbelievable that the Nazis should have gone to all this trouble to spare Martin Baum, to purify and elevate him to a position of authority, when he had been so well known for his opposition to the Third Reich. Inconceivable as Martin Baum's defection to the Nazi cause had been, it was even more inconceivable that they should have accepted him. As far as Cooper knew, Baum-Brenner had never been active in the Nazi cause and the book listed no official activities in which he was engaged. In 1943 he had defected to the Party and had moved from Warsaw to Berlin. In 1944 he went back to Warsaw and was taken to the *Vernichtungslager* at Auschwitz where he was gassed and buried in a trench. Why should the calculated glorification have ended in the ignominy of the common grave? Perhaps the answer lay in the box of papers Hawkins had sent.

Cooper closed the book and, moving to the table, began to unwrap the box. The electric light flickered spasmodically and he knew it would go out completely very soon. He removed the quilts from the closet, spread them on the floor, and managed to put on his pajamas before the light went out. He was not ready for sleep. He smoked a cigarette, aware of the single glowing coal in the darkness of the room.

He could hear the steady drumming of the rain against the outside shutters and the diminishing noise of traffic in the street and he thought about the woman in the room next door and wondered why he could feel nothing except a kind of intellectual pity for her. Perhaps they were too much alike, he decided, far too much alike. He crushed out his cigarette and lay down, waiting for sleep.

Two

1

Three days after Cooper had received the first part of the Baum-Brenner papers he had completed the translations. He took them back to Victor Hawkins to find the man in a petulant rage, sulking into the telephone as if to smother the man on the other end of the line with the enormity of his offense.

"But you promised me it would be available," Victor said, "and now you put me in a perfectly hideous position. Everything depends on that brocade, I was promised it and I will have it, and today. Otherwise I will cancel my entire order." He pursed his lips and frowned at Cooper as if to express his distaste for the whole system of commerce and bargaining. "Yes," he said into the telephone. "I mean exactly what I say."

He returned the receiver to the cradle. Removing a silk handkerchief from his jacket pocket, he wiped his hands carefully, leaning back in his chair to catch his breath, glancing wearily at Cooper again as if reluctant to plunge into another area of business so quickly. "Oh, they abuse a gentleman in this part of the world," he sighed. "They feign courtesy and they give you quick agreement, concession, but they back out on their promises. And even if you have a contract with them, a binding, legal contract, you never know whether they will honor it. And what recourse does a gentleman have when the courts are so capricious and unpredictable?"

"You're having trouble with your suppliers?" Cooper said, laying out the photostats and the translations on the long table.

"If you only knew," Victor said. "I'm redecorating one of the rooms on the second floor and I have to do everything myself. There is simply no one, my dear boy, whose taste in these matters matches my own." He placed the palms of his thick hands on the arms of the chair and slowly, with great effort, brought himself upright. He moved to the lavatory concealed behind a carved screen to wash his face. The drain gurgled noisily; Cooper only caught the general lines of his continuing complaint. Japan was simply no place for a fastidious man because it was a nation powered by coal and consequently the atmosphere was polluted with a fine dust which refused to be filtered from the air even by the elaborate air-conditioning system with which Victor had equipped this building. There was a gritty film on everything; a man simply could not escape it. And if he had a sensitive respiratory tract (as Victor did) this impure air could be uncomfortably injurious.

But someday, at an indeterminate time, when he had exhausted the aesthetic joys of this profession, Victor was going to remove himself from this dirty city and find a villa in the Japanese alps where the air was pure, a place where he would be free to concentrate and create, developing his talent for painting miniatures. Creation was everything, the purpose of life, with man created to re-create (divine extensive premise, self-reflexive), and the artist was the paragon of mankind because he brought a world into being from his imagination and his talent, involving none of the messy biological equipment.

Victor emerged from behind the screen, drying his face and hands on an absorbent towel which he dropped into a covered wastebasket. And the greatest waste in life, he continued, occurred when a man with real creative ability (himself) was forced to channel his originality, his imaginative juices, into the ebb and flow of everyday commercial decisions. "Well," he sighed again, turning his attention finally to the business at hand. "What goodies have you brought me today?"

"It's too early to tell," Cooper said.

"Too early?"

"Did you put the numbers on these documents to catalogue them?" Cooper said.

"No," Victor said. "I have given strict orders that the documents are not to be altered in any way, not to be written on."

"Then the numbering must have been done by Baum-Brenner himself," Cooper said, "although I can't see why. Because you number a series of items only when you want them kept in a certain order, and I can't see any reason why he kept most of these things at all unless they had a certain personal value to him."

"Suppose we start at the beginning," Victor said, curious. "With number one."

Cooper picked up the first photostat. "A letter from Baum-Brenner to his daughter, Mrs. Anna Klaus, dated August 17, 1944. That was about a month before he went back to Warsaw. From the heading, I gather he is in Berlin and she is in Geneva. In this letter he expresses delight over the birth of his grandson and hopes that through some miracle he will be permitted to see it. He also asks her, should she gain possession of his manuscript collection and his files, to keep them absolutely intact, with not a scrap of paper removed from

43

them. He signs the letter 'your loving father' and adds in a postscript that he is sending a key for her to keep."

"A key to what?"

"The letter doesn't say." Cooper picked up a sheaf of papers and sorted through them. "Now, strangely enough, documents two through ten predate the first document. They are carbon copies of letters Baum-Brenner wrote from Warsaw immediately before, during, and after the German Blitzkrieg of Poland. Some of them are condolence letters for nephews killed in the charge of the Pomorska Cavalry Brigade against the tanks of General Heinz Guderian; one concerns funeral arrangements he wanted made for a brother who froze to death in a cattle car among some Poles the Germans were relocating in the east, to make room for German settlers. One of the letters, as a matter of fact, wasn't written *by* him but *to* him by a member of his congregation, offering him condolences on the death of his only son, Jacob, evidently of some disease, in the Warsaw ghetto.

"There is also a letter which Baum-Brenner wrote to Governor General Hans Frank, protesting the *Asserordenliche Befriedigungsaktion*, the Extraordinary Purification Action with which the Germans purged the Jews from their homes once the army had taken over. It's written in very strong language and signed, 'Martin Baum, Rabbi.' "

He put these photostats down and picked up the next batch. "Now there is a gap from 1940 to 1943 and we have a new series of related letters, an exchange between Baum and Dr. Hans Kerrl, the Nazi Minister of Church Affairs. Apparently, at some point between the two dates, Martin Baum renounced his religion and went to work for the Germans, moving to Berlin and either taking or being assigned the name 'Brenner.' In the first letter of this series he makes an appraisal of a collection of codices and papyri removed from a monastery in Poland which was razed to make room for a Nazi agricultural experiment. The papyri are in good condition, he says; the

44

material they contain is worthless from a financial point of view—Roman tax assessments, grain inventories, that sort of thing. He says he is sending copies to Dr. Kerrl for his opinion. Kerrl tells him to keep up the good work and that he will be amply rewarded. In the next letter Baum-Brenner apparently feels free enough to complain about the supplies sent him. There's a copy of an invoice from a printing supply house in these papers, by the way; evidently Baum-Brenner refused to work without a special kind of ink, and he paid an exorbitant price for it. Anyway, he complains to Kerrl about everything. His quarters are too small and not warm enough and the humidity is too high and his daughter is suffering from a respiratory ailment. The next letter is from Kerrl's secretary, giving Baum-Brenner the name of a doctor, Kerrl's personal physician, and arranging for an appointment. And that's the last of them."

"The last of the letters?" Victor said incredulously. "That's all they have in them?"

"Yes."

Victor moaned slightly. "Worthless," he said. "Absolutely worthless."

"From your point of view I suppose they are," Cooper said.

"From any point of view," Victor said unhappily. "And if the rest of the papers are like these, I will be absolutely despondent. The Red Chinese government will not buy a pig in a poke and, much as I detest them politically, they are shrewd bargainers."

"Have you been in touch with them yet?"

"No." Victor slumped his shoulders in a shrug. "I just must bring myself to be more distrustful about people. I am too open, too defenseless. People take advantage of me. I help an old priest into freedom and in return I am given garbage." He paused, drawing a breath. "But there are some old things in the collection and they are bound to be worth something. I should have known better than to expect that a com-

45

mon priest or rabbi would really have anything of great value, so I suppose that makes it all my fault, dear boy. After all, I took the chance."

His emotions vacillated like a pendulum, Cooper realized. It was a paradox that, in so ponderous and elephantine a man, the emotions should be so agile. "We'll know better how valuable the collection is once we've had a look at the whole thing," Cooper said.

Victor pounced on this hope and immediately felt better. "Of course you're right, dear boy," he said. "But that's the price an artistic temperament exacts, reducing everything to blacks and whites, success and failure. That's one reason I discarded the Western Hemisphere in favor of the Orient. Peace of mind is simply impossible back there." He had drifted to his desk and was now occupied with taking money from the drawer, reluctantly today, since no tangible value had been received for it. He was interrupted by the telephone. Nodding an apology to Cooper, he sat down to answer it.

"Hawkins here," he said, and then listened, grimacing as he heard something unpleasant. "I do hate to discipline her," he said, "but I suppose there's no way around it. We simply cannot tolerate this sort of thing. Where are you now?" He paused and nodded. "Just bring her directly here, to my office. And by the way, did the two get off to Manila this morning? No, I'm talking about the Korean and the Chinese, the one from Singapore." He looked toward Cooper, wrinkling his nose as if his doubts of the basic trustworthiness of the world were being confirmed again. "No," he said. "He knows better than to bring up that health business. If the girls get past the Taiwan health inspectors, that's all he can reasonably ask. He's just haggling over a price which is already as generous and equitable as he can find anywhere else, and he knows it. It's ridiculous, just because one of the girls was airsick last time. What is airsickness anyway? Nausea, temporary indigestion, nothing permanent. Ito understands the

46

price is to be paid, in cash, before the girls go through customs. Don't let yourself be browbeaten."

He replaced the receiver and repeated the cleansing ritual before he went back to the money. "When it rains, it pours," he said. "Trouble on every hand, and now I face a discipline problem as well." He put the bills on the corner of the desk and turned his back on them. "You remember the girl I bought the last time you were here?"

"Yes."

"She ran away, back to her mother. Her mother tried to deny the girl had returned—she intended to sell her again, I imagine—but Itsugi found her. He's bringing her back."

"What will you do to her?" Cooper said.

"Unfortunately, it will have to be painful," Victor said, straining to his feet again and crossing to a carved wall cabinet, rummaging around on a shelf until he found a length of rubber hose. "It's the only thing a child like this understands. It will be painful but it will do no great damage, leave no marks. Her mother was quite accurate in her assessment, I have to give her that, the girl is a perfect, unblemished specimen."

For the first time in many months Cooper felt the stirrings of disgust, or anger, and the moment he recognized it he knew why it was happening to him: because Susan had been eleven, the same age as this gawky Japanese girl, and for a moment he had allowed the two to become confused in his mind, projecting Susan into this situation as if she were the one who would face this porcine man who new flexed the rubber hose in his trembling fingers. Cooper could not allow himself to become involved. There was no more Susan; he had no connection with this girl.

Walking to the desk, he put the money in his attaché case, preparing to leave, but he did not move quickly enough. As he was closing his case the door opened and Itsugi entered with the girl. Never had Cooper seen a look of such abject fear in

47

his life; the girl's face was screwed up with it and she was so frozen with terror that her breath came in convulsive little gasps and she could not cry. Obviously she had been sick to her stomach. Cooper did not move. He stood leaning on the desk, averting his eyes while she brushed by him, pushed along by the passive Itsugi.

"Tell her I am very, very disappointed in her," Victor said to Itsugi, keeping his eyes on the girl, his voice reprimanding, chiding. "She has had the very best of everything and I am arranging a glorious future for her that any girl in Japan would sacrifice anything—no, make that everything—to have. So I am disappointed and forced to extreme measures to show her how very, very disappointed I am and to remind her of her obligations." He doubled the hose in his hands and snapped it taut.

"Put it down, Victor," Cooper said quietly, not looking at him.

Victor glanced at him abruptly, quizzically. "I beg your pardon?"

"I said you're not going to beat her," Cooper said, turning to him now. "So put the hose down."

"Dear boy, do you think I want to do this?" Victor said, a curious gleam in his eye. "No, I have no desire to strike her. I abhor violence of any sort and if you can give me any sort of reason . . ."

"She's a child and you're a man," Cooper said. "I mean it, Victor."

"You don't have to threaten me, dear boy," Victor said, wounded. "When a friend wants something he doesn't have to threaten, he justs asks. I have a very high regard for you and if you don't want this girl punished in this fashion, if it offends you, then of course it simply won't happen." He turned to Itsugi. "Tell her I have decided to give her another chance," he said, "because eventually I would like her to look on me as a father, and a father always knows when a child has learned

48

its lesson and does not need punishment. Ask her if she will promise—and tell her I do not take promises lightly, they are the specie of honesty—to behave herself from now on."

He waited until Itsugi had finished the translation and then examined the girl's face expectantly. The girl said nothing.

"She's too frightened to answer," Cooper said.

"Of course," Victor said. He turned to Itsugi. "Tell her I accept her silence as agreement. And take her upstairs. See that she has a nice hot bath."

When the girl was gone Victor returned the rubber tube to the wall cabinet. "I've offended you," he said apologetically, "but I'm really not as calloused as I seem to be. I simply have no memory. Your daughter was about the same age when she passed away, wasn't she? I should have remembered that. But there are so many things on my mind, I commit one *faux pas* after another without even thinking about it."

Despite Victor's conciliatory tone, Cooper could feel the strength of his freshened curiosity, as if he had discovered a vulnerable point in Cooper that he had not seen before and had not yet determined how to make the best use of it. Victor was a tight and canny little man hiding somewhere in that gross corporeal bulk, camouflaged by his flesh and a bright barrage of persiflage, and now that he had come across something which he considered a weakness in Cooper, he could be counted on to bury that discovery in a torrent of irrelevant conversation.

"After all, my dear boy," he said with a disarming smile, "I'm really not the noxious individual I seem to be, simply because what one might class as ordinary society frowns on my enterprises. After all, I did not create the difference between the sexes and all I do is stage and make real the mystique which every man gives to the sexual act anyway, so in that sense I only preserve his illusions and enhance them. I'm sure if you would visit the second floor sometime you would

49

see exactly what I mean, because it's an extension of myself and I am not what anybody could call a sordid individual. Does that make me a criminal, dear boy, am I a worm, just because I flaunt convention in order to make people happy? And my girls—talk to them, they love me because I am good to them and they wouldn't trade the life they have here for any other. These two I decided to transfer, the little Chinese, oh, what a plum she was, she wept all last night because she had to leave here. So I don't see how you could condemn me."

"I'm not attacking you," Cooper said. "I'm not passing judgment."

"Well then, that's better," Victor said. "And I want you to know I appreciate what you've done for me, helping me to recognize that there is more than one way to solve a problem. Force never solves anything, I realize that. So we will just forget what has been essentially a lapse of taste on my part. We will overlook my gaucheries. The next batch of documents should be ready very soon and so we will concentrate on them and hope for the best." He extended a limp hand to Cooper. "Always a pleasure and an education to see you, my dear boy."

Once he reached the hall, Cooper paused outside the door for a moment to satisfy his curiosity, waiting until he heard the confirming splash of water as Victor washed his hands. Then he left the building.

2

For the next few days Cooper left his room infrequently, occupying himself with the new box of photostats delivered to him by the toothless old man who served Victor as a messenger. Ordinarily Cooper broke his routine with a walk every evening, but the weather had turned disagreeably cold and the rains continued. He stayed at his worktable, close to the hibachi which radiated a small circle of comfortable heat.

It was not only the weather that kept him in. Since the

fire he had suffered prolonged periods of extreme sensitivity
in which the most casual human contact—the glimpse of a
child tagging along behind its mother on the street—was
enough to cause him pain. It was to be expected, of course;
he was objectively rational about the aftereffects of shock and
he had been subjected to a severe one. His continued reaction
to this trauma was, in many ways, like a chronic disease in
that he was always forewarned of the attacks, and he knew he
should have seen this one coming.

Going through the random papers of Baum-Brenner had
evoked a sadness and depression within him, as if, line by
line, the portrait of a tragic figure had been drawn before his
eyes, and in this likeness he saw himself. This was something
Cooper rarely did when he was working—allow himself to
sentimentalize the documents he worked with, to re-create in
his mind's eye the personality of the long-dead human whose
hand had held a pen and made marks on paper. He would
leave such speculative indulgences to the creative historians
who took the raw material he provided and wove it into the
colorful fabric of social history; it was up to him to translate,
examine, and assess in the cold light of educated reason, to
determine the "how" instead of the "why." In this method,
subjectivity had no place; it inevitably led to distortion, inter-
polation, to a superimposition of his own thoughts over the
writing which lay before him.

He had not been able to maintain this objectivity toward
the letters of Baum-Brenner; the Jew's grief was incendiary,
sparking off his own sense of loss. In the new collection of
photostats was a long letter from Baum-Brenner to an Isaac
Silverstein. Considering the year, 1942, and the fact that
Isaac lived in London, it was possible the letter had never
been sent. From the tone of the language, Cooper guessed
that Isaac was an old friend. The letter did not try to impress
or remonstrate or implore. Instead, it seemed to reflect an
overwhelming desire to communicate the fatigue, the weari-

51

ness which followed grief, and to reveal a sense of wonderment—without rebuke—at the seeming cruelty of the God whom Baum-Brenner had served so long.

I cannot see the pattern, Isaac. I cannot see the pattern at all, why, with the suddenness of a summer storm, they are all taken from us, not only my own flesh, not only my unruly Jacob and my enduring Rachel and my father's brother and Ira—you remember him, do you not, Isaac, the cousin who saw so clearly with one eye?—and all the people of my flesh except for Anna, but not only those but the members of my congregation and their relatives as well, no, not dozens, not hundreds, not thousands, but millions, truly millions. At Treblinka and Belsec and Sibibor and many other places. I cannot put this horror onto paper. There are no words for horror as vast as this. They exterminate us. They grind our seed on the rock until there is no generation to follow us.

Obvious, Cooper thought, that he himself should be infected with despair and that this, in turn, should have led to the scene in Victor's office in which he had interceded on behalf of the girl, substituting an action now for something which should have been done a year ago, before it was too late. It was a foolish gesture, as if he had put his hand into a river to stop the waters from flowing. It meant nothing. He had spared the girl a moment's pain and kept Victor from enjoying the giving of pain and that was all. Victor was perfectly willing to return the hose to the cabinet, to suspend that punishment as a gesture of good will; it made him look good to do it.

But nothing had been resolved; the girl was still on the second floor, her whole future in Victor's hands to shape as he pleased. Nothing was changed. Nan was dead. Susan was dead. They no longer existed, no gesture of the mind could conjure them to life again. He could only succeed in wounding himself by trying to analyze and rearrange the past. This he would not do. And as far as Baum-Brenner was concerned, he resolved to remain detached.

He passed beyond the Silverstein letter to a set of new communications between Baum-Brenner and Dr. Kerrl; these were considerably less cordial than the first. Kerrl complained of the slowness with which Baum-Brenner worked. Obviously Kerrl was being pressured by his superiors, who were vitally interested in this project, and in turn he was passing that pressure on. Baum-Brenner replied with great tact and restraint. An important work like this required infinite patience; only the trivial could be accomplished quickly. The language was difficult and it required great care to translate the subtler shadings, but as proof of his constant endeavor, he was including a specimen of his work. Kerrl responded immediately, enthusiastically. He had shown it to Goebbels himself, who had been ecstatic about it. The specimen was being returned by special messenger and Kerrl reminded Baum-Brenner to mention this project to no one; the disclosure of his work could not be made until it was complete and free from any possible error.

Once Cooper had finished translating the Kerrl letter, he found he had exhausted all the contemporary material and was now confronted with a separate packet of copies of considerably older documents, one in Latin, two in Greek, one in Hebrew, and one in Aramaic. This was going to be an extremely difficult task, he realized, holding the first of the photostats to the light. The Latin was precise and correct—the work of a scribe, perhaps—but the ink had so faded as to make it almost indecipherable in spots.

The first Greek manuscript was even worse. The hand which had inscribed this had been extremely shaky indeed; there were frequent erratic scratches where a phrase had been obliterated. The second Greek manuscript was a little better. The Hebrew was an archaic form which promised to be extremely difficult, and the Aramaic, at first glance, seemed positively impossible. The papyrus itself appeared to be in excellent condition with only a few fragments missing, an

53

irregular triangle near the beginning, a few scattered holes here and there, but he had never been proficient in Aramaic and it would take considerable brushing up before he could even approach it.

By the time he came to this point it was early Friday morning and he was much too tired to plunge into these difficult documents immediately. Unrolling his bed quilts, he lay down, hoping sleep would ease his splitting headache, but he found himself too tired for sleep and his mind persisted in compiling a list of items he would need for the work ahead of him. He lay there in a drowsy state of half wakefulness until the maid came with his morning tea and the mail, then he shaved and sat down to look through the letters while he drank his tea. There was nothing of importance, nothing that required an answer. Clearing off his writing table, he put on his hat and overcoat and went out into the chill frost of a hazy morning and the crowds of people wearing gauze masks over their faces as if the air was bound to be full of contagion on a day like this.

He walked to Shimbashi Station and on impulse paused beneath the canopy which sheltered the public telephones, only to realize, once he had an operator on the line, how isolated he was by the language barrier. He tried to make her understand that he wanted the number for Victor Hawkins and in turn she kept saying, over and over, "*Moshi, moshi. Kikoemasuka?*" He was not sure he could have communicated with her even if they had happened to share a common language, competing as he was with the blaring voice of the station announcer calling the trains and the hiss of air brakes as the coaches came to an abrupt and jolting stop not fifteen feet from where he stood. In the end he slammed down the receiver in disgust and made a quick dash for the Kanda train, barely squeezing into the coach before the door hissed shut and the train began to move.

He could not locate the books he wanted. Goldsmith's *Aramaic Commentaries* was not to be had at any price, but he was able to find a couple of classical Latin and Greek dictionaries in a Kanda bookstore which specialized in such scholarly items. He also bought a rectangular magnifying glass on a short stand and a light globe of stronger wattage for his lamp. Although he did not feel up to it, he went back to the café on the Ginza for lunch with Father O'Connor, knowing that if he returned to his room now he would be unable to keep from working and the headache would become severe if he did not rest his eyes. Too, he needed information from Victor, and Father O'Connor could place the call for him, sparing him the effort of going by Victor's place.

As usual, Father O'Connor was waiting at the table near the window with the omnipresent teapot in front of him, blinking expectantly toward the door through his owlish glasses, smiling pleasantly as Cooper approached. During lunch the little priest skirted the edge of a premise which he would undoubtedly pursue as an argument once the meal was finished.

He had been having another conversation with the student who lived in Shimbashi about Victor Hawkins and his sinful establishment, he said, and the student's father—who was a clerk in the headquarters of the National Rural Police—had heard a rumor. Very shortly, under the impetus of the Westernized moralists in the government, there was to be a concerted campaign against prostitution and Hawkins would undoubtedly be obliterated in the first wave. It would make a scandal of international proportions and the very best Victor Hawkins could hope for would be deportation and confiscation of his property. More likely, he would be subjected to criminal action and imprisonment.

"And a new morality will dawn over greater Tokyo." Cooper smiled, amused at the priest's indirection.

"I know you don't believe it," Father O'Connor said ruefully. "Because you doubt everything. But it has to come."

"I think you're going to be disappointed," Cooper said.

55

"Traditionally, the Japanese don't see anything wrong with prostitution. They consider it far better than rape. And I'm sure Victor pays out a lot of money to protect himself, both above and below the table."

"But can you afford to take the chance that you might be wrong?" Father O'Connor said, ignoring the side issue altogether in an attempt to stay on his main theme. Absently, he touched the back of his hand to the teapot. The point was now on its way; Cooper could see the wave of thought cresting in Father O'Connor's mind. "Disregarding the moral implications which you apparently refuse to see, look at this in a purely practical light. The rumor just might be right. And if the police do get Victor and if you're working for him, then they will get you too. The scandal could very well ruin you. You could never go back." He poured himself a cup of tea and drank it slowly. "I'm sure it's a part of God's design for you to go back," he added.

"And at that point we come to a separation of the ways," Cooper said. "I simply don't believe there is either a pattern or a meaning to life. You can superimpose an artificial design on it with religion and give everything a significance after the fact, but there's only one real progression: birth, life, and death. And the incidents inside that progression don't follow any pattern at all."

"It's logical for you to assume that," Father O'Connor said sympathetically. "Most men don't lose everything so suddenly."

"You can't give me a metaphysical explanation for it," Cooper said. "Because there isn't any."

"To try is to question God's wisdom."

"If you admit there is a God."

"You believed it once."

"Whether I did or not isn't really important," Cooper said. He had no desire to quarrel with Father O'Connor or to upset him but he was relieved to find himself devoid of any strong feeling. The driving hours of concentration had succeeded in purging the painful sensitivity from him. He could discuss these abstractions without the least feeling of personal involvement. Evidently Father O'Connor recognized the impasse they had reached. You could not touch the soul of a man who had none. He signaled the waitress for a fresh pot of tea and used the flurry of physical activity to change the subject.

"Willa Cummings came to see me yesterday," he said. "Actually, I think I had the wrong impression about her. She's developed a rigid defense against the world but underneath it she's really a susceptible woman. And apparently you have a great influence on her."

"Oh?"

"She wanted to know everything I know about you. She thinks very highly of you."

"I wonder if you would do something for me," Cooper said abruptly.

"If I can."

"I want to make a telephone call and I can't get the operator to understand me."

Father O'Connor sighed tolerantly. "Then you don't believe me—about Willa Cummings, I mean."

"I believe you," Cooper said. "And I have an interest in her welfare. I don't want to see her hurt."

"You always look at things the wrong way," Father O'Connor said. "A negative attitude like that isn't good enough. If you were really interested in her welfare you would have the desire to see her helped."

"I have that too."

"But no desire to do it yourself."

"I couldn't do it if I tried," Cooper said. "To set out to help a person, you have to decide what would be good for them and what wouldn't. And I couldn't decide that."

57

"Because it would be a responsibility and you don't want it."

"No, I don't want it."

Father O'Connor sighed again. He thanked the waitress as she put the pot of fresh tea before him. "I'm a bad priest," he said, once she was gone. "I've never had the gift of persuasion. I've never been able to convince anyone of the truths I know to be so completely certain. That's the reason I went into teaching. I can communicate facts but not faith."

"If you were smart you'd give me up as a lost cause," Cooper said. "There's no point in berating yourself just because I'm the way I am."

"I know my limitations," Father O'Connor said, touching his hand to the teapot. It was still too hot. "It's very possible God has sent you along to point out those limitations. After all, over the years I've developed a great deal of pride in my work and now I can see I've succeeded only because I've never had a real challenge." He pushed back from the table. "I'll place the call for you now, if you like."

Victor was unavailable, Itsugi confided to Cooper. He was entertaining a very important man from the U.N. on the second floor. He could not be interrupted.

"It's all right," Cooper said. "You can get the information I want. I need to know if I can get a better set of photostats on the first document, the Latin one. I need to know if these documents are in any order. And last, I need to know if there are any more documents in the Baum-Brenner collection or if I have the complete crop."

He had only to ask the questions once and Itsugi had them. He said he would send the answers to Cooper by late afternoon.

"I suppose you need to go," Father O'Connor said when Cooper returned to the table.

"Yes."

"Then let me give you one parting word of advice," Father

58

O'Connor said. "I know you won't take it but I am required to give it to you anyway. It is one thing to commit a sin yourself, but that sin is compounded a hundred times when you lead another person into it. And sin is a reality. It is a crime against God which must be expiated or punished. It requires confession and penance. And it does exist, whether you admit it or not." He poured a thin stream of tea into his cup. "Next Friday?" he said.

"Next Friday," Cooper agreed.

Three

1

THERE was a risk involved in it, of course, because it was against the law, but Willa simply could not see the value of her thousand dollars reduced through a technicality. It was far better to pay the hundred-dollar bribe to the teller at the foreign exchange bank (he insisted on calling it a "handling charge"; she was perfectly willing to accept his terminology) than to accept the official conversion rate of Y360 to the dollar.

The transaction was accomplished off the premises, in a café down the street from the bank, but the exchange was still conducted with all the formality of a legal ceremony. The teller was a dignified, middle-aged Japanese with a severely trimmed mustache etched across his upper lip, and he handed her the papers with great stiffness, bowing slightly as he examined each requisite signature. She endorsed the cashier's check from her bank in America, then he counted out the money due her in crisp American hundreds, snapping each bill separately before he added it to the pile in front of her.

Once his business was finished, he folded the hundred-dollar bill she gave him and inserted it into the watch pocket of his black suit. He stood up and gave her a formal bow, making a speech in precisely correct English in which he thanked her for permitting him to help her and solicited any further business she might have.

Once she had the money, she went immediately to the office of a Japanese businessman in Yurakucho who made a lucrative profession of buying American currency from people like Willa at Y500 to the dollar and selling it at Y1000 to the dollar to tourists, speculators, and servicemen who had accumulated yen in excess of the Y36,000 reconvertible to American dollars under Japanese law. The transaction took less than an hour and the businessman used most of that time to make a check of her credentials, satisfying himself that she was not an employee of the Local Public Procurator's Office sent here to gather evidence against him. When she left his office she had Y450,000 in Y10,000 notes in her purse.

Despite the fact that she now had nearly half a million yen with her, she felt pressured, close to panic with the realization that this money represented the last of her savings. At one time there had been over a hundred thousand dollars in her account and now it was all gone, every penny of it, and there was no more money coming in. The Empress project had gone sour; she now knew with complete finality that she could not do it. Everything was against it and none of her contacts had come through for her.

She was not sure how much of her present incipient panic came from her financial condition and how much was due to the familiar aftereffects of a hangover, but as she walked down the Ginza she resolved to get things in hand before it was too late. She would have to stop drinking and get a project under way which offered a practical hope of reward. God, drinking had ruined so many things for her down the line, or maybe it was the other way around, maybe so many things had been ruined for her that drinking was a by-product, the only quick and practical relief from the tensions that beset her. She had never had any control over her own life. Everything that happened to her was entirely dependent on circumstance.

She had started out on a little newspaper in Kansas, fresh from journalism school, but she had never been driven by ambition. She had never really wanted to be a writer in the first place, but her father had insisted she have some profession to protect her against the almost certain weakness of the man she would someday marry—her father had never trusted his own sex because he had never trusted himself—so she had followed his advice and gone to journalism school and taken the job on the newspaper while she waited to find the man she wanted to marry.

There had been an accident on a farm near Topeka. A little girl fell down a well and Willa was assigned to the story. For forty-eight hours she stayed on the scene, drinking coffee to stay awake and whisky to dull her feelings, pounding out on her battered portable the agonizing and prolonged dying of a little girl. When that ordeal was over Willa emerged with a kind of regional fame and she received an offer from a Dallas paper, the police beat, bigger and better accidents to cover. After a couple of years of this, she was awarded the grand prize, an opportunity to report a really big slaughter, the war in Korea. *God*, she thought, remembering, *that was a war. Booze, blood, and boredom. It's a wonder our side was ever sober enough to know where to shoot.*

When the truce was declared she came home, a celebrity who had been awarded the Pulitzer prize for her reports from Korea, and there had been a movie deal and conferences and an eternal round of cocktail parties. And the glass in her hand, the magic glass, was always somehow full. And then, on top of the world, she decided to write the things she had always wanted to write: interviews at the U.N., humorous articles about women in a man's world, happy, light things

62

with no undercurrent of grimness. She had seen enough of that to last the rest of her life.

But there was no vitality to her writing then; the words came out flat and lifeless and her attempts at humor were painful. Even now she didn't know why she had failed. Perhaps she had been drinking too much—drinking always dulled her critical judgment—or perhaps her success had come only because it suited the public fancy to have a blonde in fatigues slogging through the mud at the front and grinding out the gore.

And then one spring day, the very day she was fired by the *News*, she ran into an officer she had met in Korea, Harvey Wilkins, and three days later, after a whirlwind courtship, she married him because she was ready for marriage and tired of shifting for herself and he was as welcome as solid ground after a long swim. But it was too late—God, it always seemed too late, her timing in life was completely off—and Harvey didn't want to be solid ground. He didn't want to have to control her and discipline her and help her become the kind of wife she might have been in those days in Kansas. No, he expected her immediate conformity to his mental image of an army wife, and when he could not have it he decided he had made a mistake.

The final scene had been played at a reception thrown by the wife of a brigadier general in Arlington, Virginia. As a major, Harvey was low man on the totem pole. From the minute he entered the restored ballroom of the old colonial house he seemed to shrink physically. Maybe it wasn't his fault, maybe he couldn't help it, really, because he was in an untenable position, but he expected Willa to follow his lead and remain in the shadowy background befitting a man of lesser rank.

This she could not bring herself to do, having lost all respect for the higher military echelons during her time in Korea. She had witnessed too many high-level mistakes, too

63

many weaknesses, to be in awe of the big brass, so she refused to be subdued. She circulated freely, openly, incurring the wrath of the general's wife (she thought Willa brash, too mannish), and as a consequence Willa had drunk too much and had thrown a glass of champagne in the face of the general's wife and then grabbed at Harvey's arm, demanding to be removed from this hostile atmosphere.

But Harvey did not budge. His face wore the embarrassed righteousness of a man about to make a popular choice. He told her to sober up and go home. He apologized to the general's wife and thereby dissolved a marriage which never should have occurred in the first place. She wondered where Harvey was now. In the Pentagon, perhaps, buoyed up by the rigid rules of protocol which helped him feel secure. She felt no afterglow of malice toward him now, no bitterness. He had done what he felt he had to do, as she herself had done, and even without the catalyst of the general's wife, the marriage would have ended, not so dramatically perhaps, but just as finally.

She forced her mind away from the past and kept walking along the Ginza until she found a Turkish bath. She spent the afternoon in a steam cabinet, purging the alcohol out of her system, following it with a massage, emerging into the chill, crisp evening air with a feeling of well-being she had not known in a long time. She had a steak for dinner, medium rare, and then she went on a shopping tour of the department stores, buying a new coat and shoes before she went back to the hotel.

She spent the evening polishing her fingernails and trying to wash her hair with the spasmodic supply of water provided by the tap. There was always a water shortage in Tokyo. The pipes were always spluttering and belching air at the most inconvenient times, so when she found the faucet working she filled an extra basin with water as a reserve supply. It was a wise precaution. As she was filling her teakettle to heat

64

her rinse water, the pipes shuddered and went dry. But even the reserve supply in the basin was insufficient and she was left with a slick and soapy film on her hair. God, the things she had to put up with.

Just as soon as she found a worth-while project and became sufficiently solvent again, she was going to move to one of the larger hotels. They had reserve water tanks that never went dry. As she set her hair, seated at the portable vanity table given to her by the *News* editor as a joke ("Take it to Korea, baby, can't afford to be mistaken for one of the troops"), she could hear Cooper moving around in the next room, the muffled sound of footsteps as he fetched coal for the hibachi, the muted hacking as he cleared his throat, the faint sigh of the tatami flooring giving beneath his weight as he sat down at his writing table again.

And quite suddenly she found the idea in her mind, or perhaps it had been there all along, from the moment she had discovered he was translating the Baum-Brenner papers. There was still a good bit of mystery surrounding the defection of the Jewish scholar, and if the papers helped clear it up it might very well be the kind of story she could do and do well. It would certainly be commercial.

She was not sure, however, whether Cooper would help her. They had not missed a Friday night together in the past six months, but there was little display of involvement on his part. He had never revealed anything of himself to her. She knew he had suffered a tragedy which had brought him to Japan but he had never talked to her about it. Even in bed she never had the feeling she possessed him. It was almost as if his passion were an impersonal thing, a reflex which her desire triggered in him. There was no reason to suppose, therefore, that he was going to co-operate with her out of any personal regard.

She wished she had not decided to wash her hair. She could have found some pretext to go next door and talk to him—he wouldn't have minded—and at least she could have begun to sound him out. But then again, perhaps it was better this way. There was no sense approaching him until she was fully prepared.

The next morning she called St. Justin Martyr College and made an appointment to see Father O'Connor in the afternoon. On the train ride to Sendagaya she tried to decide how she was going to handle this priest who undoubtedly knew of her affair with Cooper and could be counted on to disapprove it. She had not talked to Father O'Connor when she called the college—a nun had made the appointment as a matter of course—so she did not even have his reacting tone of voice to guide her. She had met him a week after her arrival in Japan, at a press conference sponsored by the college, and she had seen him at a number of public events, but she had only talked to him once, briefly, when by accident she had passed the Ginza café as the priest and Cooper emerged onto the sidewalk after their weekly meeting. This had happened shortly after she and Cooper began their Friday night affair and when she saw the clerical collar she turned abruptly away in an attempt to spare Cooper any possible embarrassment, but he called out to her and insisted on introducing her to Father O'Connor. It had been an awkward moment. Ill at ease, she had stammered out a few words of conversation and then excused herself, scurrying off down the street toward a non-existent appointment. Had there been a perceptive glint in the priest's eyes? Had he recognized instinctively and immediately the relationship between her and Cooper?

She was reasonably sure he had. It was possible she had been mistaken but she thought it best to assume that he did know. It would be far better to be prepared for his disapproval than to have it take her by surprise.

St. Justin Martyr was some distance from the station but it was a perfect autumn afternoon and she found the walk invigorating. It felt good to be out of the noise and smog of

66

the central district for a while. There was little traffic on the tree-lined boulevard; the houses here were bigger, and the children playing on the sidewalks seemed less wary and more spontaneous, calling out to her as she passed by.

The college itself was a group of Gothic buildings set in an imperial preserve of massive oak trees. As she walked toward the administration building she smiled at the furtive and curious glances from the uniformed boys who stood in clusters on the yellowing grass of the common. God, she thought as she went up the steps and into the building, what a virtue they made of looking grimy and sober, these vestigial remnants of a militaristic tradition.

She asked for Father O'Connor at the admissions counter and a nun in a flowing habit took her to his office, a room which struggled to look cheerful despite its spartan severity. It was bare of decoration except for the crucifix on the wall and faded blue drapes which flanked a large window overlooking the common. Her wait was not a long one. He bustled in shortly after three o'clock, wearing a cassock instead of the black suit which he wore off campus, apologizing for being five minutes late.

She was surprised to find him so cordial. He shook her hand and told her she should have given him more notice of her coming. "I would have talked you into speaking to one of our journalism classes," he said, sitting down at his desk. "It isn't every day we get a distinguished Pulitzer prize winner on our campus." He smiled, blinking as he removed his glasses and polished the lenses with a handkerchief. "Now, what brings you to our part of the city, Miss Cummings?"

"I'm not sure," Willa said, a little off balance since her estimate of his attitude had been so wrong. "I came out here to talk to you about Cooper, but—well, now that I'm here, I really don't know what to say. I feel uneasy about him, Father. He disturbs me."

"He's a very contradictory person," Father O'Connor said,

67

replacing his glasses on his thin nose and squinting at her. "There, that's better. I'm nearsighted and I get chalk dust on my glasses and between the two afflictions I get quite blind at times. But there are a number of different types of blindness and the physical infirmity is not the worst. How long have you known Cooper?"

"Six months."

"And what is your relationship with him?"

She had not been wrong after all. He did know. There was no point to being evasive. "We're lovers," she said.

"I see. You're not Catholic, are you, Miss Cummings?"

"No. Does that make a difference?"

"Only in my approach to the problem," he said, "and it is a problem. I suspect you realize that or you wouldn't be here." He looked at her sharply. She said nothing. "If you were Catholic, I would send you to your confessor, but since you're not . . ." He shrugged slightly. "You say he disturbs you. How?"

"I know something happened to him to make him jump the track," she said, "but I don't know what it is. He's never really told me anything about himself. I don't even know why he came to Japan."

"I think I can tell you that," Father O'Connor said. "He's never discussed his problems with me but I've been interested enough in him to do some basic research, what I could find out through friends and the newspapers. He's quite well known in scholastic circles, but I suppose you're aware of that."

"Yes."

"I don't have all the facts. I just have enough bits and pieces to make a calculated guess," Father O'Connor said, glancing out the window as the students in the common responded to the jangling signal for the next class period. "It's rather incredible in a way," he continued, "that Cooper is so different now from the way he used to be, when he was at Cummerland College." It was incredible, he went on, because

68

human beings were so conditioned by the time they reached maturity that it was almost impossible to effect a complete transformation in their lives.

As a priest, Father O'Connor knew a great deal about this process of transition. At one time, before he went into teaching, he had been assigned to the renovation of human beings in a gutter community in Los Angeles and it was there he had learned the practical limits of conversion. Without exception the men he had been able to reach and rescue from narcotics and whisky and all the palliatives used by the despondent had possessed a reservoir of faith from the religious training of their childhood. This was not to underrate the efficacy of God, he explained, because miracles could be worked and *were* worked, but ordinarily the strength of the foundation determined the dimensions of the structure.

Cooper's life was founded on extremely solid foundations. As the son of a Presbyterian minister, he had grown up without going through the normal revolt of the adolescent against his father and his father's faith—a condition which seemed to plague the offspring of Protestant ministers—and it was only a slight leaning toward the academic, Father O'Connor supposed, which made Cooper decide to become a scholar instead of a minister.

With a Ph.D. from the University of Chicago, he had risen rapidly through the faculty ranks at Cummerland to become head of his department, enhancing his scholarly reputation by writing a number of most remarkable books on the early Christian Era. These books were greatly respected by historians the world over, not so much for their content—they usually dealt with the tangential effects of Christianity, the Gnostics, Apologists, Copts, that sort of thing—as for the perfectly lucid and cogent style in which they were written.

Cooper had the gift of keeping himself out of it. He would start with a basic document which to the casual eye might seem totally insignificant and then he would begin to annotate

69

it, building around it, chinking in the holes with contemporary evaluations and comments, until in the end this seemingly insignificant scrap of antiquity assumed its true proportions and was revealed as the crystallized essence of a whole era of man's thought and growth. Cooper worked with facts the way a watchmaker worked with minuscule jewels and cogs and gears and the end product was finely fashioned, perfect. He was, Father O'Connor said, to use a hackneyed phrase which happened to be completely true in this case, a historian's historian.

He was not book-bound in those early days, however. He had married the year before he got his doctorate, a sparkling, charming person who was completely devoted to him. They had one child, a little girl named Susan. And then, late last year, in December it was, while Cooper was delivering a guest lecture at Yale, the tragedy occurred. His house caught fire in the dead of night and burned to the ground with his wife and daughter trapped inside.

"They died? Both of them?"

The priest nodded. "I can only estimate the shock he felt," he said. "Everything wiped out, gone. I've seen things like this before and I must say that usually a man of faith who suffers such a tragedy shakes his fist at God and then, once his bitterness fades out, returns to faith. But not Cooper. He is not bitter, not resentful. He moves and acts but he does not feel. He is alive but the most vital part of him seems dead, as if God were killed in the house along with his wife and daughter."

"So he jumped off the edge of the world," Willa said.

"Not immediately. He tried to go through the spring semester but he couldn't function. So he requested a leave of absence, accepted an offer from Hawkins, and came to Japan."

"How did he meet Hawkins?" Willa said. "It seems unlikely a couple of types like that would ever get together."

"Scholars are sometimes naïve," Father O'Connor said.

"Hawkins ran advertisements in all the academic journals. He made it appear he was running a research project on some kind of foundation grant and offered an amount of money just enough above the standard Ph.D. scale to make it seem legitimate and sound tempting." As a matter of fact, Father O'Connor continued, the advertisements never stopped running even when Hawkins had hired a qualified man because Hawkins could count on keeping a Ph.D. only a month or two before the naïve scholar realized he was being used to assess the contents and value of stolen documents, sometimes authentic, sometimes ersatz. It was a tribute to Hawkins' powers of deception that he was able to keep them as long as he did, but then Father O'Connor was sure that Victor Hawkins served Satan as an anxious servant and whatever success he had was due to this diabolic co-operation.

Hawkins was American by birth, Father O'Connor supposed, since he had an American passport, but he affected British ways and had lived in London a good many years. He had produced pornographic items for export, using as a sheltering occupation a business in rare books. When he was found out he skipped to France, where quite by accident he discovered the financial opportunities that lay in old manuscripts. It took him no time at all to become known as an outlet for unusual and significant items with no questions asked.

Once again he was forced out of a country by circumstance —knowing nothing about the manuscripts he handled, he had put up for auction a rare little Flemish history, holographic, which had been stolen from an Italian museum only the week before. He migrated to New York, where he appeared to reform, putting his ill-gotten gains into the stock market and retiring to a country estate on the Hudson to pursue his hobby of painting miniatures.

However, once again this quiet life was merely a front for other activities and within a year there was a scandal in New

York, something sufficiently heinous in a town sated with common sexual scandal to propel him to Japan. Here he established his notorious building and dabbled in manuscripts on the side, procuring some of them legitimately and all of them more carefully, hiring men who knew about such things to preclude a repetition of the French episode, contenting himself with the more minor and less recognizable items. Japan was a fertile place for such an operation; there was a vast accumulation of manuscript documents in Japan which had been taken from monasteries and research libraries by the Germans in Europe and Africa and by the Japanese forces in Asia, hidden against the time when they could be brought out and sold. That time was now.

It was fortunate for Hawkins that a man like Cooper had come along. Cooper had exiled himself from God, working with Hawkins simply because he did not care one way or the other, and Hawkins was taking advantage of this. And when the time came that Hawkins was punished for his sins—and this time would surely come—Cooper would suffer right along with him. He had allowed himself to be used; he knew full well what he was doing.

"It really boils down to saving Cooper from himself," Father O'Connor said, "and if you use the word 'lovers' in its true and larger meaning, I would say that's his first step back toward the normal world he abandoned." He looked at her quizzically, waiting for her to confirm his hope.

"No," she said. "I wasn't using the word 'lovers' like that, only in the physical sense."

"And friends?"

"I'm not even sure of that," she said. "At times he seems to be interested in me and what I think. But he really won't let himself get involved. I have the feeling I could sink in Tokyo Bay tomorrow without making the slightest ripple in his psyche."

"How do you feel about him?"

The question startled her. "I don't know," she said.

"Do you love him?"

"No," she said. "I don't think I do, anyway."

"Would you marry him if you had the chance?"

"Yes," she said truthfully, "I suppose I would."

"It would be his salvation if he did marry you," the priest said. "Somebody needs to establish an influence over him and bring him back."

"I'm not sure anybody ever will," she said. "He's pretty unreachable."

"Under present conditions, yes," Father O'Connor said pointedly, dryly. "You can't continue to be lovers in the physical sense. But I'm sure I don't need to lecture you along those lines. You're a perceptive woman. You can project a course of action to a logical and inevitable conclusion."

She nodded slightly and made no answer. She wondered if life was really so simple for the priest that he thought he could solve things by establishing a vicarious father-daughter relationship with her, giving her paternal advice against going to bed with a man, implying that happiness was a matter of abstention. He had no idea of those complex and nameless hungers which continually beset her, the tangle of emotions beyond her control which she could not even sort out, much less understand and channel into a new course.

"Perhaps," she said, returning to the original purpose which had brought her here, "perhaps I could get closer to him if I knew what he was working on. But he never mentions his work to me. Does he discuss it with you?"

"Very little," Father O'Connor said unhappily. "I have a natural curiosity about his work but I have never tried to pry. I do know he's working on the Baum-Brenner papers at present. At least, I suppose he is."

"Do you have any idea what kind of material is in those papers?"

"None."

73

"I heard a rumor at the Press Club that the Baum-Brenner papers are supposed to have the Q document in them."

"Foolishness," the priest sighed. "Foolishness. The Q document doesn't exist at all. And personally, although I don't speak for the Church in this, I think it borders on heresy to believe that it *could* exist. The belief itself is a denial of basic faith in the divine inspiration of the scriptures." A bell rang in the distance. Through the window beyond Father O'Connor she saw the buildings disgorge the black-uniformed students onto the lawn again. The priest stood up and brushed the tips of his fingers against the front of his cassock. "I'm afraid I have to be going," he said. "My schedule seems relentless sometimes. But I'm very happy you came to see me and I think our meeting has been most worth while. I'm sure God will provide the solution to all our problems."

She felt vaguely disturbed as she walked back to Sendagaya Station. She had hoped to get something tangible from the priest, information perhaps, or a germ of insight which would show her how to proceed with Cooper, but he had done nothing except confuse the issue, making her question an area of her life which she preferred to leave unexplored.

2

For the first time in months Cooper missed his Friday night meeting with Willa, interrupting his translation only long enough to go next door out of politeness and excuse himself. He had been working since one o'clock in the afternoon on the first Roman manuscript: it was tedious work and he was engrossed in it and did not want to lose his train of thought. Surprisingly enough, Willa seemed to understand. She made no attempt to make him feel uncomfortable because he had disappointed her. However, since she had already prepared his dinner, she took it to his room on a tray. He acknowledged it with a nod of his head before he turned back to peer through the magnifying glass at the manuscript that lay before him. He did not notice when she left the room.

The manuscript which he was deciphering so laboriously was not dated. It had been written by a public scribe in behalf of an illiterate Roman soldier named Lucretius Septimus who was stationed in the barracks of the Praetorian Guard in the city of Rome, serving as a jailer. "Lucretius Septimus sends greetings to Tigellinius, commander of the Praetorian Guards." Cooper had to think to place Tigellinius. Yes, of course, the infamous cohort of the equally notorious Poppaea Sabina. Tigellinius had come to power after the former commander, Burrus, had been poisoned, about A.D. 60, perhaps a little later in the reign of the Emperor Nero.

From the first part of the letter, it was obvious that Lucretius Septimus wanted something from his commander. He began with a brief summary of his service to Rome. He had served the Emperor well in the trouble stemming from the death of the Emperor's mother, Agrippina the younger, and had been responsible in part for the tremendously successful games which celebrated the return of Nero Claudius Caesar Augustus Germanicus from his residence in Campania. Only last year, Lucretius Septimus pointed out, he had survived the destruction of the IXth Legion in Britannia and had aided Suetonius Paulinus in the suppression of that rebellion, suffering in the process a most grievous wound.

Now, in recompense, Lucretius Septimus was merely asking for the privilege of drawing on the reservoir of prisoners held captive in the Praetorian barracks and surrounding quarters to establish himself as a procurer of gladiators, and to set up a school for their training. There followed a list of the prisoners Lucretius Septimus considered possibilities: a pair of Samnites, a single retiarius, a Thracian, and an assortment of Roman citizens who had been condemned to death and somehow overlooked by the officials who had combed the jails looking for men who could be sent to the arena.

Incorporated in this list was the name Gaius Claudius Paulus, and Lucretius Septimus devoted more than ordinary attention to his case, simply because he considered this man an interesting oddity.

He is a short and stocky man with a fearful countenance and is possessed of demons, a condition which has required him to be set apart in his own house. One night, when visited by the centurion Julius Octavius, who is friendly to him, he attempted to choke him to death and such was his strength that it required three centurions to subdue him. I would match him with a retiarius. It should be interesting to witness a cunning man of strength, armed with an ax against the cast net and the trident. He is convicted of murder and with dispensation from the Emperor could provide an interesting entertainment. Since his life is offensive to Hermes, I would use him in the games dedicated to his glory.

The remainder of the petition was couched in the courtly, formal language of the scribe, calling for the blessing of Tigellinius' patron god to preserve him in health and prosperity.

It was midnight before Cooper finished the translation and he was immediately aware of its implied significance. There was no question of the identity of Gaius Claudius Paulus, if the document itself could be proven authentic.

Anxious as he was to begin on the next set of photostats, he could not contemplate it. His head was splitting and he was dizzy and nauseous as well. Clicking off the lamp, he moved back from the writing table, almost upsetting the untouched tray of food Willa had brought him. He had no appetite but he used the cup of cold tea to wash down a half dozen aspirins before he unrolled his bed and collapsed on it.

He awoke the next morning with the sure conviction that he was going to be sick but he felt better once he had shaved and forced down his morning tea. He made a recheck of the translation in the bright wash of sunlight from the open shutters and then took a cursory look at the next document, which was written in Greek and signed by Gaius Claudius Paulus.

Placing it beneath the magnifying glass, he was about to begin when there was a light knock on the door and Willa came in, looking irritatingly cheerful.

"God, you look terrible," she said happily. "Big dark circles under your eyes, a living picture of the morning after." She nudged the untouched tray with one bare foot and looked at him with mock reproach. "But nobody ever accused me of lacking a big heart. I'm capable of forgiving anything."

"What makes you so cheerful this morning?" he said.

"It's a sunshiny day for a change," she said. "Harvey used to say he could tell what kind of weather we'd been having in Washington by looking at my face. Three weeks of overcast and I get bone mean. Come on to my room. I found a pound of real American coffee yesterday."

The thought of coffee appealed to him. He allowed himself to be persuaded. It was the first time he had visited her room in daylight and he found it pleasant with the shutters opened to the day and the smell of coffee brewing. Willa was humming to herself. He was feeling considerably better by the time she placed a circular cake in the middle of the table and sat down across from him.

"I knew there was a human being under that pall of gloom," she said. "Are you always like this in the morning?"

"Most of the time," he said.

"That's good to know. Now me, I get up every morning thinking it's going to be a good day. It takes until about noon for me to realize how miserable I really am." She bit into a piece of the coffeecake. "You're going to ruin your eyes, you know that, working at night with a lamp like the one you have. What time did you get to bed?"

"About midnight, I guess."

"You must be working on something interesting. Have some cake. I found a baker on the Ginza who used to work in Los Angeles."

"No, thanks." Unexpectedly, he found that he had a strong

desire to discuss what he had found, to use her as a sounding board. "It's a curious thing," he said, "but when you deal with as many ancient documents through the years as I do, so much junk for the most part, you still have the feeling that someday you're going to find one that will alter the whole history of a given era. And then, when you actually do find a document like that, you don't believe it."

"You found something like that?" she said absently. "How about some more coffee?"

He shook his head. "I'm not sure, of course," he said, "and I won't be until I get into the supplementary documents and have a chance to check the originals. It could be a forgery, a very clever one, but at this point I doubt it. In the first place, Gaius Claudius Paulus is only mentioned as one man on a list of men. The emphasis is not on him at all but on the character of the soldier who wrote the letter to his commanding officer. And yet, quite casually, this illiterate jailer knocks two thousand years of history and tradition into a cocked hat. Because he says Gaius Claudius Paulus has been condemned for murder—not for treason, not for political crimes. Not only does Lucretius Septimus call him a murderer but a madman as well. It could be coincidence, but he also mentions that this madman attacked his benefactor, a centurion named Julius, a name which is prominently connected with our prisoner in other histories. The time element is right too, because Suetonius Paulinus had subdued the rebellious Britons in A.D. 61, and the petition puts that rebellion in the past by about a year. That would place the imprisonment of our man at about A.D. 62, a date with which tradition agrees. But if he was a murderer, then that implies a victim. And the question inevitably arises, whom did he kill and why? And why was this murder so carefully concealed that this is the first breath of it?"

"It all sounds very interesting," she said, just a bit too brightly. "But I haven't got the slightest idea what you're

78

talking about. What kind of papers have you got in there anyway?"

"If I'm not wrong," Cooper said quietly, "and I don't think I am, I'm about to start translating a letter written by the same man Lucretius Septimus calls a murderer, Gaius Claudius Paulus, known for two thousand years as the Apostle Paul."

Four

1

COOPER did not go to Victor until he had translated the Pauline letter, an arduous work which took a week to complete. It was addressed to Timothy in Ephesus, contained a brief account of Paul's trouble with an unidentified man—presumably Timothy already knew his name—and ended with an appeal for Timothy to understand something which could be potentially destructive to his belief.

He first came to me in Troas, a man beset by demons, and I reasoned with him, knowing he meant to do us harm and had it within his power to accomplish it. He brought me certain papers to prove himself and so dishonored not only himself but his father as well. I reasoned with him. I told him he condemned himself if he continued and yet he did not desist and after a while the Lord struck him down and he lay as if dead.

I left the papers he had brought me with Carpus and set out on the road to Assos, leaving the others to go by water, wanting to meditate alone and consider what should be done. On the road to Assos, I was overtaken by him. Once again he came to me, not seeking the truth, but wanting only to do harm to us and our Lord unless he should receive what he demanded.

When my words availed not, once more the Lord struck him down and this time his spirit fled his body. And this was witnessed by Alexander the coppersmith, who knows the truth and yet speaks it not, bearing false witness of me to Tigellinius and to our brethren in Rome. I care not for myself. My race in the Lord is now run and I am finished but I must preserve from destruction what he has built. You must come here at once, bringing the things I asked for, not for my comfort because I have no need of comfort except in him, but to repudiate Alexander and inform the brethren here of his true nature which I cannot, being sentenced to death on his account. Onesiphorus has returned to me and Luke remains constant. Be steadfast and judge not that which the Lord has caused to be done by his most unworthy servant.

Once it was complete, Cooper put a copy of it in his attaché case with the translation of the Lucretius letter and went to Victor's place. Victor was not in his office. Instead, Cooper found him in a narrow patio garden adjoining the building on the west, his face protected from the hazy sunshine by a wide-brimmed straw hat, his neck sheltered by a white silk scarf. He gave Cooper an acknowledging glance and then turned back to the miniature mounted on the easel, daubing with a hairline brush at a composition of wax fruit.

"You must forgive me for not shaking your hand and giving you a proper welcome, dear boy, but unfortunately I am caught between the Scylla of caution and the Charybdis of necessity. It is absolutely imperative for me to utilize every second of sunlight for my painting and yet the slightest bit of sunlight has an adverse effect on my skin. I am one of those unfortunate ones, dear boy, but I try to look on the brighter side of things. Since my tolerance is so low, I accept every moment I am in the sunlight as a precious privilege. Where others squander, I hoard."

He rolled the tip of the brush into a smear of carmine on the palette and delicately edged what appeared to be an apple. "In case you might be wondering, I am striving to achieve a certain hard brilliance in a still-life miniature while avoiding the mechanical quality which always comes if you carry it to the extreme." For the next twenty minutes he said nothing at all, frowning furiously at the small enamel surface in front of him, concentrating on the edge of the apple.

Finally Itsugi appeared on the terrace. Victor looked at him with the expression of a small boy compelled to yield to a larger discipline. "I suppose I must quit," he said. Putting down his palette and brush, he stood up stiffly, looking toward Cooper. "Now, my dear boy, come along and have something to eat and we can talk about more important matters."

The food was served in Victor's office but Victor did not eat much. He made a great display of his fatigue, wiping his eyes with a silk handkerchief and examining his face in the mirror to search out the slightest flush of sunburn before he sat down at the table. Evidently there was none. He dipped his fingers in a silver bowl of water and dried them before he picked up his knife and fork to dissect the rock cornish hen on his plate. "I try to spend at least an hour a day at my painting," he said, "but unfortunately there are so many things which arise to interrupt and frustrate that desire: the exigencies of business—you can have no idea how much paperwork there is to a business like mine, veritable mountains of it, dear boy—as well as the antipathy of my skin toward the ultraviolet rays." The knife ground against bone. Delicately, Victor twisted the thigh loose from the carcass. "Do we have any problems this afternoon, dear boy?"

"No problems," Cooper said. "As a matter of fact, there's a possibility you may have picked up something extremely valuable."

The chicken thigh trembled in mid-air. Slowly Victor put it down. "We have something good after all?"

Cooper told him what he had found, opening the attaché case to hand him the translations. The papers rustled in

Victor's hands. "A hundred and fifty thousand dollars at least," he said. "At least that." A momentary cloud of doubt passed over his hope. "You are sure about this, aren't you?"

"Not completely," Cooper said. "I'd have to see the originals for that. But the documents have the right feel to them."

"Would you call it premature if I began to sound out the Red Chinese?" Victor asked.

"If I were you I'd wait. There's a connection between the first two documents so it's possible the remaining documents might be related, a continuation perhaps. And you ought to be ready to follow up, once you start the controversy."

"Controversy?"

"It should be a big one. Tradition has it that Paul was tried on a charge of treason, of agitating against the public peace, and that he was acquitted. Supposedly, he went to Spain for a couple of years. That view is supported by Chrysostom, Jerome, Clement, and a dozen other early Christian writers. Then, much later, Paul is supposed to have come back to Rome again, where he was tried on the charge of urging the Christians to set fire to the city. He was found guilty and executed. But in the documents we have there's no mention of treason. Paul has been condemned to death as a murderer and is considered so insignificant that Lucretius Septimus thinks about using him in the arena."

"Whom do you suppose he killed?"

"I have no idea."

"It really isn't important who the victim was," Victor said, stripping the meat from the bone with the gentle pressure of his teeth. "But I am frankly curious, my dear boy, to know how you really feel about this matter, inwardly, I mean. I know you are an objective person and devoted to scholarship but this does rather decimate a Christian hero, doesn't it, demoting him, so to speak? And perhaps as you get further into this you may experience a change of heart."

83

"It makes no difference to me one way or the other. I just want to make sure the documents are authentic."

"I am relieved." Victor smiled vaguely as he finished the thigh. "It's not that I doubt your honesty, understand, but I had the unfortunate experience of buying a Japanese Baptist girl—and a marvelous specimen she was too, absolutely the most exquisite mouth I have ever seen—who suddenly, at the height of her career, had pangs of conscience and decided to go into youth work or something of the sort. So you can understand my sense of caution."

Victor washed his hands in the fingerbowl again and then opened his desk to remove a stack of new bills. "I prefer new bank notes," he said, counting them out. "Can you imagine how many filthy places an American dollar must find itself in before it finally comes to you? And a Japanese bank note must be even worse. So I get all my money directly from the bank, nothing but new currency. One has to protect oneself, don't you think?"

Cooper spent the afternoon and evening using the library facilities of Meiji University, fruitlessly tracking down references to Martin Baum-Brenner. There was no published record of any work he had done for the Nazis. By the time he reached Shimbashi again he was suddenly very tired and he stopped at a bathhouse where he fell asleep on the massage table. It was nearly ten before he woke and dressed, feeling refreshed and ravenously hungry. He went to a restaurant where he had ham and eggs—which had the flavor of fish— and then he went back to his room, clicking on the light with the vague intention of working all night.

A note from Itsugi lay on the writing table—apparently the old messenger had been here during the late afternoon—and he sat down to read it. Itsugi had researched Cooper's queries with the technicians and was now responding with the answers. As far as the photostats were concerned, twelve different exposures had been taken of the documents with varying controls of light and aperture, including infrared, and what Cooper now had represented the best of the lot. The technicians were continuing to experiment and if they came up with anything better Cooper would be provided with a new set.

The photostats were in the same order in which the original documents had been found in the trunk in which they had been carried out of China. There was no guarantee that this was the same order in which Baum-Brenner had placed them. And there were no more documents in the collection. The trunk itself had been systematically dissembled in case some of the missing fragments might have sifted down into the velvet lining, but nothing extra had been found.

He shifted the next Greek document into place, preparatory to beginning its translation, and then, so he could continue his work without interruption once it was under way, he took the teakettle out of the cupboard and filled it with water, placing it on the hibachi. It was then that he heard a rustling noise and a slight exhalation of breath, almost like a sigh. He froze where he was, both startled and alarmed. Then, slowly, he turned to look behind him.

The girl sat against the wall, perfectly motionless, her eyes afraid, as if she was certain he would strike her now that she had been discovered. It was only as he twisted the gooseneck lamp to throw the light on her face that he realized this was the same girl he had saved from the beating in Victor's office.

"What are you doing here?" he said. "How did you get here?"

The girl cowered slightly. Apparently she understood nothing except the belligerent tone of his voice. Despite his irritation, he knew nothing would be gained by frightening her. He would have to get an interpreter before he could hope to communicate with her, that much was certain, so he softened his tone of voice and told her in English to stay put. He

85

would be back in a minute. He went next door to use Willa's telephone to call the desk, asking that the maid who served his room be sent up immediately.

She came to his room within ten minutes, apprehensive at being called in the middle of the night. As if by habit, she took it for granted he wanted his tea prepared and this she did, kneeling by the hibachi and never once looking at the girl as she interpreted the questions and the answers. It was a frustrating conversation; the communication was imperfect at best. The maid herself spoke faulty English and she insisted on embroidering the girl's replies with honorifics. Cooper would ask a question, the maid would nod, sighing before she transmitted the question to the girl, who would answer in frightened monosyllables which in turn would be reinterpreted in a garrulous torrent of politeness. From this halting exchange, Cooper managed to put together the skeleton of the girl's story.

Being at Victor's place had frightened her. She had been forced to stay in a small room without windows and at night there was a constant shuffling of feet down the hall past her door and she occasionally heard the voices of men, loud, drunken voices, and she had been so afraid that she could not sleep. She had run away once but her mother had forced her to go back. This time she had made friends with the old man who served as Victor's messenger and persuaded the old man to bring her to Cooper's place, since Cooper had befriended her and saved her from a beating.

"Ask her what she intends to do now," Cooper said to the maid. "As she can see, this is a very small room. She can't stay here."

In response to the maid's translation, the girl said nothing. She simply lowered her face into her hands and began to weep. How early a girl picked up the tricks of a woman, weeping at the slightest provocation. Well, he felt sorry for the girl and he could sympathize with her predicament, but he did not intend to get involved. He was not sure of the social system in Japan, but there was bound to be some juvenile authority, some facility to handle children of this sort. He was about to ask the maid to notify the Metropolitan Police when he stopped short. That would solve nothing. The police would merely notify the mother and the mother would notify Victor and Victor would fly into one of his petulant rages because Cooper had not called him first, considering his financial interest in this child. Cooper had no desire to be caught in the middle of so potentially volatile a situation, but at the same time he couldn't bring himself to turn her out.

He asked the maid if there was a vacant room in the hotel and the maid said no. He asked her if she would put the girl up for the night but this too was impossible. The maid herself slept in an anteroom off the kitchen with four other maids and there was literally no space for another person, however small, to lie down. Finally Cooper told the maid to put another sleeping mat in the corner of his room. The girl could spend this one night here and he would make other arrangements in the morning.

The girl lay down on the mat which the maid unrolled for her, making no sound, pulling the thick quilts up over her head, turning her face to the wall as if to make herself as inconspicuous as possible. Once the maid had left the room, Cooper felt uncomfortably mute, as if he had suddenly lost his voice.

Blowing his nose, pouring himself some tea, Cooper sat down at the worktable and pulled the magnifying glass into place, intending to start the translation, but his mind refused to co-operate. The girl looked so insignificantly small under those quilts, so damned small, and watching her lie there, frozen, motionless, he could not help but remember his own daughter and the fact that she was dead.

He felt an echo of the old familiar pain, a smothering sadness, and he told himself he was not going to risk going through that again, not for an unknown girl he couldn't help even if he wanted to.

After a half hour at his writing desk he realized he was not going to be able to work. He swallowed three aspirins and lay down on his own mat, but the sound of the girl's breathing from across the room kept him awake for a long time.

2

The complication of the girl in Cooper's room was something Willa could not have foreseen and did not understand. She had known nothing of the girl until one afternoon when she went next door to borrow something and found the door locked. She was sure Cooper was there—she always heard him when he went out—so she knocked persistently until he answered. When he opened the door and asked her in, the girl was cleaning the room and Cooper introduced her as My-oko Something-or-other, telling Willa it was imperative that no one should know the girl was here, not for the present. He would explain it to her later.

At first Willa indulged in all kinds of speculations about the girl and her reason for being in Cooper's room, but she could not believe that Cooper's intent was in any way immoral. She reasoned that the girl might be the daughter of one of Cooper's friends, staying with him temporarily while her parents were away, but that seemed unlikely. In the first place Cooper had no friends here except the priest and Hawkins, and in the second place the girl was a Japanese and Cooper didn't even speak the language. In any event, Willa could count on not seeing much of Cooper for the time being, so she explored in a different direction, gathering background on Baum-Brenner.

She went to the Israeli Legation in Shibuya to see if they could provide her with any information on Baum-Brenner only to find that they too were confused by his apparent political schizophrenia. It was an unofficial view, of course, expressed to her off the record by a subofficial—she could not remember his title—but the Israeli government had never established a clear-cut policy regarding Baum-Brenner. As Martin Baum, he typified the rabbinical resistance to Hitler and had become something of a folk hero for his bravery in those terrible days in Warsaw. On the other hand, as Martin Brenner, he had betrayed his people, ostensibly to insure his own safety and comfort.

These two facets of his behavior tended to nullify each other; public sentiment could not vilify a hero just as public sentiment could not memorialize a traitor. The matter would not be resolved, therefore, until the Israeli government had more information on his death and had learned why he was executed. If he had been overcome with remorse at his collaboration, repenting his betrayal, refusing to work with the Nazis any longer, if he had been sent to the gas ovens for that reason, under the name of Martin Baum, then he would be redeemed in the eyes of his people. If, on the other hand, he had been executed as Martin Brenner, simply because the Nazis had no further use for him, then his guilt was certain and irrefutable.

The Israeli government was willing to co-operate in any way to help her clarify this matter, and the subofficial volunteered to wire Tel Aviv and to initiate a search of the records for the present whereabouts of Baum-Brenner's daughter and her son. Anna Klaus had visited Israel once in the years after the war—her husband was dead and she was earning her living as a painter and interior decorator—to exhibit her work in a one-woman show in the hope of obtaining commissions. Although there had been no active hostility against her because of her father, there had been no interest in her work either. Only a handful of people came to her exhibition and nobody bought anything and she left soon after, giving her destination as Australia. Whether she was still there was doubtful, but perhaps Tel Aviv would have some information on the matter.

Once Willa had done this, she could go no further. What happened next would depend to a large extent on the information she received and on the attitude of the man next door.

3

Cooper's decision to protect the girl came about simply because he could think of nothing else to do with her. When he awoke on the morning after her arrival, he found that she had already cleaned the room and was making tea for him. When she saw him looking at her she immediately withdrew to the far side of the room and sat down, regarding him with solemn, apprehensive eyes.

"There's no need for that," he said, irritated, standing up. "I'm not going to bite you." She made no response. He groaned in frustration. "Go ahead, make the tea. The maid should be up here pretty soon and we'll try to figure out what we're going to do with you." Picking up the teakettle, he thrust it toward her in a vague attempt to show her what he wanted; when she made no move to take it he poured enough hot water into the basin to proceed with his shaving while she watched him warily, as if at any second he might turn on her. He was halfway through his shaving when, quite suddenly, she spoke aloud, so startling him that he nicked himself.

"I stay here, *ne?*" she said.

"You speak English?"

"Yis."

"I give up," Cooper said, exasperated. "Why didn't you mention this last night, when I was trying to find somebody to interpret?"

"Speak skoshi Engrish onry," the girl said. "Not much."

"Well," Cooper said, "it simplifies everything a hundred

per cent. At least I won't have to get the maid up here every time I want to say something to you." He gave her a skeptical look. "You can understand what I'm saying?"

The girl nodded dumbly.

"Then fix the tea while I finish shaving."

As they talked over breakfast, he found that her broken English, liberally salted with army expletives, was quite adequate for communication. She had the normal resiliency of any eleven-year-old child and once she realized he meant her no harm, she chattered away without the least trace of self-consciousness. It was amazing, he thought, listening to her, that a child could be so used to misfortune that she considered it commonplace.

She had lived many places, from Kobe to Sendai, and she had had many fathers, some of them American soldiers, some of them Japanese businessmen and laborers, all kinds of men, some of them nice and some of them not. Some of them had brought her presents and treated her well and some of them had beaten and kicked her. She had stayed with her mother only spasmodically, when the mother was living with a man who either liked or tolerated children. When her mother was living with a man who did not want children around, Myoko went to live with her uncle, who had a small farm in the hills near Kamakura. She enjoyed these times. Her uncle was a pleasant drunk who could not work and the land was tended by relatives who were good to her. As to brothers and sisters, Myoko knew she had at least two of the former and four of the latter. It was possible she had more but could not be sure. Sometimes after a long absence her mother would come home carrying a new baby and then the baby would disappear. Myoko didn't know what happened to them; perhaps her mother sold them just as she had sold Myoko's older sister and Myoko herself.

There was no judgment in Myoko's voice as she talked. She was not really unhappy with her mother for selling her. She did not like going against her mother's wishes and she had tried to make herself stay at the house of the Englishman, following her sister's example, but she could not do it. She wanted to stay here with Cooper for a little while, she said, until Itsugi stopped looking for her, and then she would go to her mother and persuade her to return the money and let her come home again.

To this proposal Cooper said nothing, still resisting any sense of involvement in her problem, but he knew that what she hoped for would never happen. The woman he had seen in Victor's place, haggling over the price she wanted for her daughter, would be unlikely to return any part of the purchase money. She was without maternal feeling.

After breakfast the girl cleared the dishes and then asked if he had any money, wanting to shop for food and prepare his meals. She had cooked for her uncle and he seemed to enjoy it. Cooper gave her a thousand yen and when she left he was convinced he would never see her again. He told himself he was relieved to have the problem taken out of his hands, but once the room was silent and empty around him, he felt an irrational moment of sadness, a shadow of bereavement.

He forced his mind into the patterned discipline of work and almost immediately forgot the girl as he was caught up in the contents of the document on his stand. This manuscript was written in far more coherent language than that which Paul had used, and Cooper was intrigued from the very first line.

Lucanus to Timotheus, in God our Father and in our Lord Jesus Christ. Grace, mercy, and peace from God our Father and Jesus Christ our Lord.

The letter was a recapitulation of the events which had transpired since Paul's last letter to Timothy. It contained an indirect reference to the two trials Paul had undergone in front of the Praefectus Urbi, the first on the charge of propagating a new religion (*religio nova et illicita*), of which he had been acquitted, and the second on a charge which Luke did not mention specifically but simply referred to as "that charge which was supported by Alexander the coppersmith." On this charge (homicide) Paul had faced the city prefect and the Council of Assessors and been found guilty. The verdict had been passed on to the Emperor, who confirmed it and pronounced a sentence of death.

And on the next morning, suffering the cold and the snow which had fallen during the night so that the ground was slippery underfoot, he was led in chains beyond the walls of the city and onto the Ostia road by a company of soldiers. And at the appointed place of death, even as the speculators issued forth one of their number who drew his sword, Paul was of great courage and sinking to his knees called to our Lord to prepare the way for him. And then he spoke to me, saying, "Tell Timotheus to honor that which I ask of him or I die in vain." And at that point they seized him and, leading him to a stake set in the ground for that purpose, they bound him to it and stripped him of his raiment, and scourged him with sticks until he fainted and then the soldier stepped forward with his sword and with one blow severed the head from the body. We took the earthly remains of our brother Paul and buried them in the catacombs. He is now at peace in the Lord and great is the rejoicing in heaven at his arrival and it is left to us who remain to prove the strength of our faith and the truth of our convictions. I have knowledge of that which Paul requested you to do and I can testify that the papers are both false and dangerous to the cause of our Lord, being of Satan in their origins. Satan is a wily adversary. He attempts to discredit our Master in many ways, knowing the end is at hand and his doom is fixed and sure, and he has the power to make the truth seem false and to seduce men from their rightful purpose. In all conscience I say to you, I would have done the same had John of Arimathea approached me instead of our brother, so slandering the name of him who should be exalted above all the world and attempting his defamation. I know of my own knowledge these

93

things contained in the papers to be untrue; while I stayed in Caesarea, I talked with those who were privileged to walk with him and he was witnessed when he arose from the dead on that glorious day of resurrection. Never to the moment of his crucifixion had he met Joseph of Arimathea or had there been words between them. This man had not the strength of his conviction to proclaim him openly. He believed in secret until that time when his heart was opened and through compassion he was persuaded to come forth and declare himself. I have talked with those who knew Joseph of Arimathea well in his last days and all report he was a sincere believer in our master and acted in love for him in requesting his body from the cross. He testified to the resurrection of our Lord until he was an old man and was called to be with him in heaven. Therefore the letter which purports to be in his hand cannot be his and should be destroyed. As to the other, it proves itself to be false, notwithstanding the points of truth it may contain. For it is the first rule of the liar to so mix his lie with truth that the two cannot be separated and that he who should hear the truth and know it to be true should believe the lie also. That this letter should cause doubt is not surprising. This was the reason for which it was written and the lie has been skillfully drawn. It too must be destroyed and the truth set straight again. Our brother Paul suffered the sword for this cause and we can do no less than his example, holding to belief regardless of the cost. So in the name of our Lord and through your love for him, do what is asked of you. Our brother was sorely distressed that you did not come to him in his last hours, but he held no malice toward you, only the love which we have been told to hold, one for the other. The salutation of me, Lucanus, with my own hand. Grace be with you.

By the time he finished the translation it was late afternoon and twilight had begun to set in over the city, accompanied by the characteristic blue haze of smoke and fog which was always more pronounced in the hour preceding sunset. Standing at his window, he was restless for the first time in many months. Despite his nagging curiosity about the remaining two documents he had no desire to go on working. He thought

94

about going to Willa but he needed neither the conversation nor the consuming physical expense of sex. Perhaps it was that he had now completed what Stevenson called "the withdrawal period" and was ready to go home.

The old relationships he had known there could never be the same, of course, because something had been burned out of him. But his curiosity had been ignited and these documents raised a hundred questions that needed answers and he thought how good it would be to discuss them with Stevenson and to have the resources of a large reference library close at hand. However, as the documents raised new questions, they also brought an old one closer to solution. It was becoming increasingly clear to him why the Nazis had been so interested in the work of Baum-Brenner that they should have been willing to forget his ancestry and his vocation, allowing him to carry out his research and his translations. It had been desperately important to the Nazis to downgrade the Christian religion and these documents offered every prospect of doing just that.

He was about to put on his coat and go for a walk when there was a knock on the door and he opened it to find Myoko standing in the hall, shivering from the cold, her arms full of parcels. He helped her put the packages on the table and then he took a blanket from the closet and put it around her as she knelt beside the hibachi, extending her hands to be warmed by the coals. She had blunt fingers with the nails chewed back to the quick and there was a mottled bluish cast to her skin. Obviously she suffered from chilblains.

"You damn mad at me, *ne?*" she said.

"No," he said. "And you shouldn't go around using words like 'damn.' It's not a word for little girls."

"Oh?"

"What have you been doing all day?"

The question prompted a long and rambling story which the girl told as she rubbed her hands together, wincing as the

95

circulation returned to her fingers, continuing to talk as she moved to the table to prepare a noxious-looking dinner of rice and raw fish. She had gone out to buy food with the money he had given her, but when she reached the street stalls she had decided on impulse to go home for a visit.

At the moment her mother was living with a man in Koiwa who didn't like children—he was very old and had a shop there. Myoko's mother had the status of a second wife, living in a large house with the first wife. Myoko had an idea that New Father might permit her to stay if she demonstrated how quietly useful she could be around the house.

She took the train to Koiwa and when she reached the village square with the ancient movie theater across from the railroad station, a chilly wind was blowing in off the bay and she was shivering with the cold. It would have taken no more than ten minutes to walk to New Father's house but she could not take the direct route because New Father walked back and forth between his shop and the house a number of times a day and she was afraid of running into him if she followed the main road.

So it took her about an hour to go around the village, through alleys, and along the edge of a rice paddy until she came to the high back wall which marked the boundary of New Father's property. The gate was locked and she could not ring the bell for fear New Father might be home, so she crept past the side of the house, following the narrow alley formed by the wall on the east side of New Father's house and that of the house next door. She hoped to find something she could use to climb up on to look over the wall and into the house. Ordinarily her mother spent most of the daylight hours in the room next to the garden and Myoko intended to attract her attention and have her open the back gate to let her in.

Unfortunately she could find nothing in the alley to stand on. She went through the alley to the street which fronted the

96

house, and she stayed there a long time, standing perfectly still, trying to keep from shivering as she looked down the street for any sign of New Father. There was no traffic in the street, only one car parked across from New Father's gate, and she was sure it belonged to the important son of the aging couple who lived directly across from New Father.

When she was sure New Father was not in the street she moved very slowly around the corner and approached the front gate of the house. Usually it was left unlocked, but to-day it was not. She was reaching for the bell—she had to take the chance—when she heard footsteps and turned just in time to avoid Itsugi as he emerged from the parked car and dashed across the street to grab at her. As he reached out for her she ducked and darted away and since he could not stop him-self he ran into the wall and fell down.

She ran back into the alley, scared to death, and then doubled back on the far side of the house and ran across a narrow bean field to the shed next to the rice paddy where Nomara-san kept his ox. She went in and fell down by the side of the great beast. As she lay there in the straw, her eye pressed to a crack in the boards, she saw Itsugi come out of the alley. He ran halfway across the bean field before he stopped, breathing heavily as he listened to the faint wind, and looked out across the rice paddies. She could hear him muttering to himself; he was making threats against her.

After he had stood there a long time his eye fell upon the shed and he started to walk toward it. She began to cry, hold-ing her hands over her mouth to keep any sound from leaking out. She was sure he would kill her if he found her. But he turned and went back toward the alley. Perhaps he had seen somebody at the far side of the paddy; perhaps he was afraid somebody might see him entering the shed and think he was trying to steal the ox. She watched him go into the alley and then she sank down into the straw and allowed herself to cry aloud.

She stayed where she was until the ox began to get restless, shifting in the stall, tramping his big hoofs just inches from where she lay, and then she crept out of the shed to stand next to the door, where she could not be seen from the alley. It was cold standing there in the shadows, and finally she decided to take the chance. Moving away from the shed, she ran along the edge of the rice paddy, taking the long way back to the railroad station. She was not followed.

When she reached the station she did not take a train right away. She was cold and hungry. Buying a sack of roasted chestnuts from a vender, she went into the movie theater. She could not describe the movie very well because she had seen so little of it. The theater was warm and she fell asleep as soon as she had eaten the chestnuts. When she woke up she took the train back to Shimbashi, bought the groceries, and then came here.

Cooper ate the rice and fish from a sense of duty, watching her as she wolfed her food down, her chopsticks clicking. When her bowl was empty she reached over and took the bowl which he had put to one side, finishing the food he had not been able to eat. She poured the tea and then she removed her sleeping mat from the closet and spread it on the floor, with no self-consciousness at all, apparently very much at home. He sat and smoked his pipe, thinking about what she had said. He did not know how much credence to give to her story; he was only too aware of the way children embellished things, but what she said had the ring of truth to it. It was logical that Victor would have sent Itsugi to look for her and whether the escape had been quite as dramatic as she told it was really beside the point. But one thing was certain now: what had happened this afternoon ruled out any possibility of taking the girl home and discussing the problem with her mother.

She lay in her bed, his radio tuned in to American music, and he started to ask her about her schooling, but when he turned to her, he saw that she was sound asleep. What a

98

homely, contradictory little girl she was anyway; how inhumanly she had been used. Finishing his tea and his pipe, he clicked on his table lamp and was about to go to work when he heard a knock on the door and hurried to answer it before the noise disturbed the girl. Opening the door a crack, he peered out to see a middle-aged Japanese in a business suit standing in the hall.

"You are Mr. Cooper?" the man said.

"Yes."

"I am from Mr. Hawkins."

Going out into the hall, Cooper closed the door behind him. The man introduced himself as Mr. Ito and explained that he had been assigned the task of improving the quality of the photostats. He handed Cooper an envelope. "I think you will be better pleased with these," he said. "I reduced the camera aperture and increased the illumination. So these are improved, I think."

Cooper slid the photostats out of the envelope and examined them. Even in the imperfect light of the hallway he could see that these were much better. "Yes, they are," he said. "Thank you."

Ito nodded, smiling, but something about him disturbed Cooper. It was almost as if Ito was listening for something, his head canted to one side, straining to hear the slightest sound from Cooper's room. Cooper could not be sure, of course, but he was filled with a vague foreboding. He was grateful for the covering blare of the radio.

"There wasn't any hurry about these," Cooper said. "The old man could have brought them to me tomorrow."

"He is in the hospital," Ito said. "He was involved in an accident this afternoon."

"Oh?"

"He was struck down by a truck or heavy vehicle when he crossed the Ginza. His eyesight is extremely poor and he didn't see it."

"How bad is it?"

99

"A broken leg. It is most unfortunate."

"Yes," Cooper said. "Most unfortunate."

He waited until Ito had disappeared down the stairs before he went back into his room. His foreboding had changed to alarm now, not because he believed that Victor had been responsible in any way for the old man's accident, but because it occurred to him how extremely foolish he had been to assume that Myoko would be safe in his room. Surely Victor must know by now that the old man had helped the girl escape. Apparently the old man had not told Victor where he had taken Myoko but very shortly Victor would begin to retrace the old man's route, if he had not already done so, and sooner or later he would find the girl unless Cooper did something to prevent it.

He could not keep the girl here much longer, that was certain, yet he had no idea what else he could do with her. He was on alien ground with little knowledge of either the language or the customs. He could not leave Tokyo with her; even in the comparative anonymity of a city as large as this one an American man traveling with a young Japanese girl would stand out and be easy to trace.

He decided to go to Victor's place. There were too many unknown factors to permit him to make a logical decision and he must move cautiously at this point rather than make a precipitate action that might be disastrous. He put the Luke translation in his attaché case and left the girl sleeping in the room with the radio playing. He locked the door and left the key with Willa in case she should hear the girl awaken. Then he went downstairs to find a taxi.

To Cooper's surprise, he found Victor in a buoyant mood. He welcomed Cooper cheerfully and chatted pleasantly about the great business his house was doing tonight; it was completely filled, and not by transients, those furtive and impulsive pleasure seekers, but by groups and individuals of taste and refinement who had called to make reservations and could therefore be counted on to appreciate what they found here. Even in those moments when he was forced to abandon conversation with Cooper to talk on the telephone he was completely relaxed and happy.

Cooper examined a painting on the wall. It was a pleasantly garish bird painted on black velvet, a parrot of some sort. "You must have had a good day," he said. "You seem particularly cheerful this evening."

"I should be, dear boy, because I am a sensitive man and there are those days in which all experience is a caress. I took quite a gamble, a necessary gamble, I must admit, because it was absolutely vital to preclude any possibility of fraud in a project of this magnitude."

"What did you do?"

"I had some scientific tests made on the papyri. A research team at Tokyo University subjected the manuscripts to ultraviolet photography to make sure we had no palimpsests and then took cuttings from uninscribed margins to fix a date by radiocarbon."

"You cut the papyri?"

"An infinitesimal trim, dear boy. You have no idea the giant strides that have been made in the science of radiocarbon dating. But anyway, the results of the tests were returned to me this morning and I know you will find them quite heartening. The carbon 14 tests date all the papyri at about A.D. 50, plus or minus a hundred years. The latitude is quite ample. And ultraviolet reveals no erased writing under the texts which appear on the papyri."

"Who headed the research team?"

"Dr. Ikeda."

"He's a reliable man."

"Most reliable, and he has the further advantage of being absolutely incorruptible, an indispensable attribute. So I must admit, dear boy, when I received his report, I became quite

101

excited. I made some telephone calls and let it be known in the right places that I was prepared to do business and I had my first contact with the Red Chinese government this afternoon. A Dr. Lu Hsiao-p'ing came by to see me. Perhaps you've heard of him?"

"No," Cooper said, "I can't say that I have."

"A most unusual man," Victor said, "a rare combination of politician and scholar. He is a member of the State Administration Council for the People's Republic and at the same time he is one of the leading historians in the Communist bloc. Not of your caliber, dear boy, but excellent in the field of Marxist philosophy."

"Are you going to do business?"

"Eventually, dear boy. He came to inform me the People's Republic intended to take legal steps to press for the return of property belonging to them. I was forced to remind him that this was quite impossible since his government is not even recognized in most of the world and therefore has no recourse to any law. But all of this was extremely devious; neither of us ever came out with a direct fact or opinion. It was necessary for him to test me, so to speak, seeing if I could be intimidated, and now that he knows his present course of action is impossible he will report it to his government and we'll go from there." His expression sobered somewhat now. "I'm afraid you're going to be unhappy with me, my dear boy, but I really was unable to restrain my curiosity, so I put out a few feelers, a few casual inquiries, to see what interest there would be in a Pauline holograph. I received two offers from journalistic syndicates, one from New York for a hundred thousand dollars and the other from London for a little less, sight unseen, with no question of content, providing, of course, that authenticity could be proven. I would not even remotely consider accepting either offer but I merely regard them as straws thrown in the wind, so to speak. You aren't angry with me, are you, dear boy?"

102

"No," Cooper said. "But I still say you'd do better to wait." He opened his case and produced the translation of the Luke letter.

Victor read it, his hands trembling as he laid it down, an exultant yet humble expression on his face. At first Cooper thought he was going to cry; tears welled up before they were blotted away by his handkerchief. "St. Luke on the death of St. Paul," he said. "Utterly fantastic, a priceless document. Do you suppose the other two scrolls we have are the ones he mentions in the letter?"

"I don't know," Cooper said. "It's possible." With the mention of the final documents, he now had a logical opening. "By the way, I was sorry to hear about the old man's getting hurt, the messenger."

"Oh, did Ito tell you? I was hoping you wouldn't hear about it. It depresses me every time I think about it, not only for him, poor man—the bones of the old always knit so slowly —but for myself as well. When I heard he had been hurt I developed quite a severe headache, almost migraine—it was psychosomatic, of course—because there was an element of guilt involved. After all, I was responsible for what happened to him."

"You?"

"Incredible as it seems, dear boy, I was. Not directly, of course. But I was forced to punish him for letting one of my little birds go, a charming little creature. Myoko, her name is. I think you were here the day I bought her, weren't you?"

"Yes."

"And you were here the night she was brought back after her first escape," Victor said. "Of course, I remember it all now. You were under the mistaken impression I was going to beat her. I really should have. We all would have been spared so much grief. The old man must have heard her crying and unlocked the door. It took me some time to determine how she got out, but I questioned the maids until I found one who had been negligent with her keys in the presence of the old man. When I confronted the old man with my suspicion he confessed immediately. I may not look it, dear boy, but I can assume a very stern attitude when it is necessary."

"What did you do to him?"

"I expressed my sympathy first. I know what it is to be moved by tears, to respond to a feminine cry for help, however misguided that impulse might be. But the fact remained, he opened her door and diverted the doorman's attention while she slipped out onto the street. I could forgive what he did but I could not forget and I could not allow him to forget either. So I fined him six months' wages and he was so upset when he left here, he was really quite careless. So you can see how terrible I feel about it. But then I really had no other course to follow, none."

"And what will happen to the girl when you find her?"

"Nothing."

"Nothing?"

"Nothing," Victor repeated. "That will be her punishment, to be deprived of the glorious future which I had planned for her. And maybe it's best, after all, that it should be this way, because some of the other girls were really getting quite jealous of the favoritism I was displaying toward Myoko. As a matter of fact, that painting you were admiring was done by one of my girls, ostensibly as a love token, but in reality, I think, it is a blatant appeal for attention."

"Then you'll just let Myoko go?" Cooper asked.

"In a manner of speaking," Victor said calmly. "I'll have to cash her in, of course, much as a stock that has gone sour—and by the way, stay out of the Japanese market, it is manipulated, fixed and crooked. When I say I'll cash her in, I mean there is a house in Hong Kong that specializes in young girls and, although they do not pay a good deal, I can recoup some of the money I have expended, perhaps fifty to seventy-five thousand yen."

"Then all you want is your money back."

"Oh no, dear boy," Victor said evenly. "There are really two requirements which must be satisfied by any ultimate disposition of the girl's case. I am philosophical, and I know some temperaments are ill suited to the erotic life and I would like to be able to recoup some of my investment and then let the girl do whatever she wants to do. But I know I can't permit my beneficent nature to get the upper hand in this situation, because I have founded a rather complex organization here which has a discipline all its own and is quite apart from my personal code of ethics, which is inclined toward a complete leniency. I am a very softhearted man, sometimes too much so for my own good, but nevertheless there has to be some effective method of punishment. The lion must have teeth if he is to eat meat. And much as I dislike having to enforce such measures, I look on myself in the same way that an army commander under military law must look on himself—not as an individual but as a part of a mechanism. I don't like to do business with this particular establishment in Hong Kong because the people there are heartless and insentient, but I have to think of them as being the equivalent of hell, gehenna, and just as necessary to my little world as hell is to a Christian. I mean, unless one believes that a transgressor actually goes to hell once in a while, then hell loses its efficacy and becomes worse than useless." He patted the pudgy tips of his fingers together, noiselessly. "So I shall simply wait until she turns up again. She tried to go home today and Itsugi almost had her. I dare say she will try it again before long."

"Tokyo is a big city."

"But everybody operates and moves according to a pattern. And the pattern of her life is neither sophisticated nor complex. There is really no place for her to go except to her mother or back here, and when she gets hungry enough or

105

cold enough, that is exactly what she will do. And in the meantime, of course, I shall have people looking for her. But let's talk about more pleasant things, dear boy."

He made a ceremony out of paying the money, talking about the unlimited funds Cooper would have at his disposal once the Baum-Brenner papers were sold. But Cooper was only half listening; his mind had already begun to work on the problem in the light of the new information. At the moment he himself was not suspect. Victor was content to believe the old man had simply released the girl instead of helping her to find a refuge. The best thing Cooper could do was to find a place where the girl could begin a new life outside the pattern Victor had mentioned.

As Cooper put the money in his attaché case, Victor tried to persuade him to stay the night. "We are trying something new tonight," he said happily, "and in a city like Tokyo the art of being unique is practically extinct, dear boy, because here you have a whole nation of people who are not only willing but anxious to try anything once and therefore you have a continual striving of the entrepreneurs for novelty. But they mistake novelty for newness. They overlook the boundless reservoir of the traditional past, the refinements of the ancients. In short, at midnight we are having a Saturnalia according to the classic pattern. Authentic, I assure you, down to the music and the instruments. We have rather a large group, a U.N. investigative team, some British industrialists, and an American movie star or two, but I'm certain I can make room for you if you wish."

"I appreciate the offer," Cooper said, "but I have work to do."

"Certainly." There was an expression of profound respect on Victor's face. "I wouldn't delay you for the world. I admire dedication. You run along, dear boy, and immerse yourself in your documents. They are the important things, after all, the truly important things."

106

Five

1

THE fourth document both tantalized Cooper and frustrated him. If it was authentic, it settled a long-standing linguistic dispute. It had been written by Joseph of Arimathea and on first glance the language appeared to be ancient Hebrew, but on closer examination he found it was not. The hypothesis advanced by a Professor Adolph Neubauer during the 1800s —that the common language current in Jerusalem at the time of Christ was a cross between Hebrew and Aramaic, a Neo-Hebraic language—was now proved correct. But it presented Cooper with a fresh difficulty: he could not hope to translate it until he could find a comprehensive Aramaic grammar.

Finally, with instructions to Myoko not to leave the hotel room until he returned, Cooper took the train to Kanda to make another search of the bookstalls, but by midafternoon he had found absolutely nothing that could help him. He crossed the street to the park to smoke his pipe, trying to decide whether to spend the evening in a further search or to get in touch with the priest and see if the St. Justin library might have something he could use. It was a comparatively warm afternoon, an Indian summer day which reminded him of New England with the bite of the chill air in the shadows and the swirl of multicolored leaves littering the lawns.

The park was full of college students and as he watched them eddying about the bookstalls across the street it occurred to him how incredibly alike they all were in their black uniforms, invariably rumpled and grimy, their military caps shoved down over long hair which appeared to have been cut with garden shears. Traditionally, the Japanese student lived in the worst kind of poverty, as if a prideful suffering and deprivation were a natural part of higher education. It was possible, too, that this economic grimness, the atmosphere of continual desperation on the university level, explained why so many Japanese intellectuals and government leaders had no leavening sense of humor to lighten the heavy-handed determination with which they conducted their affairs.

While he sat there he heard some girls laughing and looked through the trees to see a parked school bus at the curb. A flock of young girls in bright orange sweaters and skirts was gathered around the door, giggling and shoving as they waited to climb aboard, ignoring the attempts of a dour-faced chaperone to line them up for a more orderly embarkation. His curiosity was piqued and he drifted through the trees to watch. It was only when he came within a few feet of the bus that he realized these girls were not Japanese but South American, for the most part anyway, with a sprinkling of Nordic blondes scattered among them. The legend on the side of the bus read SCHOOL OF THE AMERICAS with an address in Ueno, and as he stood there watching, the possibility occurred to him.

Many of the girls had olive complexions and Spanish-Indian features. A Japanese girl would not be too noticeable in their midst. If he could get Myoko into this school, it was unlikely Victor could find her. And Myoko would certainly benefit by it. She was a bright little girl; he was certain of that.

He thought about it all evening and questioned Myoko about her education, only to find that she had had very little schooling. What formal education she did have had been gained spasmodically, a term at a time, during those periods when her mother was living with a man who considered education important, even for girls. She could read and write some Japanese and a simplified English which a master sergeant had taught her, but her grammar was impossible and her spelling poor. He did not mention what he had in mind, just asked her in a vague way if she liked school and wanted to go back someday. She said she had enjoyed it very much; she would like to go back.

The next day, when Cooper was having lunch with Father O'Connor, he asked about the School of the Americas. The little priest shrugged, drumming on the teapot with restless fingers while his mind sorted out all the information it had on the school and tried to correlate it with a possible reason for Cooper's interest.

"It's just what the name implies," Father O'Connor said, "a primary and lower secondary school for the younger girls of the American colony, both North and South. I should say that the families of various members of the diplomatic corps supply most of the students."

"It's exclusive then?"

"I wouldn't say that. As I understand it, they have some children of American army personnel who don't want to send their girls to coeducational institutions. And from what I hear, the enrollment has fallen off considerably in the past few years. It was a very big school after the war, but the Western community is not as close knit as it used to be." He glanced at Cooper speculatively. "It's hardly the kind of place where you would want to teach."

"I'm not thinking about teaching there," Cooper said in a

matter-of-fact voice. "I just happened to see one of their buses and I was curious about it, that's all."

"I've missed our meetings," Father O'Connor said, apparently finding the explanation acceptable. "I've thought about calling you but I didn't want to disturb your work. Are you finding anything of interest in the Baum-Brenner papers?"

"I don't know," Cooper said after a pause.

"Whether they're interesting or not?"

"Whether I should discuss it with you."

"Why?"

"Maybe because I'm in no mood to argue with you. To defend myself against a charge of heresy."

"I don't think you're a heretic." Father O'Connor smiled. "You're just in rebellion. But sooner or later you'll find that there's no sense in fighting and then you'll come around. And if you want to talk about your work, I promise not to give you any argument."

"I doubt that," Cooper said. "But I need your help, an Aramaic grammar if you have one."

"The documents are Aramaic?"

"Only the last one. The fourth document is Neo-Hebraic." He went on to tell Father O'Connor of the contents of the first three documents: the Roman soldier's letter which fixed the charge against Paul as murder, the letter from Paul to Timothy admitting it and rationalizing the act, and finally Luke's letter telling of the death of Paul and defending his actions. He added the results of the scientific tests run on the documents. To Cooper's surprise, the little priest did not seem the least bit perturbed. He poured his tea with a steady hand.

"That's very interesting," he said.

"You surprise me," Cooper said.

"Oh?"

"I expected more of an outburst from you. You're not getting objective all of a sudden, are you?"

"Not in the least," Father O'Connor said. "And you may

think I'm dogmatic but it's not that either." He sipped at his tea. "I suppose I'm like a lawyer who has been in so many courtroom fights that he really hears nothing new any more and therefore it's hard to really surprise him. That's something every young priest finds himself doing, acting as a defense attorney for Jesus Christ and the apostles and the Popes and everything he believes in, especially if he's in a position where he comes in contact with non-Christians. I've come in contact with some very bright atheists and I think I've heard all the arguments. Poor St. Paul is the most vulnerable of all because of his temper and his physical affliction. I've heard people call him an epileptic, a power-crazed madman, a rebellious Jew who created the Christ myth and founded a new sect all his own. I've read papers by scientists disproving the miracles and books by apologists trying to explain them away as parables and tracts by scholars proving that they were later interpolations put in by dedicated Christians who felt that Christ needed more deification."

"So you're convinced the papers I have are forgeries."

"Yes."

"Even without seeing them?"

"Of course."

"And it doesn't worry you that they might not be?"

"Not at all," the priest said. "Because I know what the truth is and, if your documents contradict that truth, then they must be false. Now if they were in the hands of somebody else I might be worried, realizing that there are some people on the border line of faith who might be pushed backward if documents like this were advanced as authentic. But it seems quite clear to me that this is a perfect demonstration of God's methods, that these papers should be placed in the hands of a man with complete integrity as a scholar and the skill to reveal the spurious. You might say, in a manner of speaking, that God has made you His advocate in this matter. It's quite perfect, don't you see? For instance, if I defended

111

against an attack of this sort, nobody would pay any attention to me, but you're an impartial skeptic. And however cleverly these documents have been forged, you will find the weakness in them." He raised a hand for the waitress. "I must be getting back. I'm sure we have Dalman's *Grammar of Jewish Palestinian Aramaic*. I'll see what else I can scrape up and have them sent to you."

2

"We have an enrollment of a hundred and fifty girls at the moment," Mrs. Boudreau said pleasantly. "And we currently have fifteen teachers on our faculty staff, giving us an optimum student-teacher ratio. But I don't want to bore you with our pedagogy, Dr. Cooper."

"I find it very interesting," Cooper said.

She gave him a tight, competent smile. "And now, if you like, I'll show you the music room. If you'll follow me, please."

As he followed her through the french doors which separated the library from the music room, Cooper realized why she looked so familiar to him. She was a thin woman in her mid-forties and she had a precise manner of speaking, her sentences perfectly tailored and delivered in a slightly nasal voice. The suit she wore was mannishly neutral and impeccably correct, as if somewhere she had read the specifications for a perfect headmistress and then conformed herself to those standards. The music room was in keeping with the rest of the school, spacious, charming, with the little girls grouped around a massive grand piano where a perfectly groomed young woman was attempting to teach them a scale. She glanced toward Cooper and the headmistress with a practiced smile as the lesson was interrupted.

"Say good day to our visitors, girls," the music teacher said.

"*Konnichi-wa*," the girls said in a ragged chorus.

"We try to teach our girls an elementary Japanese," Mrs.

Boudreau explained as they left the music room and crossed the paneled dining room. "Of course, we also have classes in English for our South American girls and Spanish for our North Americans. Those are the only distinguishing nationality terms by the way, North and South, and we don't even use those around the girls. All of them are taught to think of themselves as Americans, which is what they are, of course. But it's very difficult for the girls from the United States to think of *South* Americans as *Americans,* if you know what I mean."

As they approached Mrs. Boudreau's office—the walnut door marked only by a simple plaque which read HEADMISTRESS—Cooper could see that the ostensibly casual tour through the English-style house, the play yards and the stables, and the battery of bedrooms on the upper floor (severely formal, European, with just a dash of oriental décor in the form of *kakemonos* on the walls) was designed to lead inexorably to the carved oak desk which bore the name plate *Mrs. Finley Boudreau, M.F.A.,* a place for the transaction of business.

She had been trying to impress him with the exclusiveness of the school, but the tour had had a reverse effect on him and had encouraged him in the hope that he might be successful. The priest had been right. Everything here was designed to accommodate a much larger enrollment. Many of the upstairs bedrooms were vacant. It was entirely possible that the School of the Americas was having financial difficulties.

"Now," Mrs. Boudreau said, seating herself behind the desk and gesturing toward a leather-covered visitor's chair, "I'm sure you have some questions and I'll do my best to answer them."

"I think you have a lovely place here," Cooper said. "I haven't seen any better facilities anywhere in the States."

"Thank you."

"The first thing we'd better discuss is your tuition."

"Of course," Mrs. Boudreau said, as if this matter of money was really quite unimportant. "Will your daughter be resident?"

"Yes."

Mrs. Boudreau consulted a rate schedule. "Then the inclusive fee would be Y450,000 for the ten-month term. Of course, since she would be a late enrollment, we can deduct a proportionate amount from that total. And, as I say, the fee is inclusive: books, laboratory, riding lessons, everything except, of course, any spending money you might allow her for our weekly outings. We try to persuade our parents to limit these allowances to Y3000 a week, something under ten dollars American. And the inclusive fee can be paid in quarterly installments if you prefer."

"I see," Cooper said. Was she reducing the fee through anxiety that he was intimidated by the sum? Was she making concessions? He could not be sure. "Now," he said, "I'd like to know about your entrance requirements."

"They're very simple," she said. "We'll give your daughter the standard tests to determine where our program might be of the most benefit to her. We have no facilities for the mentally or physically handicapped, but I'm sure that's not what you meant."

"My daughter is perfectly healthy, mentally and physically," Cooper said.

"Of course. And we require that our girls' parents be native-born citizens of one of the American countries."

"Both of them?"

"Beg your pardon?"

"Do both parents have to be native-born citizens?"

"Oh no," Mrs. Boudreau said. "Some of our most distinguished South American diplomats have European wives. I take it that's what you want to know. Is your wife European?"

"She was Japanese," Cooper said evenly. "She is no longer living."

For the first time Mrs. Boudreau was momentarily thrown off stride, caught in the same instant by the need for an expression of sympathy and the adjustment in her thinking required by his disclosure. "I'm truly sorry," she said, covering any confusion she might have felt.

"Since her mother is dead, I feel it's very important for Myoko to be enrolled in a school like this," Cooper said, continuing before she could summon up any objections to the enrollment. "I think you can understand what I'm going through. I married a Japanese woman twelve years ago and took her back to the States with me, but unfortunately I lived in a New England town that refused to accept her, simply because she was oriental. Prejudice is an ugly thing, especially among educated people who should know better."

Mrs. Boudreau concurred vaguely.

"Anyway," Cooper continued, "my wife came back to Japan. My child was born about the same time my divorce became final. I never saw my daughter while she was growing up. And then, two years ago, my wife died. I didn't know it at the time, as a matter of fact. I only heard about it the early part of this year. So I came over here to see if I could find my daughter and do something for her." He paused for effect. "Do you mind if I smoke?"

"Not at all," Mrs. Boudreau said, fishing through the top desk drawer for matches. Lighting his pipe, he gave himself time to gauge her reaction to his story. So far, she seemed sympathetic but he could not be sure whether this sympathy was personal or professional. "I won't bore you with all the details," he said. "I'm sure you've heard a dozen stories like this before, but anyway, when I found Myoko she was living with her aunt, who was, in turn—how shall I put it?— well, she was living with an American soldier. I took Myoko away from there immediately, of course. I want to take her back to the States with me but all of her documents, her papers, were destroyed by her aunt and it will take me some time to have them replaced. Until then—and it's possible it might take a year—I would like to know she's receiving the best of care and a proper education."

Mrs. Boudreau sighed. "That does present certain problems," she said.

"I hope you don't have a racial exclusion policy here," Cooper said without rancor. "I'm trying to convince her the climate has changed, that she will get a better reception in the States than her mother did."

"We don't have an official policy like that," Mrs. Boudreau said. "But I'll be quite frank with you, Dr. Cooper, the policy of any private school such as this is determined to a large extent by the attitudes of the parents."

"I shouldn't think that would be much of a problem," Cooper said, a little ashamed of the oblique pressure he was about to exert. "It seems to me that the parents, especially those in the diplomatic service, would be forced to have a liberal attitude in matters of this sort. It wouldn't look very good for them to support prejudice, privately or otherwise, against a representative of their host country."

Mrs. Boudreau's eyes flicked to his face, assessing his intentions, and then moved to the blank application form on her desk. "No," she said. "Of course not. And we pride ourselves on the democratic attitude we encourage in our students, the complete lack of any prejudice, racial or otherwise. So we wouldn't refuse to admit your daughter for that reason. But certain forms are required by the government. You have no papers, birth certificate, government documents, anything?"

"Nothing," Cooper said. "I've made application to the proper government agencies but, as I say, it could take a year. However, I can provide you with an affidavit of parentage and some of the particulars concerning her birth. I can bring it to you when I make the financial arrangements."

He could tell that she was wavering, balancing the trouble she might have if she accepted the girl against the implied trouble she would have if she did not. And perhaps the mention of money made some difference; he was not sure. In any case, she inserted the application blank and an assortment of brochures and mimeographed sheets into a manila envelope and handed them to him. "I'm sure we will enjoy having your daughter with us," she said in a sincere voice. "And I'm sure she will enjoy it too."

Leaving the school, he was more hopeful than he had been in some time. On the train back to Shimbashi he looked through the material in the envelope and the list of articles Myoko was expected to bring with her (underclothes, uniforms, overcoat, raincoat, toilet articles, etc.) and those which were forbidden (television set, traveling iron, etc.) and those which were optional (transistor radio, typewriter, etc.). With any luck, he could complete his shopping tomorrow morning and take her to the school in the afternoon. If he handled it cautiously there would be no chance of Victor's tracing the girl beyond her brief stay in Cooper's room, should he succeed in getting that far. By tomorrow night the girl would be safe and Cooper could get back to work.

It was not to be that simple, he discovered as he reached the hotel. Willa intercepted him in the corridor. She was upset but calm. There had been some trouble while he was gone and she knew what had happened but she had no idea what it was all about.

She had been working when she heard somebody pounding on Cooper's door, so she looked out into the hall to see a middle-aged Japanese in a business suit who showed every sign of being drunk. His face was flushed and when his pounding on the door prompted no response from inside Cooper's room he began to kick the door with the side of his foot, bracing himself against the wall to keep from falling on his face.

Fearful for the girl in Cooper's room, Willa dashed to her telephone and called the hotel manager, who rushed upstairs and accosted the drunk. At first Willa was sure there was going to be a bloody fight; there was an angry argument which ended in a flurry of scuffling but as Willa opened her door she saw that the manager had the situation well in hand. He was dragging the drunk toward the stairway while the drunk flailed his arms in a feeble gesture of resistance. Once the two men were gone, Willa had heard Myoko crying quite hysterically in Cooper's room, and she had gone to see what she could do.

"How did you get in?" Cooper interrupted.

"The door locks are all the same," she said. "Any room key will open any lock. A prime example of Japanese efficiency."

"All right. Go on."

She had gone in, she said, and Myoko was so terrified that she refused to be consoled, certain the man had come for her and would therefore return. This was only approximate, Willa could only guess at what Myoko was trying to tell her because the girl spoke only a few sentences in English before she lapsed into a torrential outburst of Japanese. In the end, Willa took Myoko to her room where she would be safe in case the man did come back.

"She's there now?"

"Yes."

Cooper opened the door to her room and went in. The girl was nowhere in sight. "Myoko," he said quietly, "don't be afraid."

He heard the sound of weeping from beneath the bed and moved to it, pulling up the concealing drape of bedspread as she emerged, coming into his arms and clinging to him while Willa closed the door. Cooper said nothing for a long time, feeling the tightness of the thin arms around his neck. "Nobody's going to hurt you, Myoko," he said quietly, trying to calm her. "Nobody at all. But I have to know what happened and only you can tell me. Did you recognize the voice of the man in the hall?"

"Yis."

"Who was he?"

"I don't know his name. The Engrishman's house, *ne,* he works there."

"I see," Cooper said. He turned to Willa. "Do you have any aspirin?"

"I think so."

"Dissolve two of them in a teaspoon of water," he said.

When she brought the aspirin to him he held out the spoon to Myoko and she took the medicine without a protest. "Now," he said, "I want you to lie down for a while and close your eyes."

She nodded and climbed into the bed, looking up at him with wide and somber eyes. "Everything aw right now, *ne?*"

"Everything's all right," he said.

She closed her eyes. He sat down, smoking his pipe, trying to think his way out of the situation, trying to put down the rising emotion he felt within him. He looked at her lying on the bed, one arm over her eyes, her breathing regular as she went to sleep.

"Coffee?" Willa said. "I have it made."

He nodded. When she brought it to him he drank it slowly.

"You want to tell me about her?" Willa said, sitting down across from him.

"She's from Victor's place," Cooper began. He told her the whole story. She listened in silence. When he had finished talking she put her cup down.

"God damn him anyway," she said. "He's a real monster. You think he knows you have the girl?"

"I don't know," Cooper said. "But I think I can find out soon enough." He picked up the telephone and asked the hotel switchboard to get him Victor Hawkins. To his surprise, the call went straight through and Victor was on the line in less than a minute. Cooper gave him no time to develop a defense.

"I just want to know what you think you're trying to do," Cooper said angrily. "One of your men came over here and tried to break into my room this afternoon."

"Break into your room, dear boy?" Victor said. "You must be mistaken."

"I'm not mistaken," Cooper said adamantly. "From the description I have, it sounds like Ito. I won't put up with it, Victor. You can send your man for the photostats any time. I'm through."

From Victor's response, Cooper could tell the man was really shaken. His voice quavered as he made an obvious attempt at mollification. He could not let Cooper quit, he insisted, not over something so inane as the mistake that had been made, proceeding from an error in judgment, perhaps, but totally without malice. He hurried to cover himself with ashes; it was his fault because he had misjudged his own employees and given them the wrong incentive. He had come to the conclusion that the old man had not merely released the girl but had taken her someplace where he thought she would be safe, to one of his relatives or friends perhaps; the Japanese were as fortunate as the Jews in this regard, in that they were so inbred, herded together on this small island, so to speak, that each one of them had a nebulous network of relatives.

To cut down the time required to trace the old man's steps, Victor had simply offered an incentive plan to his employees, ten thousand yen for the one who found the girl. It had caused quite a commotion and had created more problems than it was worth. Three of his maids had not shown up for work today—relatives had called in to report them ill—and Victor knew this was an untruth. They were out looking for Myoko. "Greed, dear boy," Victor complained. "It makes people forget their responsibilities. It reduces them to animals." As for Ito, Victor continued, he was a drunk and a troublemaker anyway, and since Cooper's room had been on the old man's itinerary, Ito had leaped to a wrong conclusion and made a fool of himself, jeopardizing a really fine relationship, the friendship Victor felt he had established with Cooper. For this, Ito would be reprimanded, severely punished. If Cooper could bring himself to overlook this example of poor behavior, he could rest assured he would not be troubled again. Victor was contrite, he wanted to make amends. Cooper allowed himself to be persuaded and then put the receiver back on the cradle.

"I think he knows I have the girl," he said quietly, after he told Willa what Victor had said.

"Oh?" she said, surprised. "Then why doesn't he just take her?"

"He's in a tricky position," Cooper said thoughtfully. "He wants her but he needs me, at least until the translations are finished. I think Ito heard the girl the other night and told Victor about it. And Victor had to find a way to have the girl taken from my room without being personally responsible, so he set up an artificial system to put the responsibility on his employees. That way, he could blame Ito if I kicked up too much of a fuss about having my room invaded."

"Then why didn't Ito follow through?"

"I don't know. Perhaps because he was drunk, befuddled. But I do know I can't keep her here any longer, not even tonight. Will you help me?"

"Sure," she said without hesitation. "What do you want me to do?"

"I don't know. I have to think about it."

Telling her to keep her door locked, he went to his room. He sat down at the writing table, opened the drawer, and began to count the money he had accumulated, jotting down the subtotals as he finished one stack after another, then adding these once he was through. Y610,000; that was his final figure. It would be enough but just barely; it would wipe out the reserve he liked to keep on hand.

His bluff at the school had depended to a large extent on the affluent aura he projected. He could not afford to take the cut rate he was offered and he could not pay the tuition in installments. He did not fool himself for a moment that all of Myoko's problems would be solved once she entered the school, but if he paid the full amount it was going to be far easier for the headmistress to retain the girl and work out the difficulties than it would be to send her back to him and return the money.

He would pay the Y450,000 and set up a reserve of Y45,000 on deposit with the headmistress to be doled out to Myoko at Y3000 a week for fifteen weeks. That left him Y115,000. Out of that he owed Y20,000 on his bill at the hotel. Putting Y75,000 into his attaché case, he went back to Willa's room.

"Have you hit on anything?" Willa asked him.

"I think so," he said. "But I'm not very good at things like this so if you can think of anything better I'll appreciate it." He sat down and lighted his pipe again. "If Victor's offered a general reward to his organization, then I can pretty well count on being watched whenever I go off this floor. So I'll go down to the lobby. You wait until I've been there five minutes and then take the girl down the back stairs."

"What do I do when I get her out of the hotel?"

"You take the train to Yurakucho Station," Cooper said. "Find a small Japanese-style hotel and get a room. If you get that far, I don't think you'll have any trouble. One more thing: if you do have any difficulty on the way to the station, if anybody tries to take the girl away from you, let them have her."

"Let them take her?"

"You couldn't stop them and I don't want either you or Myoko to get hurt. So, if that happens, let her go and come straight back here. I'll take it from there."

"All right," Willa said. "If I get to Yurakucho, what then?"

"Tomorrow morning, find a beauty shop somewhere, a

hairdresser. Have her hair lightened a shade—not much, not to blonde or anything like that, but I want her to look as if there's a Caucasian in her background someplace. Have it set in an American style, a pony tail."

"You're behind the times," she said. "The latest pre-teen fashion is to look as much like a tired call girl as possible."

"Most of the girls at the school wear pony tails."

"Then a pony tail it will be."

He took the mimeographed sheet out of his pocket and handed it to her. "After the hair, I want her outfitted with everything the school will allow her to have. You'll find the things listed on the 'expected to have' and 'optional' lists. And get a leather suitcase for her clothes, something that looks expensive." He handed her the attaché case. "Do you think you can do all that on Y75,000?"

"That's about two hundred dollars," she said. "A woman who can live on nothing can do miracles with an amount like that."

"Good," Cooper said. "Once you get these things, take the train to Ueno and go to the entrance of the Imperial Museum. Have lunch first, but be there by three o'clock. I'll meet you." He looked at the girl. She was still wearing the light green dress she had been wearing when she first came to his room. "She'll freeze to death on a night like this. Do you have a coat you can lend her?"

"Sure," Willa said.

Cooper approached the bed and sat down beside the girl, touching her arm gently to awaken her without alarming her. She came awake quickly and looked up at him.

"Myoko," he said, "Miss Cummings is going to take you to another hotel tonight. I would like to keep you with me but we don't want Hawkins to find you. Can you understand that?"

She nodded.

"Now, tomorrow, I'm sending you to a very nice school

123

where you can be with other girls your own age," he explained patiently. "You'll be safe there. In order to get you in, I have told them that you are my daughter, that I was married to your mother and that your mother is dead. It's like a game, but you'll have to remember it all the time. You will have to pretend. Do you think you can do that?"

The girl blinked at him. "You are my new father, *ne?*"

"No, I'm your only father," he insisted. "You have been living with your aunt for two years. She is a bad woman. You don't like her. If anybody asks you about her, that's all you will say, just that you don't like her."

"My aunt?" Myoko said, trying to grasp what he was telling her.

"We'll go over this again tomorrow," Cooper said. "But I wanted to tell you tonight so you can be thinking about it. It's a game. But you have to remember it."

"You are my father," she said slowly.

"Yes," Cooper said. "That's it." He turned to Willa. "Give me five minutes and then leave. When you reach Yurakucho, call here and ask for yourself. The operator will ring your phone and I'll be here to answer it. Don't identify yourself, the operator could be listening in. Just ask for Miss Cummings and I'll know you've made it."

"All right."

He went down to the lobby and sat on a low modernistic sofa near the registration desk where a diminutive Japanese in heavy tortoise-rimmed spectacles was arranging artificial flowers in a vase. There were few people in the lobby. A heavy-set old man in a gray kimono occupied the couch near Cooper, reading a Japanese financial journal and smoking a tiny pipe which held no more than a pinch of tobacco. Cooper recognized him as a resident. A cleaning man was sweeping the floral carpet with a tiny broom, whisking the dust into a pan on the end of a long handle, completely oblivious to Cooper's presence. On the far side of the lobby, partially concealed by a clump of artificial bamboo, was a British officer, looking properly awkward and ill at ease as he waited for a girl.

None of these people could be connected with Hawkins but Cooper felt tense nevertheless, glancing every few minutes at his watch and trying to imagine where Willa was at that moment. Five minutes and Willa was leaving the hotel. Ten minutes and she was approaching Shimbashi Station. He would give her another ten minutes and then he would go back to her room to await the call.

He picked up a copy of the English edition of *Asahi* from the table in front of him but he could not concentrate on it. As he turned the page, he was startled to find that his hands were trembling. Folding the newspaper carefully, he put it down, occupying himself with tamping tobacco into the bowl of his pipe, not wanting to smoke but needing some physical act to absorb his restlessness.

He wondered vaguely if the people in the lobby were really as placid as they seemed, if the desk clerk who now picked up a flower from the stack on the registration desk and inserted it in the bowl, canting his head to one side as if to see the arrangement in a new perspective, was not just occupying himself to keep from thinking about the precarious hold he had on his job here. And perhaps the old man with the passive face who squinted at the rows of figures in the journal held close to his eyes was at the moment suffering in the grip of some inner panic at seeing his money evaporate and disappear in the shifting patterns of the stock market.

When it came right down to it, there was little external torment in the world any more; the whole advance of civilization was predicated on keeping the physical man from being uncomfortable. Most of a man's torment was internal, proceeding from anxieties and fear of the unknown, the future, the elements which were gathering to affect and change his life and over which he had no control.

125

At the end of another ten minutes he went upstairs and let himself into Willa's room, just as the telephone rang. He answered it and a moment later heard Willa's voice on the line.

"Is Miss Cummings in?" she said.

"No," Cooper said. "Would you like to leave a message?"

"Just tell her everything's fine. I'll be in touch tomorrow."

"I'll tell her," he said. "Good night."

When he got back to his room he clicked on his lamp and, sitting down at his table, began to write out the fictional facts he would need to include in the affidavit for Mrs. Boudreau.

Six

1

By MIDAFTERNOON Willa was tired, irritated, and ready to wash her hands of the whole business. During the night and day she had been with the Japanese girl, Myoko had not said a dozen words to her, neither approving nor disapproving the things Willa bought for her but merely enduring the experience of shopping and the hairdresser with a passive attitude Willa found intolerable. She had gone to a lot of trouble to help this girl and Myoko treated her like a jailer. At the dress shops, the girl could not be persuaded to express an opinion one way or the other, standing listlessly in front of the mirror while Willa tried to communicate with the clerks in pidgin English.

This was not all that was bothering Willa, of course, and she knew it, but it was not until quite late in the day, as she and Myoko were standing in front of the museum, watching Cooper approach across the park through the rain, that she realized fully why she felt such an antagonism for the girl. She was jealous; Cooper had done for this girl what he had refused to do for her, taking an active interest in her welfare and risking something he valued in order to help her.

She knew it was true but the insight did nothing to increase her liking for the girl or to lessen her irritation with Cooper for being late. By the time he arrived she was furious and she started to tell him so, but he was so obviously pleased with what she had done to transform Myoko that she didn't mention it.

"You've done a fine job," Cooper said as he looked at the girl. Myoko's features were still unmistakably Japanese, nothing could change that, but the metallic blue-blackness of the hair had been relieved by a brown undertone, and with a pony tail, bobby socks, and American-style clothes she looked Nisei instead of native-born. It was a subtle difference, perhaps, but an important one as far as the school was concerned. "I don't know how you did it," Cooper said, "but I'm relieved. Let's go someplace and dry off. I've had a terrible afternoon."

In a tearoom near the museum Cooper took a sheaf of papers from his inside pocket and handed one of them, written in Japanese, to Myoko. "I want you to read this and remember it," he said. "It's the same information I'm giving the headmistress at the school and it's quite important that we keep our stories straight. Can you understand it all right?"

"Yis," Myoko said.

He handed the affidavits to Willa with a sigh. "I should have had you do these for me," he said. "I simply don't have any gift for invention."

She could not stay angry with him. He looked very tired, as if he had slept even less than she had. She examined the affidavits. They had been typewritten on official-looking paper and at the bottom of each was a melted dab of red wax which had been impressed with what looked like a notary's seal, although the inscription was in Japanese. There were Japanese signatures brushed along the sides of the pages and romanized at the bottom.

The first affidavit certified that George Cooper had been married to Akiko Kawamura on August 2, 1948, in a civil ceremony in the city of Fukuoka and that the ceremony had been witnessed by the man whose name was affixed to this document. The second testified to Myoko's birth and registry and the last was what amounted to a death certificate for the fictitious Akiko. "You've done a hell of a good job," Willa said. "Remind me to call on you when I need a new passport. What's the seal down here at the bottom?"

"I don't know," Cooper said. "I think it has something to do with the Bureau of Fisheries. The public stenographer I went to used to work for the government and when he left he took the seal with him. He uses it on everything. He threw in the red wax for a touch of color and to keep the characters on the seal from being too readable. The people who signed the affidavits were pulled in off the streets and given five hundred yen apiece for their signatures."

"Can't beat that," Willa said, amused.

"Were you able to get everything on the list?"

"Everything except the typewriter," Willa said. "I did a lot of haggling but I still didn't have enough money. The rest of her stuff is in the suitcases."

"I appreciate what you've done," Cooper said, "and now I'd better get her over to the school. I take it you didn't run into any trouble?"

"None," she said. "And since Myoko's going to school, maybe you'll have time to have dinner with me on Friday?"

Cooper folded the affidavits and returned them to his pocket. "If you're free," he said.

"As a bird. Good luck."

She waited with them until they caught a taxi and then walked back to the railroad station in the rain, feeling sleepy but not depressed, more hopeful of Cooper's co-operation now that the old schedule had been re-established.

As she sat on the train for Shimbashi, watching the rain sweep across the buildings and walls which pressed close to the elevated tracks and occasionally gave way to the larger view of a village square or congested street, she allowed her mind to entertain the prospect of success. She wondered how Harvey would feel when he saw her return to prominence with all the old bugaboos and weaknesses conquered once and for all. She wondered if he would feel the slightest pinprick of regret, the slightest sense of loss.

She hurried from the train station to the hotel, getting inside the door just as the lightning flashed and the slanting rain became a heavy downpour. She was wet and uncomfortable and she wanted nothing more than to soak in the public bath for a couple of hours and then go to bed. But as she approached the desk to ask if there was any mail she realized she was not to be granted this luxury. The clerk was agitated, disturbed. He rolled his eyes as he handed her the one letter in her box. "Porice," he said, whispering, nodding vaguely toward the divan behind her. "Porice are here."

It was indeed a policeman and she wondered how she could have failed to notice him when she came in. He was a lean man in his early thirties and he wore a trench coat and a snap-brim hat. *All the sartorial elegance of Dick Tracy*, she thought as he approached her. He bowed slightly as he opened his wallet and exhibited his credentials.

"I am Mr. Taiga, Miss Cummings," he said. "Public Procurator's Office."

"So I see," Willa said, smothering the alarm she felt. "What can I do for you?"

"This is a routine inquiry only," he said, pronouncing his *l* distinctly. "If you will come with me, please."

She had no desire to go with him; she was tired, wet, and nervous and her mind sorted through all the reasons he might want to talk to her. The possibilities were endless. A country like this had a thousand laws she knew nothing about; she undoubtedly broke a dozen of them every time she walked down the street.

"Are you arresting me?" she asked.

"No," he said.

He bowed to the clerk and the clerk returned it, giving Willa covert sympathy with his eyes as she followed the investigator out of the hotel and onto the street. An unmarked police car drove up in the rain to meet them, the rear door swinging open.

She had no idea where the car took them except that the building was in the central district, about ten minutes from the hotel. It was a squat, modernistic, no-nonsense building and they parked behind it and walked through the rain to the rear door, with Taiga hurrying ahead to open it for her as if she were an honored guest. The driver remained behind, in the car.

It was only as they entered Taiga's office on the second floor that she began to relax. The room was pleasant, even cheerful, not at all what she imagined a Japanese interrogation room would be like. There was a vase of fresh flowers on the desk, peonies, next to the framed portraits of a smiling woman and children. The chair in which he seated her was upholstered in a brightly patterned fabric. He flipped the switch on an intercom and said something in Japanese. Then he turned to her. "Tea?" he asked.

"Yes, thank you."

He said something else into the intercom and then proceeded to remove his raincoat, using a sponge to wipe off the excess water, folding it with the precision of an army corporal making a bed before he placed the coat on a shelf behind his desk. He dried his hat with the sponge and then placed it on top of the raincoat.

"I don't like so much rain," he said, "but it is necessary to the agriculture, so whether I like it or not is unremarkable. Do you like rain?"

"Sometimes."

"Sometimes I like rain too," he said, sitting down behind his desk, "but not so much. Have a cigarette?"

131

"Thank you."

He pushed a box over to her and removed the lid, then stood up and came around the desk to light her cigarette. "I like American cigarettes very much," he said. "They are unavailable sometimes and very expensive, but I like them."

She knew he was using her to practice his English and it was hard to keep from mimicking. She had to keep reminding herself that this was not a social occasion. A uniformed policeman brought in a small lacquered tray with a teapot and cups and proceeded to serve her. "I hope you are able to drink tea without sugar," Taiga said.

"I am able," Willa said with a smile. "Where did you learn your English?"

"In a rapid course," Taiga said, "with a private tutor. While at Tokyo University, it was my attempt to learn the speaking of English, but all which was taught was English literature and American literature. So it was necessary for a rapid course in speaking the language as you do."

"You do quite well," Willa said.

"Thank you. At least my meaning is known to English-speaking people whom are contacted by my business." He sipped his tea. "May I see your passport, please?" he said.

"Certainly. Would you mind telling me what this is all about?"

He nodded as if he heard her and understood her, but he said nothing. He studied her passport in silence, raising his eyes only once to compare her face with the picture. He flipped through the rest of the pages, then closed it with a snap and handed it back to her. "So you are a journalist."

"Yes."

"With which paper are you working, or with a wire service, perhaps?"

"At the moment I'm free-lancing. That means I don't work for any particular publisher."

"You recently received monies from the United States?"

"Yes."

"One thousand dollars?"

Of course, that had to be it, the transaction at the foreign exchange bank, the conversion of the dollars into yen. She made no outward sign of her discovery. She placed the cigarette on the extended lip of the ashtray and picked up her cup of tea. "Yes," she said. "One thousand dollars."

"And this was monies from the sale of your writing perhaps?"

"No," she said calmly. "I transferred funds from my bank in New York. They sent me a cashier's check for a thousand dollars. I took it to the foreign exchange bank and had it converted into yen."

"Three hundred and sixty thousand yen," he said. "Am I not correct?"

"I think that was the amount, yes."

"In what notes were the monies? Ten-thousand-yen notes? Fives? Ones?"

"I really don't remember," she said.

"But you have then spent all of this monies?"

"I can't really say," she said, refusing to be cornered into something that might constitute an admission.

"But you have monies now, in cash."

"Yes, of course."

"And if it is from the foreign exchange bank, then one could know in what notes the original transaction was made?"

"Not necessarily," Willa said. "I have other money coming in from time to time."

"Oh?" he said, interested. "And from what source?"

"Different sources," she said, her mind fluttering now. She had evaded one admission only to find herself confronted by another. "Loans," she said. "From friends."

"In what amount?"

133

"I couldn't say."

"Would you like more tea?" he asked abruptly.

"No, thank you."

"I am sorry there is no sugar," he said. "Many Westerners prefer sugar to their tea, I hear."

"Yes," she said. "Many Westerners."

"It is necessary to have comfortable for interrogations," Taiga said, sitting quite stiffly in his chair. "Have you comfortable?"

"No," she said, deciding the time was right for a little diverting righteous indignation. "I don't think you're being fair to me. I can't quote laws to you, but I sure as hell don't think you can hold somebody without charging them with something. Now am I being charged with something or did you have me down here to drink tea and practice your conversational English?"

He looked blank for a moment and she thought at first he was shocked into some kind of oriental anger, but then she realized he looked blank simply because she had been speaking so fast he could not follow the meaning of her words. "Have another cigarette?" he said.

"No. I want to know the charge against me." She spoke very slowly, trying to pick basic words he could understand. "I will not answer any more questions until I know the charge."

"Ah, so desu-ka?" he said quietly, lighting another cigarette for himself before he launched into an explanation, preceding it with an apology for his shortcomings as an investigator. He had been an investigator a very short time and, although the procedures were quite definite for the interrogation of a Japanese national, they were entirely different when it came to a foreigner, especially a Westerner. It was not only a difference in language, but the Japanese government was anxious not to offend tourists or members of the Western press or business, and it was difficult to question a Westerner without offending him. "But I mean to offer you no offense," he said. "That is why I say this is routine inquiry only."

"You offend a Westerner more when you beat around the bush," she said. "When you don't get to the point."

"So?" he said. "I remember that for future times." He removed a sheaf of papers written in Japanese from the drawer and placed them on the desk in front of him, putting on a pair of reading glasses before he began to translate them for her. She could not tell whether everything he said was a translation or whether he slipped in a few side comments on his own—he did not raise his eyes from the papers—but she suspected that much of what he explained came from his own personal opinion.

First, the official conversion laws were necessary to protect the yen against inflation, because if there was an unlimited open exchange the people of Japan would soon trade all their money for a more stable foreign currency and this would lead to bidding and very soon the yen would be worthless. For the same reason, individuals were forbidden to cash in more than a limited amount of Japanese currency when they left the country, because this would contribute to the same inflation.

These laws demanded strict supervision and sometimes a foreigner, through pity for a Japanese perhaps, or through fondness, or sometimes through a desire for profit, assisted a Japanese in making an illegal financial transaction. The government had recently been investigating the foreign exchange bank at which Willa had cashed her check from the United States and they had uncovered a number of men there who were engaged in illegal currency transactions. A Mr. Genda was one of these men and found in his papers were receipts signed by a number of Americans, who had supposedly availed themselves of his services. Miss Cummings' name was on one of these receipts.

Mr. Genda had retained these records, hoping that when he was caught he could use them as a bargaining point with the

135

Public Procurator's Office, because he could not very well be prosecuted without the names of the Americans being revealed, and the Americans would be embarrassed and the Japanese government would suffer mortification at this. It was Genda's contention that he had given Miss Cummings nine one-hundred-dollar bills (American), retaining one for himself. Basing an investigation on that presumption and having the serial numbers of those bills, the police had discovered a businessman named Fukuzawa in Yurakucho who had a flourishing business in illegal currency exchange when he was intercepted. The American bills which had been given to Miss Cummings, according to Genda, were among those confiscated. Fukuzawa had confirmed this. He had purchased nine hundred dollars in American currency from Miss Cummings, giving her five hundred yen to the dollar.

"It's ridiculous," Willa said.

"Then you deny?"

"Yes."

"And the papers which were given you by Genda-san which bear the writing of your signature? Are you deny you write this?"

"I signed some papers," she said, "but I didn't read them. As I recall, there were quite a few of them and they were all in Japanese."

"And are you deny you are dealing with Fukuzawa in Yurakucho?"

"Yes," she said.

"Then you will produce some bank notes given you from the foreign exchange bank, yes, to show good faith?"

"No," she said. "Not that I don't want to help you. But I may or may not have any of the bills I received at the foreign exchange bank. And I sure as hell don't intend to start trying to prove I'm innocent."

"The book of appointments in Fukuzawa's office is bearing

136

your name for"—he consulted the paper again—"for October 16. Are you denying this represents a fact?"

"Not necessarily," she said. "I'm a journalist and I have to interview a lot of people in my business."

"Then you were not there?"

"I may have been."

"You don't remember?"

"Not at the moment, no. I don't remember being there."

This was unfortunate, Taiga continued quietly. Things would be so much simpler if she could bring herself to remember visiting that office in Yurakucho—if indeed she had *really* gone there—because even though Japanese law was different in many ways from occidental law, it was still necessary to establish a case before it could be prosecuted. A witness, somebody who had actually sold American currency to Fukuzawa, would be most useful.

"I'm not saying that I did sell him anything," Willa said cautiously. "But I'm curious. What would happen to a witness like this?"

"The witness, if American national, would be returned there, I think," Taiga said.

"Deported, in other words."

"Deported with gratitude."

"And suppose this witness did not testify?"

"Ah," Taiga said with a mournful sigh. "A most unhappy circumstance." Under the Japanese law as under Western law, such a person could then be accused of complicity and tried right along with the primary defendant, if there was sufficient evidence to warrant this. However, under Japanese law, this evidence could be anything: hearsay, gossip, even one person lying against another; all of it would be heard and examined by the three judges who would decide the case.

For example, Genda's testimony implicating Willa was sufficient to bring her to trial; it would be up to the judges to decide whether that testimony was true or false. If they decided it was true, Willa was likely to share the fate of Genda and Fukuzawa, a fine or imprisonment, possibly both. "So your right decision is most important to your welfare," Taiga said, opening the box on his desk. "Another cigarette?"

"No, thanks," Willa said. "You said I'm not under arrest."

"Yes."

"Then I can leave?"

"Yes."

She stood up. "How soon will this case come to trial?"

"After the new year begins," he said, taking off his reading glasses. "The accused will suffer arrest in December, perhaps. So if perhaps a witness does not wish to suffer arrest, an early coming in would be advisable." He pressed the intercom button and said something in Japanese before he crossed to the door and held it open for her. "The car will return you," he said. "Many thanks for your presence."

During the ride back to the hotel she controlled herself very well, but once she reached her room she found that her hands were trembling. She wanted a drink badly, she needed one, but she refused to indulge herself. She needed no false hope, no artificial confidence. She thought about retaining a lawyer but decided against it. No, she was guilty and they would have little trouble proving it. This meant she had about a month to get the Baum-Brenner business wrapped up before the roof fell in on her.

She emptied her purse out on the bureau, looking for an aspirin, and found the letter the clerk had handed her. It was from her contact at the Israeli Legation, reporting Tel Aviv's answers to his queries. As far as Tel Aviv knew, Anna Klaus had been in Sydney, Australia, until late in 1950 when she had gone to the Fiji Islands. Her trip had something to do with a commission to decorate a new tourist hotel or a sightseeing ship, but where she went when she left the Fijis was not known. She had not forwarded her new address to Tel Aviv and when official government mail was sent to her at

138

Suva it was returned with the notation, "Not Deliverable."

She sat down at her typewriter and wrote to the *Fiji Times* in Suva, asking for any information they might have on Mrs. Anna Klaus or her son, hoping the editor would recognize the name Willa Cummings and put forth the effort from a spirit of fraternal co-operation, free. In case he would not or could not, she sent the text of a search advertisement which she wanted run in his classified at his usual rates with the bill and any subsequent correspondence to be mailed to her in Tokyo.

Once she finished writing the letter and addressing the envelope, she was quite sleepy. The anxiety generated by the interview with the detective was now subsiding. She had been in worse trouble than this before and somehow she had survived it. She would do it again. She left the letter on her desk to be mailed first thing in the morning, then she took two sleeping pills and went to bed.

2

From the moment Cooper conceived the plan to get Myoko into the school he had dreaded the first encounter between the girl and the headmistress, anticipating the expression on Mrs. Boudreau's face when she saw through the deception and demanded an explanation. He was both pleased and a little startled when this did not happen. The enrollment was effortless.

In that first meeting, as Myoko bowed to Mrs. Boudreau, awkward, ill at ease, Cooper realized that behind Mrs. Boudreau's prim and efficient exterior lay the instincts of a woman who truly loved children. There was no artifice in her smile, no cloud of doubt, and as she asked Myoko to come and sit by her at the desk, Cooper felt grateful and relieved.

The formalities were brief; the application form and the affidavits slid beneath Mrs. Boudreau's eye; she gave them no more than a cursory glance to make sure they contained the information she needed. Cooper signed the entrance forms, paid the tuition, and set up the allowance fund, then Mrs. Boudreau ushered them upstairs to meet Myoko's roommate, a dark-skinned Bolivian girl named Maria Romo who took Myoko by the hand and led her off to inspect such intriguing things as closets and bureau drawers. Mrs. Boudreau beamed after them.

"You have a beautiful child, Dr. Cooper," she said. "And I don't think there will be the slightest problem of adjustment."

"No, I don't think there will be," Cooper said, pleased that everything was going so well. It seemed the most natural thing in the world for him to be here, enrolling Myoko in this school as his daughter. She was quite pleased by the room and she kept turning to Cooper as if to make sure she was really going to be allowed to stay here. Before he left the room he picked her up and kissed her, telling her to remember all the things they had talked about.

On the way downstairs he told Mrs. Boudreau he would visit Myoko as often as possible and would call at least twice a week. If there was an emergency she could leave a message for him with Father O'Connor at St. Justin Martyr College. He could provide her with no direct address at the moment; his research required him to travel a great deal.

On his way to the train station he stopped in a public urinal to make an assiduous search of his pockets, tearing the receipt Mrs. Boudreau had given him into small pieces and flushing them down the toilet, making certain he had nothing that would connect him with the school.

He had thought that, once the girl was safe, his mind would be released from the problem, but even as he presented his day ticket to the conductor and boarded the coach, pressing into the tight jam of people trying to get inside before the door hissed shut, he realized it was not going to be so

140

easy. She would be safe for the next few months, but what would happen to her when the school was recessed for vacation? He would have to provide some place for her to spend her summer and he would either have to stay in Japan or find a way to take her back to the States with him.

A consideration of this latter possibility presented enormous problems, not only practical—how to arrange her emigration from Japan and entry into the United States, a minor girl over whom he had no legal control—but emotional as well. What was his true feeling for this child? Was she simply a transitory phase between the old and the new? Was he prepared to take the full responsibility for her life, assuming he could find a way to do so? He was not ready to answer that question.

Once he was back in his room, he went to work immediately, realizing there would be no more money from Victor until he could complete a partial translation of the Neo-Hebraic. And now, for the first time since he had begun his work for Victor, he felt not only the pressure for money but the excitement of anticipation as well. Assuming the authenticity of the document which lay before him, it was the first discovery of a holographic document written by a man who had not only seen Christ in the flesh but had played an important part in his tragedy and triumph, claiming his body from Pilate and placing it in a tomb he had made for himself.

But as Cooper began the translation, using the grammar the priest had sent him, his anticipation began to dull. The letter was not a narrative history, a chronicling of events which Joseph of Arimathea had witnessed and felt compelled to describe. Instead, it was an abusive discourse which Joseph was directing at his son.

My wrath sits upon you like the dust. You cannot escape it wherever you go, for you find it on the road and it is in the air you breathe and you cannot rid yourself of it. Your loyalty is like water held in a broken jar. It seeps away and cannot be held for long. You disgrace the seed from which you grew and trample it underfoot. You profane the name which you carry among men and cause sorrow in the heart of him who begat you. You heed not the voice which calls you from error and directs you in the right path. If it had been meant for us to fight, then he would have returned to lead us. That he did not was a sign from God we were not to do it. And yet you turn your head and proceed to wickedness. Was it this for which you were born? Was it for destruction that you were created?

An unfolding scorn—this was what the letter represented, a wrath which gained momentum even as the old man committed it to paper, an anger superimposed over a deeper anguish. By reading between the lines and studying the indirect references in the manuscript, Cooper could approximate the area of conflict between father and son. The son had been raised in the Essene school and had become a dedicated Jewish nationalist, a firebrand anxious for rebellion and the overthrow of the oppressive Roman legions in Judea. Evidently the father had at one time shared these views, but something had happened to throw them into discord. There had been a split between them and now Joseph was writing this letter to bring about a reconciliation, not through love or persuasion, but through the brute force of indignation. His son would either come back into line or be damned; that was the essence of the letter. Human nature never changed, Cooper realized. Joseph of Arimathea was like any number of stubborn fathers Cooper had known.

He had gone only this far in his translation when the lights flickered and went out. He lighted a candle to give him enough light to get ready for bed and went to sleep the moment his head touched the hard pillow, awaking the next morning with a feeling of extreme well-being. Opening his shutters to the day, he found the sunlight soft and the morning remarkably clear and he delayed his translation long enough to write a brief note to Stevenson, asking him to use his influence to keep Adams from filling his chair right away.

"I'm tied up in a project which has all the earmarks of something really important," he wrote, "and it should give us something to argue about for a long time to come. There's no way I can possibly come back for the spring term but you can tell Adams I will definitely be there for the fall semester, and if you can persuade him to hold off until I'm through here, I don't think he'll regret it. I value your friendship and appreciate all you've done for me."

He addressed an envelope just in time for the maid to take it with her when she finished cleaning his room and making the tea. Then he cleared off his table and went to work on the Neo-Hebraic again.

3

She watched him as he lay beside her on the bed, his passion spent, his hands laced together over his chest, his eyes closed, his mind woolgathering. She lay there, making no attempt to cover her nakedness, her head rolled sideways on the pillow as she looked at him.

"Will you light me a cigarette, please?" she said.

He reached out for the pack of cigarettes on the night stand and lighted two of them, handing her one and placing the bronze fish ashtray on the bed between them. She lay back, blowing a plume of smoke toward the ceiling.

"It's been a long time," she said.

"Yes."

"I've missed you." She looked at him again, his profile silhouetted against the lamp, the long, thin fingers cupped around a cigarette, bringing it to his mouth, retreating as he exhaled the smoke. "God," she said abruptly, without rancor, "the power of the associative reflex. You're in bed with me and you're thinking about her."

143

"Who?" he said, startled.

"Your wife."

"I suppose I was."

"I've often wondered about her, what she was like. Were you happy together?"

"Normally so, I suppose. I never gave much thought to it when we were together. I was absorbed in my work and she didn't make many demands on me, so I assumed she had everything she wanted."

"You sound as if you feel guilty about it."

"I suppose I do."

"Maybe you wouldn't feel that way if things had ended differently."

"You know about the fire?"

"Father O'Connor told me."

"I keep thinking that it needn't have happened," he said quietly, "if I had just been a little more aware of what was going on."

"What could you have done? You weren't even there."

"I might have changed the sequence."

"The sequence?"

"Of events. But I wasn't astute enough to know what was happening, to recognize it. Maybe I would have lost Nan anyway, but not like that, not by default." He talked slowly, punctuating his story with long stretches of silence while he smoked one cigarette after another, resurrecting his own personal tribe of ghosts.

He had planned to take Nan with him to New Haven when he went down to deliver his lecture at Yale, but at the last minute Susan came down with the sniffles and a light fever which presaged any number of childhood diseases and he decided it would be best if Nan stayed behind to take care of Susan instead of leaving her with a baby sitter. Nan was extremely upset about this and when she drove him through the snow to catch his train she did something she had never done before. She asked him not to go, to call the dean of the Theology School and make some excuse, any excuse. Cooper had attributed this temporary weakness on her part to an attack of nerves—after all, Susan wasn't feeling well and Nan was always upset whenever Susan was ill; Nan was a very overprotective mother—and he had soothed her as best he could, assuring her that he would catch the first train back after the lecture was over. If anything went wrong, she could always call him. She did not press the matter and he caught the train for New Haven without giving it a second thought.

He gave his lecture the next morning, intending to catch the one o'clock train back to Cummerland, but the dean had arranged for him to conduct a seminar that afternoon and in the evening a dinner party had been planned in his honor. The invitations had already gone out and he couldn't very well back down, so he called Nan to tell her he would be staying over. He got no answer when he called the house, so he sent her a telegram informing her of his change in plans.

The seminar was equally as successful as the lecture had been. Dinner was at eight, and Cooper had just finished the soup when a maid came into the dining room to tell him he had a long-distance call. It was odd how he remembered all the details of that telephone call as if they had been struck into his memory with the force of the blow around which they centered. He had the taste of clam chowder in his mouth; there was a bowl of geraniums on the telephone table, a silver bowl with blossoms floating in the water. There was a note pad next to the bowl with a mechanical pencil sticking to the metal rim, magnetized; the top sheet of the pad was covered with doodles in the dean's distinctive hand. There was laughter in the room behind him; obviously, the dean had just said something funny.

As Cooper picked up the telephone, he was a trifle uneasy, certain that Nan was calling to tell him Susan's cold was worse. Of course, it was not Nan at all; it was Cooper's colleague, Stevenson, his deep voice sorrowful as he tried to pick the most solacing words to carry the message. But no words could possibly soften the impact of a house burned down, a wife dead, a daughter not expected to live.

One of the men at the dinner drove him back to Cummerland, four hours on the road, and Cooper could remember neither the man's name nor his car, only the arrival and his first glimpse of Susan in a hospital bed, heavily bandaged, under sedation, whimpering in her drugged sleep. She died shortly after he arrived. In a daze, he stumbled out of the hospital, determined to go back to the ruins of the house, but Stevenson dissuaded him. The next day Stevenson told him what had happened, making no effort to conceal the truth, knowing that sooner or later Cooper would find it out anyway.

The fire department wasn't sure how the fire started but they suspected a short circuit in the wiring of the old house, probably in the wall next to the entry hall. In any event, the fire had spread very quickly and within ten minutes the stair well had become an inferno. When the smoke poured under her door Susan must have awakened and tried to get out, only to find that her door was locked. She must have pounded on it, screaming until Nan heard her and rushed up the burning staircase in her nightgown to unlock the door and let her daughter out, but by that time the whole floor was ablaze. Nan unlocked the door before she collapsed, but Susan had already turned away from it and was trying to get out the window. She finally did get the window open and jumped to the snow-covered lawn below where the neighbors extinguished her burning pajamas.

When Cooper had heard this account he could not grasp it. It was as if, in his shock, his mind was too muddled to make sense out of anything and he had argued with Stevenson in an attempt to clarify what had happened. "It couldn't have been that way," he said. "Nan never locked Susan's door."

And then Stevenson had given him the final bit of information which was enough to bring the walls of his world crashing in around him. Nan had locked Susan's door because she was entertaining a man in the bedroom downstairs.

At this point in his narrative, Cooper's voice trailed off. He lay on the bed in silence, smoking his cigarette, staring at the ceiling while Willa looked at him incredulously. "She had a man in the bedroom? They're sure about that?"

He nodded. "He was still there when the firemen arrived. He was in pretty bad shape himself, severe burns on his hands and arms. He'd tried to get Nan down off the second floor but she was too hysterical and he barely got out himself before the stairs collapsed. There was nothing he could do."

"Who was he?"

"A salesman of some sort, life insurance, I think. He sent me a letter a couple of months later saying how sorry he was about the whole thing. Evidently he had been with Nan quite a few times during the six months before the fire, when I was away or working late. I blamed myself more than I did him. I think Nan really tried to break it off. Looking back, I can see a dozen times when she tried to tell me about it, to ask for my help, to keep me from going off somewhere and leaving her alone. But I was too non-committal."

"Do you know why she did it?"

"Not completely," Cooper said. "I wasn't a good husband, I know that. She needed to be caught up in someone else's life. She needed someone to make her feel loved and worth while. She needed a man to give himself to her completely, to merge with her, and I never did that. No, I never gave myself to her, not even partially. And it took a tragedy to make me aware of what a complete failure my marriage was. I had to be jolted out of my illusion." He crushed out his cigarette. "A strange thing happened to me the day I found out the truth. I didn't feel any grief at all, no anger, no despair, just an overwhelming lethargy. So much had happened to me and

I didn't feel a damn thing. Nothing was important to me. All I wanted to do was sleep."

"I've seen that," Willa said. "In Korea." He was silent again now. She reached over and touched his arm, lightly, feeling the need of contact. "Where do you go from here?" she said.

"Home, I guess."

"Back to the college?"

"Yes."

"How soon?"

"I don't know. Next fall at the latest."

"And you'll go back to doing what you did before," she said. "Just like that."

"No, it won't be the same. I know that. But I think I belong there. I'm a plodder. I do best when I'm in a rigid pattern, getting up at the same time every day, working, eating, sleeping, all scheduled, the same day after day. A life like that would bore you, wouldn't it?"

"I don't know," she said. "Maybe it would. But then, everything else bores me too, or almost everything. God, I've spent my whole life trying to keep from being bored."

She sat up on the bed now, straightening her hair, the rapport between them bringing her close to the point of honesty. *All I want is another chance and you can give it to me. We can help each other and this time will be different for both of us because I'll be open with you. And when I get up there again I'll conserve my resources and find myself.* She could not risk it. Even though they were close now, he might misunderstand and she might lose not only her chance but the affection he was beginning to feel for her.

She stood up. Coming around the bed, she leaned down to kiss him, her hair falling about his face like a musky curtain. "Why don't you sleep for a while?" she said. "I don't see how you get any rest in that Japanese bedroll of yours anyway."

He smiled up at her. "I'm a creature of habit, remember?"

She shrugged. "Can you stretch your habit pattern enough to include a cup of coffee?"

"I think it's that flexible," he said.

As she put the coffeepot on the hot plate, it occurred to her how nice it might be to marry a man like this, to have the security of a disciplined life for a change, to say to hell with the frustration of ambition once and for all. *God*, she thought, checking herself. *How foolish can you get? Don't get off the main line. Don't muff the big chance by getting all confused.* She rinsed out the cups for the coffee and put the thought out of her mind before she went back to join him.

4

The next morning Willa received a cable from Moss Hardwick, her agent in New York, offering her an assignment from Leon Warren at *World Today*. Warren was willing to pay her $2750 for an article on Japanese war veterans and how they felt now about their former American enemies. He wanted to run Willa's article back to back with a piece developing the same theme from an American point of view. "Must have five thousand words by December 29," the cable said. "Urgent, firm deadline. Much luck."

She was both pleased and terrified by the assignment. Moss had at least a dozen clients who could have done the story and, considering her present reputation, it must have been a hell of a job for him to sell her in a tight deadline situation like this one. She couldn't afford to let him down, she had to prove that she still had her old competence. Stifling the strong urge to have a drink, she sat down to think, to develop an angle.

Over the years she had developed a writer's ability to become interested in almost anything and she found herself stimulated by the idea, remembering immediately a trio of mutilated men she had seen only a few weeks before, Japanese veterans in ragged army uniforms, standing on a street corner and begging yen from the people who passed by. There were surprisingly few beggars in Tokyo—she supposed there was a law against them—and she didn't think it would be too hard to find them. The first had a stump where his right leg had been; the second was blind; the third exhibited a ragged and hideous scar across his face and neck. But it was not their multiple afflictions that made her remember them, it was the incongruity of Japanese veterans standing on street corners, playing American instruments (mandolins and guitar) and singing American military songs ("The Halls of Montezuma," "Anchors Aweigh") in the hope of exploiting the generous charity of American servicemen. If she could find them they would be perfect for her article, crystallizing a point of view.

She called the Japanese Travel Bureau and hired a guide who arrived at the hotel within ten minutes. He was a neatly dressed and gregarious young man and seemed to know his way around. She told him about the three men. She was almost certain she had seen them on the Ginza, but after she and the guide had spent half a day searching for them through the Ginza bars she began to think she had made a mistake. Maybe she had seen them someplace else.

The guide was in favor of taking her back to the hotel— there was no point to her paying another half day's fee, he said—but she refused. After all, she insisted, there was only a difference of four hundred yen between the half-day and the all-day rate and the beggars were indispensable to her story. This was not completely true—she could develop another angle if she couldn't find them—but she had no desire to go back to the hotel.

By midafternoon they had covered most of the bars down to the Kyobashi Bridge and Willa was enjoying herself immensely, stimulated by the traffic and the crowds and the garish colors of the shops. In the warm sunshine she felt relaxed and pleasantly lethargic, as if she had left all her anxieties back at the hotel. The guide stopped at a camera store which catered to servicemen and tourists—PICTURES OF YOUR EXPERIENCE IN JAPAN IS YOUR MOST ENJOYABLE REMEMBERANCES—and while he went in to ask the proprietor about the three beggars she waited on the sidewalk.

As she stood there in the broad doorway, looking at the people passing by, she had the uneasy feeling she was being watched, and in a moment a bespectacled little Japanese swooped out of one of the canvas stalls along the curb to approach her. It all happened so quickly, she had no chance to be alarmed. He bowed slightly, then, removing his hat, thrust an envelope into her hands, bowed again, and scurried off into the crowd. At first she thought he was either a solicitor for a pom-pom boy or a sidewalk photographer but when she glanced at the envelope she saw her name written across the front in a flowery, Spencerian hand. In the upper left-hand corner, engraved in opulent black letters, was the name of Victor Hawkins. When she opened the envelope she found three crisp new ten-thousand-yen notes and a letter:

My dear Miss Cummings:

As a long-time admirer of your journalistic skills and talents, permit me to pay my respects to you, hoping you will not be offended by the inclusion of this monetary token of esteem which will demonstrate my desire to discuss a business proposition which I trust you will find interesting, challenging, and remunerative. If you will join me tonight at eight for dinner at the Meiji Club, I shall be most gratified and do my best to explain the reasons for this request, other than the natural personal delight I shall feel at making your acquaintance.

Sincerely yours, dear lady,
Victor Hawkins

P.S. For your convenience, I am including the address of the Meiji Club in Japanese, which, if you will give it to any taxi driver, will enable him to find the place.

At the bottom of the sheet was a string of Japanese characters.

She put the envelope in her purse and when the guide came out of the shop she told him she had decided to abandon the search for the rest of the day. He gave her his card. If she wanted to try again at a later time he would be delighted to make himself available. She said she would call him.

5

The Meiji Club surprised her. She had expected it to be small, discreet, and properly conspiratorial in its atmosphere, but she was wrong. It was huge, gaudy, and expensive, with a large dance floor surrounded on three sides by terraces of tables. It was set apart from the rest of the splashy night clubs on the Ginza by the most spectacular lighting she had ever seen. The ceiling was deep black, designed to give the impression of an open and unclouded night sky studded with millions of brilliant stars. The illusion was perfect.

The headwaiter eyed her warily; she was quite obviously the only Caucasion in the crowd of formally dressed Japanese waiting behind the velvet rope, but once she gave her name and asked for Victor Hawkins' table, he became solicitous and ushered her past the rope immediately, leading the way up the carpeted stairs to the topmost tier of tables.

As she had been wrong about the Meiji Club, she also found she had underestimated Victor Hawkins himself. From all she had heard of him, she had expected a bloated, dissolute man with a thin façade of effeminate mannerisms. But as he stood up at her approach he radiated warmth and an infectious charm. He had dressed in dinner clothes for the occasion and looked like a successful and urbane businessman. He took her hand in his with spontaneous warmth.

"How extraordinarily nice of you to come," he said, blocking the adroit movement of the headwaiter in order to seat her himself. "And if you will pardon the presumption, may I tell you how lovely you look, what a perfect gown that is for you. The color is absolutely perfect."

"I will pardon the presumption," she said, smiling. "That's always nice to hear."

"Would you care for a drink?"

"No, thanks. But go right ahead."

"Alcohol has never agreed with me," Victor said unhappily. "I have often rued this particular allergy because there are so many rare and exquisite tastes and bouquets to be found in the alcoholic catalogue, but then, one doesn't always have a free hand in matters of nature. One takes, so to speak, whatever nature gives." He sat down now, easing himself into his chair. "I took the liberty of ordering dinner but I don't want you to feel bound by my choice if there is anything you would especially like to have. I feel I must warn you in advance that the food I have chosen is quite basic, thoroughly American, nothing exotic."

"That's fine with me," she said.

"Good." He nodded slightly. The headwaiter disappeared down the stairs.

"This is an unusual place," she said appreciatively, looking down toward the distant dance floor. "I wonder why I've never heard of it."

"Presumably because you are an American, dear lady," Victor said pleasantly. "The Meiji was founded on reverse snobbery. It's reserved exclusively for socially prominent and wealthy Japanese who have no desire to mingle with foreigners. And by 'foreigners' I don't mean Caucasians specifically, but other orientals as well. A very rich Korean—they are quite good businessmen, you know, the Koreans—has been trying to come here for months, but he can never get past the entrance rope because, after all, he is not Japanese. Of course there isn't any problem with Americans because the sign outside is quite small and written in Japanese and few of them even know what this place is. And in case you might wonder how I come to be here, I had the good fortune to invest in this concern when it was established, so in that sense I am considered one of the owners. Too, most Japanese don't look on me as a foreigner. I'm rather like Lafcadio Hearn in that regard, in that I have a genuine interest in these people and their customs, and so I have been more or less assimilated. And speaking of prejudice, I have often wondered if there isn't stratification in the minority groups, if the Negroes don't have prejudices too, for instance. By that I mean, do you think a Chicago Negro looks down on an Alabama Negro? And does an Alabama Negro look down on an African Negro?"

"I haven't got the slightest idea," Willa said, a little awed by the incessant torrent of words and thoughts.

"I should think so," he said. "Everybody has to have somebody to look down upon, to feel superior to, so to speak. And in most truly ancient cultures a class has been created specifically for that purpose—the untouchables, the *eta* class in Japan, so that even in his relative poverty the average Japanese feels elevated above something."

The dinner was excellent and American—steaks and potatoes served with a flourish—and Victor's monologue was interrupted by a brassy floor show which erupted all over the dance floor, an extravaganza replete with sequined nudes and fire jugglers and startling visual effects. Once the final act was over and the Japanese master of ceremonies had abandoned the field, Willa tried to discover what had prompted Hawkins' invitation, but without success. He was simply too glib, flooding the silence with discourses on everything from prejudice to art. But gradually she began to see that his monologue was neither so random nor so pointless as it seemed. Evidently he felt it necessary to lay a broad foundation of words and ideas before he could explain why he had asked her here.

It was only when dinner was over and the coffee had been

served that he began to approach his point like a bird coming to roost, talking around it in ever diminishing spirals. "I know the stories which are circulated about me, dear lady," he said, spooning sugar into his cup. "And it wounds me, it truly does, to have anybody think badly of me, but I consider it the price which has to be paid for being an individual, for trying to create beauty of an unorthodox nature, for attempting to rescue that particular kind of beauty, so to speak, from where it has fallen. If I could, I would sell everything I have and invest that money in the creative people of this world, but unfortunately I know this would be a hollow and useless gesture. Because the price must be paid by the artist, not by somebody else, because the price exacted by art is a part of the creative process. It is for that reason I try to be as business-like as possible, because art is speculative, business concrete. Art transports you; business lets you know where you are."

"And just where are we?" Willa said. "You lost me somewhere along the line."

He seemed to take no offense at her bluntness. "We are at a point where our interests coincide, dear lady. At the risk of giving offense, I shall be quite frank with you. I am aware of your present circumstances."

"What circumstances?"

"Financial, having to do work which is beneath your talent simply because you need the money. I know you are capable of truly great writing—you have done it in the past—but I also know that you need something to put you back into the top rank." He raised his cup; a diamond cuff link glittered in the subdued light. He looked at her speculatively as he sipped his coffee. "I have it within my power, dear lady, to be of enormous assistance to you. But the mere fact that I make this offer constitutes a certain risk on my part, so I would like your word, if you decide not to take my proposition, that you will discuss it with nobody."

"All right," she said. "That's fair enough."

155

"I'm glad to find you co-operative," Victor said. "But before we go into the details, let me describe the benefits which you will receive. First, I will give you the sum of five thousand American dollars or its equivalent in yen—your option—as a retainer. Should you follow this project through to the end, a matter of a few weeks, dear lady, no more than that, then I will give you exclusive rights to the story of the Baum-Brenner papers. You're familiar with them?"

"Yes," she said, trying to cover the surprise she felt. "Cooper has told me something about them."

"The exclusive rights should bring you quite a large sum of money," Victor said. "And it goes without saying that this should re-establish your reputation."

"Why should you offer this to me?" she asked.

"Because I am not a greedy man," Victor said. "And I realize full well that the proper publicity will only enhance the value of the physical manuscripts. And I should tell you now, there is considerably more to these papers than you might imagine."

"Oh?"

"Cooper simply has no idea what he is about to uncover."

"And you do?"

"Of course," Victor said evenly. "I had a rough translation made by my Japanese scholars before I even sent the photostats to Cooper."

"Then why bother with him at all?" she said, confused.

"My dear lady"—he smiled indulgently—"I use him for the same reason I use you, because a proper promotion requires a blend of talents, not just one. I use him for the same reason the Germans used Baum-Brenner. People might vilify him for renouncing his faith and joining the Nazis, but as a scholar he was above reproach, absolutely meticulous. The Nazis knew what they had and were simply using Baum-Brenner to establish its validity, just as I know what I have and am using our friend Cooper to do the same thing. The documents are authentic beyond the shadow of a doubt. Later, when I allow him to examine the papyri, he will discover that."

"I don't want you to think that I go around looking gift horses in the mouth," she said wryly, "but you know and I know that you could have bought my journalistic services for whatever you wanted to pay. So I have the feeling you want something more than a writer."

"Quite so," he said. "You are very perceptive, dear lady. And being perceptive, I'm sure you recognize in our friend Cooper a quality of mind which, under other circumstances, would be most laudable, but in this situation, as you will see, could very well prove disastrous to me. There is, beneath that cold exterior, the soul and heart of a martyr. He thinks he is only interested in the facts, devoted to the truth, whatever it happens to be, but he is basically constructive by nature, not destructive. And that could make a difference."

"I see what you're getting at," Willa said, "but I think you're wrong. He's talked to me about what he's done so far and he's never expressed any desire to cover it up, to call it off."

Victor sighed patiently. "And what is there to cover up? That Paul was considered a madman by the Romans? That's nothing new. I doubt there was a single Christian in the early centuries who was not considered a madman by someone. That Paul was convicted of murder and executed for it? I can show you a thousand such murders in the history of any church which are now considered holy acts because they were committed to preserve the faith. No, it would change the emphasis, perhaps, proving that Paul so loved Christ that he was willing to kill anyone who denigrated him. It would humanize a saint but it certainly wouldn't destroy him."

"Then what do you think he would try to cover up?"

"The next two documents," Victor said bluntly. "The first is a letter from Joseph of Arimathea to his son John, the same man Paul killed, by the way. The bulk of it is nothing more

157

than a long and dreary reprimand and general condemnation, heaped on the head of a recalcitrant son by an angry and vindictive father. I must say in passing that I agree with the father most emphatically. The son deserved everything he got. It seems that the son was a skeptic, angry because he had been fooled, because he had put himself wholeheartedly into a movement based on a false premise. It appears from the two documents that Joseph of Arimathea was one of the sponsors of the messianic movement, a secret supporter of Christ, and that the son was allied in the movement. I am not a biblical historian, dear lady, so I cannot supply you with all of the political background, but suffice it to say that the plan was for Christ to rally the people behind him in an armed uprising to throw off the yoke of Rome. In the beginning he was simply a mystic, a semi-political leader who had really gathered a considerable amount of support from the simple people. But at some point—when he became involved with John the Baptist perhaps—he began to think of himself as something more, the Messiah as a matter of fact, the son of God. The Aramaic document, by the way, was written by Jesus himself, in his own hand, a record of his sayings and some of the precepts of the heavenly kingdom he intended to establish with the overthrow of Rome."

"A document written by Christ himself?" She felt very cold now.

"Quite so. It's a long thing, obviously the Q document which was used as a source for the gospels. The papyrus is in excellent shape, priceless, absolutely magnificent. But to continue. John of Arimathea was to be in charge of the armed forces for the rebellion, which was to come about when Jesus entered Jerusalem for the feast of the passover. But this didn't happen, dear lady, because in the interim Jesus had come to identify himself with the prophesied Messiah and this required a sacrificial death and resurrection. Since John of Arimathea was an immensely practical young man, he had no belief whatsoever that this could be accomplished. His father, having implicit faith in Jesus, never doubted for an instant. The resurrection would certainly guarantee success; there could be no public doubt of a man who had been crucified before them and then come back from the dead. The people would rally to him instantaneously. The Roman legions would stand no chance. So Jesus was crucified and John of Arimathea had his men ready to distribute arms on the morning of the third day." He paused again, sipping his coffee. Down on the dance floor the band had begun to play a rhumba.

"And then what happened?" she said quietly.

"Dear lady, it's quite obvious," Victor said evenly. "On that third morning there was no rebellion because, simply put, Jesus did not rise."

She said nothing. His coffee cup clinked against the saucer as he put it down.

"Joseph removed the body from the tomb and had it buried secretly, hoping people would assume Jesus had risen. And some of his disciples did believe it, of course, the more suggestible ones. But there was no possibility of an insurrection now, no rallying point. John of Arimathea was naturally bitter and wanted to expose the whole thing and that was the reason his father sent him such a strong letter and the Q document too. I rather think, although this is only conjecture, that the reason John of Arimathea went to Paul was to seek financing for a new army, the old one having faded away in the years after the death of Jesus, and to get the physical support of the Christians. But by that time what had begun as a political movement had become an eschatalogical one. John threatened to reveal the truth if Paul didn't help him. Paul couldn't tolerate this. So he killed him."

"I don't believe it," she said after a long moment. "I simply don't believe it."

"I know how you feel," Victor said sympathetically. "I was most distraught when I first received the translation, most upset, because I am a Christian, dear lady, and the last thing I wished in this world was to see my faith destroyed. But then, it's morally wrong to believe in something which is demonstrably untrue, now isn't it? Abhorrent as I find it, the documents withstand every test of verification."

"And you think I am going to be able to talk Cooper into accepting this?" she asked.

"No," he said. "I have no doubt you are a very persuasive person, but you will have absolutely nothing to do with that. The documents are authentic and he is going to prove that for himself. But I must admit there is a question in my mind as to what he will do when the full implication of what he has hits him, whether he will accept it calmly in the light of reason or whether he will try to protect the faith he pretends not to believe. There is nothing tangible he can do, of course, not as far as the eventual verification of the documents is concerned, but if he chose to publicly denounce the documents as being false, then it would take me a considerable amount of time to submit them to other scholars who would refute him. So I want you as a stabilizing rudder, so to speak. As the only person truly close to him, you can keep him on an even keel, emphasizing the direction in which his duty lies— to truth, to scholarship. And of course it does, dear lady. That is exactly where his duty lies."

"You have a good pitch," she said, suddenly tired, wishing she had never accepted his invitation, "but I don't believe you're willing to pay such a price for a stabilizing influence."

He smiled tolerantly. "It is also imperative for me to know what Cooper is thinking, his mental climate, so to speak, as he threads his way through the final two documents. I shall expect you to call me every day or so just to let me know how he is getting along. If he suddenly decides to reverse himself, to refute these documents in the public press, I have to be forewarned. I have to know before he does anything."

God, she thought, *why does he have to pick me?* She was

tired and sick to her stomach and she wanted to tell him to go to hell.

The band was playing a twist now. A woman in a silver-sequined dress was in the middle of the dance floor and as the spotlight glinted on her Willa remembered a time when she was walking with her father and they came to a stream in the pine forest and she saw something glittering in the water, alive with fire; when she approached, ever so cautiously, she saw it was a silver minnow, struggling against the rushing water, working furiously to get upstream but doing no more than stand still against the current. And she wondered at the time, being a child with an inquiring mind and an innate skepticism beyond her years, why that beautiful silver minnow should be struggling so hard to get upstream when the creek appeared to be the same upstream as it was down. *Let go, little minnow,* she found herself whispering. *Let go and find quiet water and be beautiful like you're supposed to be.*

"I think I'd like a drink now," she said at last. "Scotch and water."

Victor raised a finger; a waiter appeared from nowhere. Willa said nothing while she drank, giving him no answers, angry because he had known what her answer would be before he invited her here. He knew the right points of pressure to touch; he had a chart of her weaknesses.

"I'm not going to give you an answer tonight," she said stubbornly, fortified by the drink. "I'm going to give this whole damn project a lot of thought."

"Of course, dear lady," Victor said, relaxing now. "I think you should. But I want you to know, in advance, whether you accept or reject my proposition, what a great pleasure it is for me to be with you this evening. And it will always have a prominent place in my catalogue of memories that I had dinner with Willa Cummings, a fine talent and a truly charming woman."

Seven

1

FATHER O'CONNOR's stomach was giving him trouble again. During times of strain and confusion he felt a visceral agitation; his whole digestive tract trembled violently and uncontrollably within him. He felt it now. It was unfair, he thought, that Cooper should have put this problem in his hands. He turned toward the fireplace in his sparsely furnished room, aware that Cooper was waiting for his comment and opinion on the translation he had just finished reading.

"Well," Cooper said, "what do you think?"

"I think it's a monstrous fraud," Father O'Connor said, placing his hand flat on his stomach in a futile attempt to still the quaking. "A blasphemous hoax. It has to be. There have been attempts to fictionalize the life of Christ before this. The Wolfenbüttel Fragments, the Natürliche Geschichte —I could name a dozen of them, just offhand. This is the same kind of thing. The story is fraudulent and fictitious and the documents have been forged, either for profit or out of some warped hatred for our Blessed Lord. I don't know how you can be deceived by something so patently false."

"Is it?" Cooper said.

"Of course it is," Father O'Connor said, his stomach trembling so violently now that it approached the edge of pain. "What do you want me to say, that Christianity is the offshoot of some ancient and unsuccessful rebellion, that Jesus Christ was nothing more than a political leader with delusions of grandeur?"

"No," Cooper said heatedly. "I came here for an objective opinion because I'm disturbed and upset and I can't trust my own judgment. I can't wish this away and neither can you, and we're not going to smother it by all the protestations of faith and blanket denials that either of us can think up." He grabbed up the photostats and banged them on the table, frustrated. "You talked of yourself as a defense attorney for Christ; all right, act like one. If there are holes in this, help me find them. If all this is false, help me prove it."

"On the spur of the moment," Father O'Connor said. "Just like that."

"Just like that," Cooper said firmly. "I've put Victor off as long as I can. He knows I'm stalling. And as things stand now, any objective scholar in the world would back him up."

"I'm not the man for this," Father O'Connor said, shaking his head, tired. "If we could only get somebody else . . ."

"I'll ask you straight out," Cooper said. "All I want from you is a simple yes or no. Will you help me?"

"Yes," Father O'Connor said. "I'll do the best I can." He poured himself a glass of water from the carafe on the table. It was stale. He had asked the housekeeper to change the water in the carafe at least twice a day whether he drank any of it or not. *I'll have to remind her,* he thought illogically. *The human memory is a faulty instrument.* His eyes fell on the crucifix mounted on the bare white masonry wall. He took a deep breath. *Be objective,* he told himself. *The truth is obfuscated by emotion.* He removed his reading glasses from their worn leather case and put them on, moving back to the photostats on the table. "All right," he said. "What can you tell me about the scientific tests? Is there any possibility Hawkins could have paid for a favorable report?"

"No," Cooper said, obviously relieved by the priest's change in attitude. "I've seen the reports and I've talked with Dr. Ikeda. The radiocarbon tests were witnessed by a dozen men and the ultraviolet tests revealed no trace of an earlier writing that had been bleached off. As far as I can tell, the texts on those papyri are original."

"Then you've examined the physical papyri yourself?"

"Yes," Cooper said. The translation of the final Aramaic had been completed at two that morning, he explained, and he was so disturbed by it that he could not sleep. As soon as he heard Willa stirring next door, he used her telephone and called Victor to make arrangements to examine the final papyri, giving as an excuse his inability to make a translation from the photostat. Victor grunted his assent and Cooper went to his place, where Itsugi had been instructed to meet him.

The document rooms lay to the rear of the building and they were the most elaborate facilities for handling papyrus manuscripts that Cooper had ever seen. The air pumped into the antiseptic room was filtered and humidified, the light was perfectly balanced; it was quite apparent Victor was equipped for a volume operation. The Neo-Hebraic and the Aramaic manuscripts had already been laid out on the broad worktable for his inspection, the sections fitted together and pressed between glass.

There was a difference between the papyri on which the two documents had been written. That used by Joseph of Arimathea was the superior of the two, made from the broad middle sections of the papyrus plants. The papyrus of the Q document—Cooper used this only as a descriptive title, not as an expression of opinion—was of an inferior quality. The polishing process, by which the finished sheets were smoothed with ivory or bone to give them an even surface, had been badly done. In places the ink had run into the grain and the writing was smeared.

He had thought the two documents were separate. This would have given him more latitude in interpreting them, making possible a supposition that one might be authentic and the other forged at a later date, the second building, so to speak, on the information contained in the first. This was made impossible when he found that the last phrases of Joseph's letter had been written on the top of the first sheet of the Q document. Whether Joseph had done this to link the two together purposely, or whether he had simply run out of writing space and utilized that area which Jesus had left blank could be no more than conjecture. From the condition of the fragments, Cooper concluded the two scrolls had been rolled together, the Q document forming the inner core and protected by the more durable sheets of Joseph's letter wound around the outside.

While he was in the room, after spending the morning examining the Neo-Hebraic and the Aramaic, he was permitted to examine the originals of the Lucretius Septimus, Pauline, and Lucan letters. Again, Cooper could find nothing in the quality of the papyrus to cast doubt on their authenticity. The Lucretius letter was written on *charta hieratica,* the best-quality papyrus produced by Rome, a choice in keeping with the attitude of a subordinate addressing his superior. The writing itself had obviously been done by a competent and practiced scribe.

The Pauline letter was written on a low-grade papyrus, someplace above the *charta emporetica,* the lowest grade of packing paper. The sheets were not uniform. Obviously Paul had been forced to write on whatever paper he found available, in this case the end sheets of inferior quality from a number of different rolls, the *eschatokollion.* These sheets had been pasted together to form a *scapus.* Luke, having access to a better-quality paper, put his message to Timothy on a standard roll of papyrus, approximately fourth quality if you were using the scale of eight described by Pliny, or fifth if you were using the scale of nine established during the reign of Claudius.

"Then there's nothing there," Father O'Connor said with a sigh. "What about the paleography?"

"The script is authentic in all the documents," Cooper said. "I'd stake my reputation on that. It would take some comparisons with other manuscripts of the same period to establish that absolutely, but I'm sure it can and will be done."

"Then let's examine the chronology," Father O'Connor insisted.

They dissected the Roman soldier's letter for two hours, taking it point by point, but they could find no error. The chronology was logical, accurate. There had been a rebellion of the Iceni and the Boadicea in Britain in A.D. 61 and the IXth Legion had indeed been destroyed, and this insurrection had been put down by Suetonius Paulinius. The trouble stemming from the death of Agrippina was historically authentic; Nero had issued orders for the death of his mother in A.D. 58 staying in Campania until the deed was done and he could gauge the reactive violence of Agrippina's supporters. There was no such violence. Had Lucretius Septimus taken part in the suppression of Agrippina's followers? There was no way to prove he had not. The games which he described, celebrating Nero's return to Rome, had been held in September of A.D. 59.

The facts in the document were unshakable and only at one point could Father O'Connor raise any kind of objection. Lucretius had written that Paul's life was considered offensive to Hermes, possibly because at one time the people of Lystra and Derbe had referred to Barnabas as "Zeus" and Paul as "Hermes." Wasn't it logical that Lucretius, being a loyal Roman, would have used the name "Mercury" instead of

"Hermes"? Cooper refused to take this point seriously enough even to discuss it. "Nero was a Hellenist," he said, dismissing it, picking up his translation of the Pauline letter.

They discussed the Pauline letter until dawn, but once again everything seemed to fall into place. According to Acts, Paul had walked the nineteen miles from Troas to Assos alone, leaving his companions to go by boat. It was an obscure scriptural point which most Bible scholars dismissed as being self-explanatory. Paul had left his companions because he wanted time to think, to meditate. But if this letter was to be believed, he had a much more logical reason for his solitary journey.

John of Arimathea had approached him in Troas and Paul had taken the lonely road to Assos either to escape him or to assure a private meeting place if the young man followed him. John had followed him, the earlier argument was resumed, and John had been killed. Whatever had happened there had been witnessed by Alexander, the coppersmith, who, according to scripture, had testified against Paul.

From Paul's statement that Alexander had perjured himself, three possible versions of what happened on the road to Assos could be theorized. First, it was possible John had died of natural causes, a stroke perhaps, a heart attack in the heat of argument. In this case, Alexander had lied against Paul. Second, Paul could have struck John in self-defense, in an exchange of blows, and Alexander could have misinterpreted or distorted what he had seen. Finally, it was possible Alexander had testified accurately and Paul was lying in his letter to Timothy, trying to justify what had happened.

But Paul's letter was ambiguous and it took the Lucretius letter to make it clear. Lucretius, in turn, was indirectly supported by Luke. The letter from Joseph of Arimathea to his son supplied the motive and some of the background but only when it was supported by an interpretation of the Q document. At no point, for instance, did Joseph mention

Jesus by name. Instead, he used the term "Bar-Nasha," an Aramaic word meaning "man" or "son of man," an indefinite noun which was also used as a pronoun when a man was speaking of himself in the third person. "That we were not to arm ourselves and rise up was proven when the man did come forth," Joseph wrote to his son. Was this man (Bar-Nasha) Christ? Was this statement a reference to the hoped-for resurrection? The contiguity of the two documents made the meaning perfectly clear; "Bar-Nasha" was the term Jesus used to refer to himself as the "son of man."

The reason Joseph sent the Q document to his son could only be inferred, but to Cooper it seemed perfectly valid. Joseph hoped to dissuade his son from his determination to rebel and what better method could he choose than to allow the leader of that rebellion to condemn himself in his own words, to let the promises ring hollow, the hopes vain? If God had not seen fit to raise Jesus from the grave, was not this sufficient proof that God was against the planned rebellion? From Luke's letter, it appeared that Joseph had come to believe in Christ again in his later years—Luke's letter included him among the faithful Christians in Jerusalem—but that later state of mind had nothing to do with an interpretation of this letter.

The thread of continuity went from one document to the next, an interlocking sequence of events which were supposed to be facts. Father O'Connor was dizzied by them, angered by them because he knew the whole thing was false, it could not be true, and he could demolish the whole structure if he could shake one of these facts loose and disprove it, but he could not do it. The visceral agitation had been replaced by a dull ache now. He raised a last argument without any great strength behind it, knowing Cooper could knock it down. "It's impossible," he said wearily, having to push the breath out of his lungs to form the words. "There's no way these documents could have been preserved in any monastery for two thousand years. They would have been destroyed as heretical a long time ago."

"We don't know for sure they came from a monastery," Cooper said. "The Germans may have uncovered them during the fighting in North Africa."

"All in one tidy group?" Father O'Connor said testily. "Neat and tidy. And why didn't the priest in China destroy them?"

"He probably didn't know what he had."

Claim, counterclaim, argument, refutation, all ephemeral conjectures, flights of oral fancy, insubstantial, inconclusive. A bell rang in the distance and the little priest looked up with a start. It was time for early mass. Quite without his knowing it, the black night had faded into a gray day. He was so tired he could no longer think clearly. Once mass was over, he would plead illness . . . no, he could not do that. The question was bound to be asked and he could neither equivocate an answer nor let this knowledge spread. He would have to get through his classes somehow. He took off his glasses. "I have to go," he said, "but I can't leave it here. I have to know what you're going to do."

"Stall for more time," Cooper said.

"I don't mean now," Father O'Connor said, wishing he had something to clear his head, to make his perception more acute. "I mean to say, if you can't disprove these documents, then what will you do?"

"I don't know."

"Does that mean you won't do anything?"

"I don't know."

The summoning bell rang again, insistently. "Can you sit by and watch Christianity destroyed?"

"There's never been any guarantee that once you uncover truth it's going to be pleasant or constructive," Cooper said.

"Don't give me any of your classroom generalities," Father O'Connor said irritably. "Something has to be done to stop this blasphemy and I give you fair warning right now. If you don't do it, then I will." He turned away, blinking, determined not to carry this anger into the chapel. His eyes fell on the crucifix again, the tortured Christ in walnut, and he felt suddenly chilled to the marrow. How infectious was disbelief; how contagious was doubt. He forced his mind away from the thought. Wheeling toward the door, he left the room without looking back at Cooper. He hurried down the hallway, half running toward the sanctuary of the beginning mass.

2

In her mind, Willa set a line of demarcation beyond which she would not go. It was an artificial limit, of course, a rationalized behavior, and she knew it, but it enabled her to keep her self-respect. She had agreed to take Victor's money and keep him informed of Cooper's state of mind, but she told herself that if the time ever came when Cooper was jeopardized by her actions she would stop immediately.

Cooper had become far more important to her by now than the projected results of any of Victor's promises. In the back of her mind, the way of life Cooper had prescribed for himself began to appeal to her. A disciplined, routined life might be just what she needed, she decided, but even in her most severe moments of panic and despair she knew she could not marry Cooper as a failure seeking a refuge. When she retired from the arena, it could only be after one final and absolutely stunning coup, and the Baum-Brenner collection was going to be it.

She told Cooper about the lead she was developing on Anna Klaus and was relieved to find that he was neither upset nor irritated that she should have undertaken this research on her own. On the contrary, he was quite interested

170

and asked her to let him know the minute she had anything specific.

In turn, he had now become completely open with her, using her as a sounding board as he tried to assess the material he translated. He had been forced to tell Victor of the contents of the Neo-Hebraic and the Aramaic and evidently Victor had put on a good show of surprise, weeping at the magnificence of the find and its commercial potential. Apparently Cooper was not pleased by what was happening, but as far as she could see, he was going to do nothing to stop it.

And then, one Thursday night when he returned from a particularly frustrating session in Victor's manuscript room, Cooper gave her a real fright. "Those documents must be false," he said. "They have to be!"

"Oh?" she said, keeping her voice even as she continued to clear the dishes from the table. "Did you find something today?"

"No, I didn't find a thing. And that's the trouble."

She left the dishes on the table and went over to sit by him on the bed. "So you're one of those," she said with a smile.

"One of what?"

"I don't know what you call them," she said, "but I've run across more than one in my time: people who damn something if it's faulty and suspect it if it's perfect."

"I suspect this all right," he said. "Look at it from a purely objective viewpoint. Each of these documents supports the others. Here in one convenient little bundle we have a perfect and full progression, from a quasi-official description of Paul as a murderer, to a confession of the crime, to a rationalization of it, to a reason for it, to an exposé of Christ as a political bungler. From A to B to C, it's that simple. And having A makes it easier to believe B, and so on down the line. There is literally too much here. I can understand, for instance, how the Luke and Paul letters might have been preserved together

171

—after all, they were both addressed to Timothy—but both letters ask him to destroy the Joseph letter and the Q document. He was a true believer and he should have done it, but he didn't."

"But maybe he—"

"Let me finish, please. All right, granted that for some reason Timothy preserved all four documents. What about the first one, the letter to Tigellinius? It was addressed to a Roman commander by a subordinate. Logically, once Tigellinius had read it, it would have been thrown away. There was no reason for him to keep it. No action was taken on it as far as I can determine. Then how did this one significant and relevant letter find its way into the collection?"

"Somebody put it there."

"But who? When?"

"Is that important?"

"Very important," he insisted. "It disturbs me. The odds are, I'd say, a million to one at the very best that Baum-Brenner or the Nazis could have pieced this collection together from different sources, say the Q document from Oxyrhynchus and the Lucretius letter from someplace else and so forth. So these documents must have already been a collection when they were discovered. Do you follow me?"

"Yes," she said.

"All right, then. Suppose they were assembled by an early scholar. Now, if he was a staunch believer, like Father O'Connor, for instance, he would have destroyed them immediately. Or his faith might have been destroyed by them, and if this happened he wouldn't just sit on them, keep them quiet. On the other hand, if a non-Christian scholar had assembled these documents they would have been used in an all-out attack against the Christian church."

"Maybe they were," she said, "and maybe we just don't know about it. A lot of early writings were lost."

"But nothing of this importance," he said. "If these doc-

172

uments were ever used as a basis for an attack on Christianity, we would have refutations and arguments and defenses against them. We would have dozens of references to them and we could get a pretty good idea from those references what information the documents contained, even if they had been destroyed. But there's nothing, absolutely no mention of them in any of the sources I'm familiar with. As far as I know, Baum-Brenner was the first man to see these documents in two thousand years."

"This is very hard on you, isn't it?" she said. "You don't want this to be true, do you?"

"If it is true, I want to be convinced beyond the shadow of a doubt. I've never enjoyed the work of the scholarly assassins."

"Perhaps something will come along, darling," she said. She did not want to talk about his work any more. His attitude depressed her. She patted his hand and then stood up to finish clearing the table. "That's one thing I've learned in my business. Something always comes along. It may not be good, but it comes along."

"How's your veteran article doing?"

"It's not," she said. "I need something to hang it on and I can't find it. I went out to interview a retired Japanese admiral yesterday. He's supposed to be hell on Americans and I thought I could get some potent stuff there, but he's only bitter because his granddaughter is having an affair with an American staff sergeant. And that's not the kind of material Warren is interested in." She sighed. "It's going to take longer than I thought it would, but I'll get it. I don't have any choice. I have to."

Cooper left early and she put a fresh sheet of paper in the typewriter and placed her notes to one side of the machine, looking forward to the first stroke of the key which would break the mesmerizing blankness. Sharpening a half dozen pencils, she laid them beside her notes and then removed her reading glasses from her purse and held them up to the light, detecting a smudge which called for finding the box of tissues before she could begin her work. She sat down in front of the typewriter and picked up her notes, reading through them to refresh her memory, hoping that she would somehow come up with something.

In the old days, in Korea, she had written with a galloping disregard for syntax or grammar, allowing her impressions to spill out on the paper, anxious to get one thing finished so she could start the next. She had never been a stylist and she lacked the ability to find the perfect phrase, the indispensable word, the befitting cadence, but there had been a freshness to what she wrote, a spontaneity which evoked the feel of battle, the confusion and the boredom and the almost impersonal mayhem of an artillery war. Now, sitting by herself in this hotel room, faced with the task of piecing together an objective article, a job of craftsmanship rather than an expression of intense personal feeling, her mind refused to work.

She sat in front of the typewriter a full hour and then said to hell with it. She was tired. She needed rest. She would start over again in the morning, when she was fresh. She had a drink and went to bed.

It was somewhat easier the next morning. She managed to suffer through an opening page which, even if it seemed static, at least gave her something to work with, a beginning. She was interrupted by the morning mail and a letter from the *Fiji Times*. As she read it she felt that it was an omen, that things were beginning to break for her again. The editor apologized for taking so long to reply but he had waited for a local businessman—who had employed Mrs. Klaus—to return from Singapore. Now that the businessman was back, the editor could offer specific information. Mrs. Klaus had indeed been at Suva, where she had redecorated a local hotel—doing a splendid job of it, the editor commented parenthetically—

and about six months ago she had gone to Singapore, where she had a number of commissions to do private residences. When she finished her work in Singapore, she had gone to Japan. As far as the businessman knew, she was still there, near a mountain town named Taguchi; she was doing work at a resort hotel, the Akakura Western Lodge. And the editor did indeed recognize Willa's name, closing his letter by wishing her well and offering to assist her in any way he could.

She considered the letter important enough to take next door, using it to interrupt Cooper's work. She found him studying an Aramaic grammar but when she told him about the letter he seemed more enthusiastically interested than he had in weeks.

"I thought I'd write her a letter," Willa said, "to see if she'd be willing to give me an interview."

"If she will, I want to go with you," Cooper said. "There are a lot of things I want to ask her."

"Such as?"

"The most important thing is whether or not she has any other manuscripts that belonged to her father."

"Are you looking for anything specific?"

"I don't know what I'm looking for," he said. "Would you like me to write her?"

"I'm looking for any excuse not to go to work," Willa said with just a trace of a smile. "I'll let you know when I hear anything."

Eight

1

THERE was a reply from Mrs. Klaus within a week. Her letter was full of a gentle melancholy. "It has been a long time since I have heard my father's name spoken or even seen it written," she wrote, "and I am reluctant even now to talk about him. He drank his cup of bitterness a long time ago, as I have drunk mine. And now that the cup is empty, I do not wish it to be filled again. He has been judged many times and I have no answers to the charges made against him. I offer no explanation of the things he did or did not do. I can say only this: he was the most gentle man I have ever known. He was a kind father and I loved him." There was no mention of any manuscripts.

Now Cooper wrote to her directly, a long and detailed letter in which he described his interest in her father's work and denied any concern with his politics. "I have always held the greatest respect for your father as a scholar," he wrote, "and I would not presume to judge him for what happened during a time when all moral values were upset by war. I wouldn't disturb you except that this is matter of the greatest

176

importance. I am currently working on what seems to be the last project which occupied your father before his untimely death, a project which could influence a reshaping of religious thought in the world. It is urgent, therefore, that I know if there are any pieces to his manuscript collection which I do not have. I would appreciate hearing from you. And I assure you, nothing I do will serve to rekindle any of the old controversies concerning your father."

Her final note came by return mail. "I will be at this hotel through February," she wrote. "I do have a small number of old manuscript fragments which my father left in my safe-keeping. You are welcome to examine them, if you will come here."

He replied that he would come as soon as he could get away, possibly in mid-December. He would let her know the exact date later.

There were, however, a number of complications he had to resolve before he could leave Tokyo and the first was Victor. Cooper did not intend to let Victor know about Anna Klaus or his projected trip to Akakura and there was no way he could just take off for a week. Victor's joyous buoyancy had begun to sag and his bright confidence to tarnish.

"I think I am being played for a fool, dear boy," Victor confided to him one afternoon in the manuscript room. "They expect to bring the price down, I presume, reducing it through a series of delaying tactics."

"The Red Chinese?"

"Dr. Lu Hsiao-p'ing," Victor said petulantly. "I have co-operated with him in every way possible. I gave him a copy of Dr. Ikeda's findings. I provided him with a précis of the material and allowed him in here to examine the papyri, on the presumption that all these preliminaries would lead inevitably to a bid on the part of his government."

"And they haven't made one, I take it?"

"No," Victor said. "He vacillates. He seems undecided as to the authenticity of the documents. I am afraid, dear boy, at the risk of imposing on you, that I shall have to ask you to meet with him one day soon. He can't refuse to accept your certification, surely."

"I don't know that he'll accept my opinion," Cooper said, "but I'll meet with him, after I've finished my study of the papyri."

"I appreciate it, dear boy, I truly do," Victor said. "And I am sure I can count on you to proceed with all possible speed."

No, Cooper thought, Victor was going to tolerate no delays at all.

A second and unexpected complication concerned Myoko. Cooper found out about this on a Friday when he was having lunch with Father O'Connor. The priest had received a call from a Mrs. Boudreau who needed to get in touch with Cooper concerning his daughter's plans for the Christmas holidays. Since the school operated on a Western schedule, it recessed for ten days during the Christmas season to allow the children to participate in all the gala festivities planned by the embassies and the legations. Therefore it would be necessary for Cooper to pick Myoko up on the twenty-second, as the school would be closed and the staff personnel would be away.

Father O'Connor had been completely at a loss to know what to say to the woman. At first he was sure there had been some mistake and was about to tell her so, but then he remembered vaguely that Cooper had mentioned the School of the Americas and decided to ask Cooper about it. If there was some mistake, Father O'Connor could call her back.

"No, there's no mistake," Cooper said. "I gave your name as a contact. I meant to tell you about it, but so many other things have happened, it slipped my mind." He briefed the

178

priest on the girl, expecting some comment, some word of caution about getting involved in a matter of this sort, but the priest said nothing.

As Father O'Connor picked up the teapot Cooper noticed with some surprise that his hand was shaking; the tremor was sufficient to splatter the tea outside the cup. He looked terrible, Cooper decided. His eyes were dull; there was a liverish cast to his face.

"You don't look well," Cooper said. "Have you been sick?"

"I don't sleep well." There was a twitch of irritation in Father O'Connor's voice. "But I don't suppose I could expect to sleep well, not with something like this hanging over me. Have you discovered anything new?"

"No," Cooper said. "But there's been another development." He told the priest about Victor's contact with the Red Chinese and his difficulties with Dr. Lu Hsiao-p'ing.

"Then perhaps we have hope after all," Father O'Connor said. "If the Red Chinese are balking, it may be that Hawkins will have trouble finding a buyer."

"I think Victor has a pretty good idea what's going on," Cooper said. "The Red Chinese will quibble awhile and then they'll make an offer."

"Will he take it?"

"He has no desire to get tangled up in a prolonged scholarly dispute. If they make him a reasonable offer, I think he'll take it."

"He can't be permitted to do it."

"I don't like this any more than you do," Cooper said, "but I can't foresee anything that will stop him."

"God will prevent it," Father O'Connor said, his voice no more than a murmur. "God won't let it happen."

To this Cooper said nothing at all.

After lunch he decided on impulse to go out to the American Embassy. As the taxi carried him through the congested streets past the Diet Building he realized there was only one course of action open to him now. He would have to find a way to leave for Akakura on the twenty-second and he would have to find a way to take Myoko with him. He couldn't keep her at his hotel over the holidays and he couldn't take the chance that she would stay put if he made other arrangements for her. Ten days was a long time for an eleven-year-old to remain cooped up in a hotel room and the pull of family ties might very well prove too strong for her to resist. If she went back to her mother's house she would certainly be returned to Victor and this time there would be no chance for Cooper to help her again.

It was only as the taxi approached the embassy grounds that Cooper realized what an untenable position he was in. It was foolish of him to approach the American government with a problem he knew they could not resolve. There was no way they could help him take a Japanese minor back to the United States, especially when he had no hope of obtaining legal custody of the child. At best, he could only complicate an already complex situation. As the taxi slowed down, Cooper leaned forward and tapped the driver on the shoulder.

"I've changed my mind," he said. "Take me back to Shimbashi."

The taxi driver shrugged, nodded, and wheeled his cab around.

2

Father O'Connor's dreams varied from night to night but they were all centered around the same motif. In one of his dreams he was kneeling beside his bed, contemplating the crucifix on the wall, praying fervently, when suddenly, quite without warning, his throat constricted and his mouth went dry and he became mute, unable to call out the name of Christ which was on his tongue. And before his eyes the walnut crucifix became translucent. The arms stretched in agony

180

along the transverse bar of the cross sagged as if the implied bones had been dissolved; the strong lines of victory in the face became distorted, melted out of shape, and the legs shriveled and dissolved and ran down the wall like liquid wax until there was nothing but a stain on the wall, the color of blood. In some of his dreams he left his room, running down the hall in search of the sanctuary, and found himself in an endless maze; in others, he ran into the city and found the churches in ruins, no sign of the cross, as if in a single instant a faceless enemy had laid siege to Christ and obliterated all signs of him. From all these dreams he awoke in a cold sweat and, once awake, refused to go to sleep again, spending the rest of the dark hours in prayers that these hallucinations would be lifted from him, that God would show him what to do. But there was no answer and the dreams continued.

He finally decided he could no longer carry this burden by himself and made an appointment with Father Laurent, the head of the school, going to his office one afternoon after his final class for the day. Father Laurent was in his midsixties, a powerful figure of a man who held himself straight as a ramrod and was considered just as inflexible by his subordinates. It was rumored on the campus—primarily by the students, who felt free to speculate on such matters—that Father Laurent had become a priest late in life, after serving a number of years in the French Foreign Legion, and that he had carried into the priesthood all the discipline and rigidity of his former profession.

Father O'Connor knew this was an illusion which the boys chose to maintain. They had a great fondness for absolutes, for militant certainties in life, and they felt better having a strapping big man with an army background as their spiritual commander, leading them in the battle against the temptations of the flesh and Marxism. As far as Father O'Connor knew, Father Laurent had never been in any army, but his spiritual strength was undeniable and it was for this reason Father O'Connor chose to approach him.

Father Laurent was occupied with paperwork when Father O'Connor was admitted. The older priest glanced at Father O'Connor briefly and then waved him to a chair while he continued to write, not wanting to lose his train of thought. Once he had finished, he put down the pen and leaned back in his chair, removing the rimless spectacles from his craggy face and placing them on his desk, smiling toward Father O'Connor to put him at his ease. "Whenever one of the students complains about paperwork," he commented, "I'm tempted to make him wade through mine for a day."

Father O'Connor smiled slightly, dutifully.

"Now," Father Laurent said, "what can I do for you?"

Father O'Connor shifted uncomfortably in his chair. "I don't know," he said vaguely. "I know something needs to be done for me, but I don't know what it is."

"Then perhaps I had better tell *you*," Father Laurent said sympathetically. "There is no guarantee that simply because a man devotes his life to God he can work day and night without feeling it. Sister Angela came to see me about you last week. She's quite concerned about you."

Father O'Connor only half heard what his superior was saying. His eyes were fixed on the crucifix on the wall, sidelighted by the late afternoon sun streaming in through the window. It threw a bank of shadow against the whitewashed surface.

"So I was going to ask you to come in anyway," Father Laurent said, his smile fading somewhat now to be replaced by a quizzical concern. "Are you feeling all right?"

Father O'Connor removed his eyes from the crucifix. "No," he said. "I haven't been feeling well."

"How long has it been since your last physical?"

"My health is all right," Father O'Connor said. He glanced at the crucifix again and then looked out the window. "Have you never doubted?" he said abruptly.

"Doubted what?"

"Everything," Father O'Connor said vaguely. "Christ, the Church, God, everything."

"Is that your trouble?" Father Laurent said.

"I don't mean metaphysical doubts," Father O'Connor said. "I don't mean doubts based on deduction or presumption or inadequate physical evidence. I mean doubts approaching heresy, doubts of the divinity of Christ and his resurrection, doubts of the existence of God." He shrugged. "It could have been so easy, you know, for the Christ myth to grow in a superstitious society. Every man wants a father. Every man wants a savior. It would have been easy for the facts to be replaced by fiction."

"I suppose you have a point," Father Laurent said. "It's possible."

"And Christ may never have existed at all," Father O'Connor said. "Jesus may have, but not Christ, not as Messiah. That's possible too."

"No," Father Laurent said calmly, "that's impossible."

"But what if I showed you indisputable proof?" Father O'Connor said. "What if I brought you authentic documentation that proved Jesus to be a political leader who failed in his mission, was executed for it and buried to remain buried?"

"You've seen such proof?" Father Laurent asked.

"Yes," Father O'Connor said. He went on to tell the full story of the Baum-Brenner documents. "When I first saw the manuscripts I told myself they were ridiculous. I told myself they were forgeries, specious blasphemies against Christ, specifically designed to degrade the Church. I told myself I could defend against these charges, discover the flaws, the holes, the contradictions. But I couldn't. I'm a scholar and maybe that's my trouble, my weakness, because if I believe in the human ability to disprove, then I must also believe in the human ability to prove. And those documents simply cannot be disproven."

183

"You mean *you* can't disprove them."

"Nobody can. I am truly sorry, Father, I would cut out my tongue if it would help, but the fact remains, nobody can disprove them."

"What you mean to say is that in the time you have had to study these documents you have not been able to marshal enough evidence to contradict those points which appear to be facts," Father Laurent said firmly, pressing the tips of his fingers together, thoughtfully. "That's one of the basic flaws with us as men. We assume that simply because something *seems* to be impossible, because everything contributes to the appearance of impossibility, that it *is* impossible. We have developed the powers of logic to a fine art and we rely on them. We assume that, if logic can prove something, it is true and that, if logic cannot prove it, it is false. But under that method all Christianity is false because the facts of Christianity suspend logic. It is not logical that Christ should have been born of a virgin. It is physically impossible. It is not logical that Christ arose from the dead. This is a contradiction of terms. It is not logical that a whole civilization should suspend belief in logic to worship a Christ who defied all logical analysis. And the worst offender against Christ is the intellectual Christian who attempts to break down the component parts of his faith and analyze them and rationalize them and identify them." He paused, pouring himself a glass of water from the carafe on his desk. "The Church has withstood assaults from all directions for two thousand years," he said. "Her adherents have been slaughtered, persecuted, reviled, subjected to alien persuasions and unassailable pagan logics, and yet she still stands. Perhaps these documents will cause a temporary setback. Perhaps it will take a hundred years or more for irrefutable evidence to be uncovered to prove them false. But it will be done, I have no doubt of that."

Words, phrases, syntax and rhetoric, using logic to disprove the nature of logic, that was what he was doing, platitudes, formulas, old wives' tales, myths, traditions, the massive and unassailable continuity of the Church, the omnipotence of God, power through longevity.

But I am a priest, Father O'Connor wanted to say, a man whose faith should be unshakable, and don't talk to me about the progression of centuries because my Christ has been killed, wiped out, and the murderer is still at large and he will kill Christ in countless others unless he is stopped.

He sat silent a long moment, blinking in the warm sunshine. Father Laurent continued to study him sympathetically, seeing nothing. "We all go through our time of doubt," he said. "Even St. Peter himself went through it and he eventually conquered it with a great and overpowering victory. I would suggest, if you can get copies of those documents, that we forward them to the bishop."

"The bishop?" Father O'Connor said sharply, shrilly. "You'd send them to the bishop?"

"Of course," Father Laurent said. "We can't hope to deal with this matter on our level."

"On our level," Father O'Connor echoed, shaking his head. Father Laurent did not understand at all. "The bishop will take the problem under advisement and then pass it on. Up, up, up. And then finally, perhaps, a decision will be made, but even if it is, it will be much, much too late."

Father Laurent's frown carried a reprimand but he did not put it into words. "I know you're distraught," he said. "And when a man is distraught he has trouble seeing things in their true perspective."

"And you don't think I see this for what it is?"

"I don't know," Father Laurent said. "I know it's upset you, that much is sure. And maybe I'm mistaken, but I don't see that there is anything we can do about the sale of those documents. If he wants to sell them to the Chinese we can't stop him. But if you have any realistic suggestions I'll be glad to listen to them."

Suggested line of attack: evil should be destroyed, swept out in righteous anger, showers of gold from the hurtling tables of the money-changers, divinely propelled; suggested approach: direct action, the fig tree shriveled, leaves curling, branches withering, roots withdrawing, capillary action suspended, osmosis ossified, transpiration blocked, no conciliatory discussion—*gentlemen, the question before the seminar concerns the productivity of this specific specimen fig tree (Genus, Ficus; family, Moraceae) as contrasted with the average productivity of similar fig trees, calculated over a ten-year period, such contrast indicating barrenness as compared to copious fecundity, with conditions to be considered including (A) acidity of the soil, (B) pestiferous blights, rots, fungi, and parasitical afflictions of root and branch.* He thought all this and said, "No, I don't have any suggestions."

"Then I'll make a few," Father Laurent said, rising from his chair and walking over to Father O'Connor, laying a paternal hand on his shoulder. *Manual ministration, digital reassurance.* "First, I want you to have a complete physical examination. I'll make all the necessary arrangements for you to go into St. Luke's during the Christmas recess. Secondly, I'm going to cut down on your schedule for a while in the hope you will avail yourself of the opportunity to rest and meditate. And third—this is most important—I suggest you put this problem in God's hands for the time being."

Father O'Connor nodded, hearing only patches of words and sounds, staring at the wall where the crucifix had been. The wall was blank. Christ had been blotted out. He closed his eyes, opened them, blinked, looked again, indirectly, from the periphery of his vision. The crucifix was still there. He had been staring at the reflection of the sun glittering in a cut-glass bowl on Father Laurent's desk, a miniature glaring light captured in an angled facet, burning a temporary blind spot into his vision. Turning his head slightly so that Father Laurent could not observe, he closed his eyes. Gradually the luminous spot faded from his retina. "Yes, yes," he said in a soft voice. "Of course. That's exactly what I will do."

He stood up with effort, shaking Father Laurent's hand and making his way back to his room. He laid out his writing things on the table, preparatory to writing a letter to his mother, but he could not bring himself to make the effort. Devout woman, stout competent fingers pressing the beads of the rosary, onyx and gold, stone and metal, blessed by Pius himself. *Hail Mary, Mother of God . . . Ave Maria . . .* Fifth grade, six weeks' report card, comment from Sister Theresa: "Philip has a gift for expressing himself but he has the tendency to dramatize." Maternal inquisition: "And what does that mean?" Mama's voice, hard, thin, probing, "Just what does that mean? Have you been making up lies again?" Defense, projection of sincerity with watering eyes, trembling voice: "I don't tell lies, Mama, you have to believe that." Resolution, imploring feminine eyes looking to heaven for supernatural guidance offered widows, orphans, the lame and the halt, the meek and the poor, the put-upons. "There's only one truth, one heavenly truth, and you break the heart of the Mother of God, you make her weep when you tell lies. If you're going to be a priest, you have to learn to accept nothing but the truth for yourself and in yourself. You have to be on guard all the time because Satan is the master liar and, if you keep on lying, then what you're doing is following him."

He put the writing materials back in the drawer and sat down in the chair next to the fireplace. He would be logical in this. He would not be intimidated by the vagaries of his own mind. He had not slept in a long time, he had a tendency to hallucinate. Very well, he would proceed very slowly, examining each thought as it came to him, building with the utmost care the structure upon which he would base his actions. He would put down the rebellion of his mind and consider the problem prayerfully and deliberately, seeking guidance from God. First question: "Are these documents genuine and do they reveal the truth?" He formed his answer carefully. "I think they're false but I can't prove it. Therefore I'll proceed on the assumption they're false."

The answer did not entirely satisfy him but he filed it away. Next question: "Assuming these documents are false, knowing them to be the work of Satan, what can I do about it?" The first answer—that he should leave it to men better qualified to disprove this attack—was unacceptable. No, the proper answer was personal intervention. He would have to do it himself, taking matters into his own hands, attempting persuasion and, should this fail, applying force. At the risk of his own soul, this had to be done. The documents had to be suppressed.

But prerequisite to force was a weapon of some sort, and prerequisite to the employment of a weapon was the obtaining of it. It came to his mind, there was a man, a member of the congregation, a Colonel Fitzgibbons, who had volunteered last spring to conduct a class in marksmanship for the boys of St. Justin's—"There's nothing like a session on the pistol range to clean out the mental cobwebs, develop the reflexes, eh, Father?—and he had been dissuaded with infinite tact. Was he still in the parish? Father O'Connor had not seen him at mass recently. He would investigate. He would find a way. He had no doubt of it.

He approached the telephone, called Victor Hawkins, and made an appointment to see him. Then he lay down on the divan and for the first time in a long while he slept soundly, without dreaming, awakening only as the evening bells sounded to call him to vespers.

3

One of Cooper's problems was solved when Willa volunteered to take Myoko to Akakura on the twenty-second. She could use the vacation, she insisted, and perhaps the trip to the mountains would restore her fading objectivity toward the magazine article. He picked up a railroad timetable one evening on his way home from Victor's place and after dinner sat down with Willa to plan a schedule.

188

"You might be better off on the seven o'clock train," he said.

She consulted the timetable. "That would get us there in the middle of the night."

"It's not very convenient," he said, "but there's less chance of anybody noticing you if you leave during the rush hours."

"You're right there," she said. "A murder could be committed in Tokyo Central during rush hour and nobody would ever see it. All right, seven o'clock it is. What next?"

"You'd better make reservations at the Akakura Inn," he said. "It's a quarter mile from the Akakura Western Lodge, smaller, less crowded from what I've been able to find out about it. Take two connecting rooms in the name of . . . give me a name . . ."

"McCauley."

"Mr. and Mrs. Matthew McCauley and daughter Pamela."

"Pamela?"

"They'll be too polite to question the disparity between the name and the girl, once you get there."

"All right."

"I think it might be safer if you go out to the Shinjuku office of the JTB to make the reservations," he said. "And it might be better if you don't get to Tokyo Central until just before train time."

"Do you think all this is really necessary?"

"I don't know. Victor hasn't mentioned the girl in weeks, but that doesn't mean he's given up. Do you mind going to all this trouble?"

"I suppose not. When will you be up?"

Cooper shrugged. "That depends on Victor," he said. "I can't leave until I'm sure the deal won't go through before I get back."

"Do you want me to contact Mrs. Klaus when I get there?"

"Not until after the twenty-seventh," he said. "I'll try to call you, but if you don't hear from me by then, you can assume I'm not coming."

189

"God," she said, "that has an ominous ring to it."

"I don't anticipate any trouble," he said, "but Victor isn't the most stable man I know. And I want us to be prepared for anything."

4

Father O'Connor passed through the gate in the snow, feeling unreal, his mind focused on a prayer as he followed up the path and approached the doorman, who bowed slightly but made no move to let him in.

"I'm here to see Victor Hawkins," Father O'Connor said, lifting his eyes in the swirling snow toward the solid and windowless bulk of the second floor. "An appointment. Father O'Connor."

Now the doorman opened the door and led him in, down the hallway to Victor's office, rapping on the door and then retreating, leaving him alone when Victor called out, "Come in." Father O'Connor turned the knob, pushed, and entered. Victor was sitting in front of a vaporizer at the desk, inhaling the plume of steam which hissed from the plastic spout, wrinkling his nose and grimacing as if to loosen his head passages to the mist. He glanced toward the priest and then jangled a silver bell before he came forward to shake Father O'Connor's hand, helping him with his coat and hat, handing them to a houseboy who appeared from nowhere.

"Beastly night for you to be out, my dear fellow," he said. "Perfectly beastly, but I want you to know how delighted I am to meet you at long last. Cooper has told me about you. Have a chair. Would you care for tea?"

"Yes, thank you," Father O'Connor said, sitting down, looking around the office. *Sodom must have had its quiet rooms,* he thought.

Victor gave orders to the houseboy and then returned to the vaporizer, holding his fingers in the steam until they

190

were beaded with water, drying them with a silk handkerchief. "I hope you don't mind the hiss of the vaporizer, Father, but the central heating in this building is simply atrocious. Not that it doesn't heat the air, no, it does that all right, but it purges the air of moisture in the process, dries it out. And I have either been blessed or cursed with a delicate respiratory system—it has something to do with the membranes lining the nasal passages—and dry air is simply something I am unable to tolerate. I know that seems impossible, my dear fellow, but my lungs are abused by it. A half hour in a hot, dry room and my lungs are parched. They hurt physically. Breathing becomes a painful process." He lowered himself into a chair across from Father O'Connor, folding his hands in his lap. "Now, in what way can I be of service to you?"

"The documents," Father O'Connor meant to say, but his throat was dry and no sound came out. He cleared his throat and spoke louder. "The Baum-Brenner papers."

"Yes, of course. I take it that our friend Cooper has talked to you about them?"

"I've seen the photostats."

"I'm sure they must have distressed you, Father, just as they distressed me."

"Distressed you?"

"Of course. I know you have probably heard some terrible things about me—I have a great many detractors—and I will admit that my life has not always been what I have wanted it to be, the pressure of circumstance can sometimes be overwhelming, but beneath it all, I like to think of myself as a Christian."

"A Christian?" He was having trouble hearing. The words registered but somehow lacked meaning. He shifted slightly in his chair. The pistol in the side pocket of his suit coat was uncomfortably heavy. He closed his eyes briefly, trying to pray that he could understand and know what to do, but his mind was blank and Victor's loquacious torrent swept over it, giving him no chance to form thoughts of his own.

"Yes, at one time I was a Catholic as a matter of fact, born to it, but as a child I was not allowed instruction in the faith, due to the negligence of my parents. Very few parents accept their responsibilities any more, in any culture, and unfortunately mine belonged in this category of laxity." He was interrupted by the arrival of the teacart and excused himself to wash his hands, insisting that Father O'Connor should go right ahead. When he reappeared from behind the carved screen he resumed his remarks at the exact point where he had left them, popping a small tea biscuit into his mouth while he continued to talk. "Not that I blame my dear parents, no, on the contrary, I think it is up to every man to seek his own salvation whether the rudiments of faith were given to him as a child or not."

Father O'Connor poured himself a cup of tea, cradling the hot china cup in his hands, breathing the aroma before he sipped it, trying to clear his mind, to find the right words. "Is it true that you are selling the Baum-Brenner papers to the Red Chinese?"

"I've had some discussion with them," Victor said.

The tea burned his tongue. He could not taste it. "You know what they'll do with the documents if they get them."

"That's conjectural, after all," Victor said.

"They will attack the faith with them. Not just the Church, but Christ himself."

"I try not to think about such things," Victor said. He reached for another tea biscuit. His teeth pulverized it with a slow, grinding motion. "I must admit that I am in no position to judge the validity of these things one way or the other since I can never hope to attain the high level of understanding that you have, my dear fellow. But I dare say that the Christian faith will be strong enough to withstand any attack mounted upon it by a nation of professed atheists."

Father O'Connor closed his eyes again. This was not the way it was supposed to be. He was not supposed to be in the position of having to confess the weakness of his faith. The positions were reversed, he had to set them straight. "You're not an ignorant man," he said, trying to make his words firm. "Surely you must realize that if you persist in this you're placing your immortal soul in danger. You have the most destructive power in your hands the world has ever known."

Victor studied him now, his eyes faintly quizzical. "I take it you've made a study of these documents, Father?"

"Yes. I know what I'm talking about."

"I am concerned about my soul, of course," Victor said. "But when it comes right down to it, all I can do is accept on faith one way or the other. I mean by that, dear fellow, that on the one hand I am told by you that these documents are absolute in their destructive power. And on the other hand I have come to an overwhelming conviction in the certainty of Christ, and—meaning no disrespect to you, Father—being compelled to choose one or the other, since the two are contradictory, then I must stay with my original faith. And doing this, I can't see that my soul is in jeopardy. I mean by that, one's soul can't be in jeopardy simply because one believes so firmly in Christ as to know that he can't be destroyed."

Dissembling, Father O'Connor thought. *He is dissembling and I can't follow him.* He placed the teacup back on the cart. "Then you do intend to sell the documents to the Red Chinese." *Yes, that was it, back to specifics.*

"They have not offered to buy them."

"But if they do make an offer you will sell the papers to them?"

"If the offer is equitable," Victor said. "You must understand, my dear fellow, that when I aided the unfortunate priest in his escape from Red China it was not without its

193

financial aspects. It required a rather substantial expenditure, and although I regarded it as a privilege to be able to help, it was something of a drain on my resources."

There, it was now clear-cut. He had no choice now. He had made an attempt at persuasion and it had failed, because he was too weak, perhaps, or because his conviction lacked the power to pierce the defensive screen of words. He shifted in the chair again, his hand going to the pocket, his fingers touching the metal, the cold, smooth cylinder of the barrel. His thumb hooked around the butt. He pictured in his mind the removal of the pistol from his pocket and Victor's response, the fear, the thin line of glistening beads popping out on the forehead, the mouth slack and wordless, the eyes perplexed.

Father O'Connor had seen fear many times before, he knew its symptoms, its effects, and now he remembered a young man lying on the street near the mission in Los Angeles, a gunshot wound in his stomach, a grocer standing nearby with a pistol, waiting for the police and the ambulance which would arrive too late for this young thief who was leaving adolescence and would never arrive at manhood. Father O'Connor remembered the face, the dying eyes aware of dying and terrified by it, the face blanched with it, the flesh sour and rancid with the smell of it. Remembering, Father O'Connor faltered. The fingers tightened and relented, withdrew from the pocket, leaving the pistol behind.

"Are you all right, my dear fellow?" Victor said, concerned.

Father O'Connor nodded, soundless, picking up the teacup again. "I'm tired, that's all. Tired."

"I know how that can be," Victor said sympathetically. "That is one of the prices exacted from us by time, the increasing fatigue." His thick fingers formed a pincer to pick up another tea biscuit. "A thought occurs to me, Father, an inspired thought which might solve both of our problems at the same time. After all, I can see your point of view in this matter. I can understand your natural repugnance at the thought of these crucial papers going into atheist hands." He chewed the biscuit thoughtfully, ruminating, his face gleaming now as his new thought gained impetus. "Yes, it might work out very nicely, I think." He turned his face toward Father O'Connor now. "Do you suppose, my dear fellow, that the Vatican might be interested in buying the collection?"

"The Vatican?"

"Yes."

No, he wanted to say. *The Church cannot be blackmailed, pressured, coerced.* "I don't know," he said quietly.

"I do think it would be worth a try, my dear fellow. Of course, I can't approach the Curia Romana myself, they wouldn't listen to me, I'm afraid, since I am so unworthy of their consideration. But I am sure if a distinguished scholar and dedicated man such as yourself contacted them, apprised them of the circumstances, they would certainly give you the benefit of their attention."

"You want me to do it?" Father O'Connor said.

"You are in a perfect position to do it after all," Victor said brightly. "You have studied the collection."

No, I won't do it. I'm a poor priest but I won't compromise myself and my Church. "How long would I have?" he asked.

"I hate to have to impose a deadline, Father. But unfortunately, due to the exigencies of the current situation, I'm afraid I would have to have some word within, say, two weeks."

Father O'Connor sipped his tea. He nodded, slowly. "All right," he said. "I'll try."

5

The snow completely demolished Willa's schedule. She had intended to reach Myoko's school at four but the traffic was impossible in the central district and by the time the taxi deposited her at the gate it was close to five. Even then Myoko was not ready and Willa was forced to make inane conversation with one of Myoko's teachers in the downstairs parlor.

When Myoko finally appeared with her packed bag, it was six o'clock and darkness had set in. As they hurried down the sidewalk toward the street Willa slipped and almost fell. The temperature had dropped, turning the afternoon thaw into a treacherous glaze underfoot. She knew there would be no chance of finding another taxi in this weather; they would have to catch the electric train. She allowed Myoko to carry her own bag and clutched the girl with her free hand to steady herself as they approached the street, pausing just inside the gate while Willa looked out to see if anybody was watching the school.

If there was, she decided, he would be frozen stiff for nothing. She couldn't see any farther than a few feet in the swirling snow. Towing the girl behind her, she set out at a cautious pace toward Ueno Station, arriving there to find it packed with people who milled around the train platforms, pressing forward in an unruly mob to lay siege to coaches which were already filled to the bursting point.

Willa had one advantage. She was taller than most Japanese men and was wearing heels as well, so she was able to see over the heads of the crowd. This gave her a temporary head start. From this perspective she could almost chart the currents in the human tide, and when a coach screeched to a stop the crowd immediately in front of the opening doors was pushed into it by the young men hired by the railroad for just that purpose. She missed one coach and when the next arrived she thrust her suitcase out in front of her, banging a Japanese businessman on the shins. He jumped away and she yanked Myoko into the breech and then held on as she was propelled into the coach by the insurgent force behind her.

She was a little luckier at Tokyo Central. Since she already had the tickets to Taguchi, she was able to avoid the congested ticket windows. After considerable jostling she towed

Myoko onto the train and found seats in a coach filled with skiers, most of them young and boisterous, all of them wearing gaudy sweaters and square-toed boots. As she settled down, putting her arm around the girl, who nestled against her, Willa had never felt more miserable in her whole life. Her feet were soaking wet from the snow which had packed around her shoes and was now melting. Her coat was soggy. Her ears were tingling with the cold and she knew she was going to get no sleep at all on the long ride. From somewhere in the coach came the discordant wheeze of a concertina. She looked at her watch. Ten minutes to seven. She wondered if there was any place in the station where she could get a drink in ten minutes. She thought not. Well, there was bound to be a bar at Akakura and that offered her some consolation. She could certainly hold out that long.

6

The evening had been hard on Victor, Cooper decided. For the first time in their relationship, Cooper had seen Victor completely unsettled. Even now, Victor had lapsed into a fretful silence. He lay back against the upholstered seat of the limousine, his restless gloved fingers drumming on the polished surface of the attaché case held across his lap, his lips pursed loosely in an attitude of speculation.

"What did you think of him?" he said finally, in a sober and reflective voice.

"He wasn't what I expected," Cooper said.

"What he was doing tonight was perfectly obvious to me," Victor said with a faint petulance. "He was trying to intimidate me, trying to prepare me for a lesser price when the time comes that his country decides to make an offer. The People's Republic is notoriously tightfisted, you know, absolutely penurious, when it comes to money matters. And I must say, dear boy, at the risk of offending you, that you did absolutely nothing to help matters tonight."

"I won't certify the documents until I'm convinced," Cooper said.

Victor sighed, apparently unwilling to press an issue which might cause further dissension on an already unhappy evening. "I should never have agreed to this conference tonight in the first place, not on his terms in any case. To go to his place in weather like this, carrying an absolutely priceless document—that was a great mistake, but I hoped to demonstrate a certain willingness on my part to get along, to be co-operative with him in a matter of such great importance to both of us." He fumbled in his coat pocket for his cigarette case. He offered Cooper one and then lit his own from the car lighter. "But I am sure now that he misinterpreted my gesture as a sign of weakness. I am constantly violating my own rigid standards of behavior, my dear boy, relaxing them at the most inopportune times."

Cooper said nothing and in a moment Victor sank back against the seat again, brooding at the perfidy of his fellow man, nibbling at the cigarette in short, nervous puffs. The limousine had entered the Ginza by now and the snow, which had stopped about nine, began to fall again. Even at this time of night and in the worst possible weather, the Ginza was crowded. The traffic was relentless; the kamikaze cabs did not seem to be affected in the least by the condition of the streets. They followed the same erratic courses through the staggered lines of more cautious drivers, chained wheels clanking, horns blaring.

Cooper had never seen the lights in the neon spectaculars more beautiful; the great loops and whorls of flashing color, ordinarily garish and tasteless, were muted by the falling snow and projected a whirling aura of color on the wind-borne flakes. Over the din of the traffic came the recorded brassy blare of Christmas carols. It seemed a little incongruous to hear Christmas carols in a country filled with people who didn't have the slightest idea what Christmas was all about. Ironic, he thought, that what had begun as a pagan celebration was returning to paganism once again. Full circle, and if the document in that briefcase were released and faith shriveled, would it really make any difference as far as Christmas was concerned? Would the lights in this street be any dimmer, the music diminished, the revelry subdued?

He closed his eyes, trying to quiet the incipient headache that had been threatening him since their arrival at the headquarters of the Red Chinese trade mission in Shinjuku. It was a mistake, he thought, to have allowed Victor to persuade him to go along, but he had been curious to meet this Chinese scholar and had hoped to be able to delay any negotiations long enough to make the trip to Akakura.

He had presumed, from Victor's description, that Dr. Lu would be a functionary, more politician than scholar, and this had led Cooper into the error of underestimating the man. Dr. Lu Hsiao-p'ing was a solid, dumpy man with a square face and high cheekbones, in his late fifties, Cooper supposed. He was partially bald and what hair he had left on either side of his receding hairline was gray. He wore an ill-fitting gray woolen uniform which was rumpled and baggy, as if he had slept in it. He was a compulsive smoker, consuming one cigarette after another and always down to a final quarter inch, pinching the last remnant of tobacco between thumbnail and index finger, his face screwed up against the heat while he extracted the last shred of smoke.

He chatted amiably while his servant brought in tea and cakes, conversing intelligently enough in a nasal, unmusical English on the general subject of the weather in Peking, but once the formality of a preliminary refreshment had been dispensed with, he turned to Cooper and began a general questioning of Cooper's background and the methods he had used to translate these documents.

When Victor removed the Q document from the attaché case and partially unrolled it on the table, the questioning became a verbal aggression, a subtle attack not only on the document itself but on Cooper's scholarly capabilities as well. How could he believe this was authentic? How could he allow himself to become persuaded when there were so many areas of doubt concerning this document? For instance, the carbon 14 tests dated the Q document at A.D. 50, plus or minus a hundred years. What made Cooper believe that this document had not been forged at the near end of that chronological range, around A.D. 150, as a part of the mounting activity against the early Christian church? Too, the content and tone of this document was at complete variance with all the evidence of the first two Christian centuries.

At first Cooper was irritated and then he realized that to Dr. Lu this was no more than a dialogue to test the demonstrable strong points of the Q document, a sham battle along the same lines the real battle would follow once the Q document was subjected to the scrutiny of Christian historians. In this mock war, Dr. Lu was attacking, leaving it up to Cooper to defend.

He began with a comparative consideration of the two papyrus fragments discovered by Grenfell and Hunt in Oxyrhynchus, the controversial "Sayings of Jesus" which had been dated by experts at about A.D. 140. Many historians believed that these sayings came from a book known as *The Gospel According to the Hebrews* which had been circulated in Egypt in the first century after the death of Christ. The content and tone of these fragments were totally different from the Q document. Was Cooper now prepared to describe the "Sayings of Jesus" as spurious or unreliable? And if this Q document was truly representative of the thought of Jesus, then how was it that his aberrant personality was so successfully hidden from the great majority of his followers? Was Cooper prepared to say that Jesus did not reflect the Essene philosophy as revealed by the manuscripts found in the caves of Wadi Qumran? Did not this Q document have certain aspects in common with the Coptic manuscripts of Manichaeism and Gnosticism?

He wound his way through increasingly obscure references which Cooper only vaguely remembered and could not quote without the texts before him. Consequently, Cooper's answers were general and not specific. In the first place, the script used in the Q document was one which predated that used in the "Sayings of Jesus." It was closer to a script found on a papyrus fragment and a potsherd which the Israeli archaeologists had uncovered in their excavation of Herod's palace at Masada in 1956. Herod's palace had been destroyed in A.D. 73. The script in the Q document also exhibited a great lack of elegance and was similar to the crude graffiti or inscriptions found on Palestinian burial chests. These two comparisons tended to date the Q document in the early part of the first Christian century.

As far as aberrations were concerned, Cooper went on, in many early cultures divinities were often considered mad, and the only way aberration could be judged was in the context of the time in which the aberration occurred. All that anyone could say with any certainty was that various followers of Jesus saw him in different lights. For proof of this, Dr. Lu had but to look at the multiple Christian sects which sprang up in the early centuries, many of them radically different, all of them basing their beliefs on an interpretation of something they had not seen and which, from a historical point of view, had been imperfectly witnessed and recorded.

As far as the Oxyrhynchus fragments were concerned, their connection with the Q document had never been more than hypothetical. The most logical explanation was that the *Gospel According to the Hebrews* was another version of the *Gospel According to Matthew*. Matthew had written his work in Aramaic and it was translated into Greek to meet the needs of Hellenic Christianity. But it was not to be assumed that this was the only translation of his work. It was equally possible his gospel had been changed slightly to meet the spiritual needs of a Jewish-Christian sect known as the Ebionites and translated into Greek with a different emphasis altogether. The Oxyrhynchus fragments could very well be a part of this second translation.

At the end of four hours of discussion Cooper had absolutely no idea what Dr. Lu was thinking, whether he had come to any conclusion and, if so, what he would do about it. Dr. Lu concluded the evening by asking Cooper point-blank if he was ready to certify the documents. Cooper said he was not.

When the car stopped in front of Victor's place Cooper was about to beg off from any further discussion and go back to the hotel, but he allowed himself to be persuaded to go in for a nightcap. Once they reached the office, Victor's spirits began to improve. He rang for the houseboy and divested himself of his coat, hat, and gloves, then he placed the attaché case on the desk and walked up and down the room, balancing himself on the balls of his feet, rubbing his hands together briskly while he considered his order to the houseboy. "Are you hungry, dear boy?" he asked, turning to Cooper.

"No," Cooper said. "But I could use a brandy."

"Cold weather always increases my appetite," Victor said. He turned to the houseboy. "Bring a bottle of brandy for Dr. Cooper and have the kitchen prepare me a top sirloin of Japanese beef out of the shipment we received from Osaka. And caution the chef that I wish no pink showing, none, since I find nothing more nauseating than underdone beef."

The houseboy departed and Victor sank into the chair behind his desk. "How comforting it is to have a chair that fits the body," he said, fitting a cigarette into his holder. "I must say that, along with the mental strain this evening, I also found it physically exhausting. Chinese furniture is especially abominable to me. It has a certain classic elegance, I will admit that, but it is made for very slight people with absolutely no corporeal bulk. I have often thought of having a special chair made for myself, something easily transportable, that I can take with me when I am forced to go out of the building. Do you think that would be gauche, dear boy, to carry one's own chair?"

"If I were you, I'd do what I wanted to," Cooper said.

"How very right you are," Victor said. The telephone on his desk rang. He grimaced at it but it continued to ring. "Excuse me, dear boy," he said to Cooper. He picked up the receiver and held it slightly away from his ear so that there was no physical contact. He listened with a frown. "Give him a word of caution," Victor said. "Remind him where he is. Be tactful, of course, but explain that even in pleasure there must be a certain discipline." He put the telephone down and glanced at Cooper ruefully. "We have a very high-ranking English statesman on the second floor tonight. He is a veritable master of the polished phrase, dear boy, a renowned orator, but I must say he doesn't know how to behave himself. One can never really tell about people, of course." He exhaled a puff of smoke which formed, for an instant, a cloud in front of his forehead before it dispelled. "Did I tell you about my visit from Father O'Connor?"

"No," Cooper said.

"He said you had consulted him about the documents."

"Yes, I did."

"You really shouldn't have done that," Victor said chidingly. "You really should have asked my approval before you consulted him. But I suppose, after all, that it was a good thing because he wouldn't have come to see me otherwise. And his presence gave me a truly remarkable idea, dear boy, an inspiration. He has written to Rome to see if he can arouse any interest in our collection on the part of the Curia."

"Have you heard from them?"

203

"Unfortunately not," Victor said with a sigh. "But then it is still early and I haven't given up hope altogether in that direction. A complex organization such as the Roman Catholic Church moves very slowly. And should they display no interest, I have some other thoughts on the disposition of the manuscripts which should either force the People's Republic to the point of bidding or open an entirely new and potentially lucrative market."

The telephone rang again. Victor picked it up grimly and listened for a few moments. "Very well," he said. "Simply take the girls out of the room for the time being. I'll handle it myself." He replaced the telephone on the cradle and then crushed out the cigarette and raised himself to his feet, slowly, reluctantly. "I shouldn't be long," he said. "I hope you will forgive the interruption."

"Of course," Cooper said.

The moment Victor left the room and closed the door behind him, Cooper stood up. The thought had been in his mind since the first telephone call and now it urged him to action. He crossed to the door and tried it. It was not locked. Taking his coat out of the closet, he crossed quickly to the desk and picked up the attaché case containing the Q document, then he opened the door into the hallway and looked out. It was deserted.

He moved down the hall at a half run, slowing down when he reached the front entrance, emerging from the building at a normal pace, nodding to the doorman, who bowed at him and smiled. Cooper did not look back. Only when he reached the first side alley and ducked into it to rest against a wall, his heart pounding, a little dizzy from the sudden exertion, did he take the time to look at his watch. It was twelve thirty-six. The next train to Taguchi left in twenty-four minutes. With any luck, he could make it. He put on his overcoat and walked briskly down the narrow lane through the snow, heading in the general direction of Tokyo Central.

Nine

1

COOPER dozed fitfully during the long night and came awake as the train attendant shook his shoulder. *"Taguchi tsungi desu. Taguchi."* Now he became alert, emerging from the dream which still lay heavy on his mind, reaching out reflexively to touch the firm bulk of the attaché case wedged between him and the wall on the narrow seat. "Taguchi," the train attendant said, grinning. "Next. You wish Taguchi, no?"

"Yes, thank you," Cooper said. "I get off at Taguchi."

"Ha," the train attendant said, bowing, repeating himself just to make sure Cooper understood. "Taguchi next stopu."

Cooper was totally unprepared for what he found when he left the train. He had left Tokyo at night and here the sun was so brilliant against the snow that he was momentarily blinded. He stood on the platform, blinking, exhilaratingly awake now in the sharp mountain air. To his left, the tracks receded in the distance, flanked on either side by high banks of snow thrown up by the plows, and beyond the bend where the tracks were no longer visible he saw the snow-crested mountains sharply defined against a cobalt sky. Carrying his attaché case, he walked through the cut in the snowbank to the station house, which looked more Swiss than Japanese, the snow heavy on its pitched roof, a spiral of smoke emerging from the chimney to rise in a plume into the windless sky.

In the station he bought a pair of sunglasses and tried to get information concerning transportation to the Akakura Inn, but the station agent could not understand what Cooper wanted. He listened closely, attentively, a strained smile on his face as he tried to grasp what Cooper was saying. In desperation, Cooper turned to a group of skiers waiting on the benches for the next train back to Tokyo and asked if anybody spoke English. He was rewarded by the response of a shaggy-headed young man, obviously a university student, who was delighted at the opportunity to practice his English.

If Cooper was relieved to be able to communicate, he was depressed by the information the student gave him. The snows were very deep between here and the hotels on the rim of Hakama Crater, the student said, and of course there was no way to keep the summer roads open; therefore, there was no ordinary vehicular traffic at this time of year. However, the hotels operated what the student referred to as "wesaru"—which, Cooper supposed, was the Japanese way of pronouncing "weasel," a cross between a jeep and an army tank—to carry the guests back and forth from the trains.

"How often do they run?" Cooper asked.

The student produced a timetable written in Japanese and ran his finger past an asterisk to an explanatory note at the bottom. "Ah," he said unhappily. "Ah." Unfortunately, he explained, there were complications. Now the Akakura Western Lodge, the larger of the two hotels, had two vehicles and a maintenance garage, and one of these vehicles was available at all times to take guests down (departing) or to pick them up (arriving). It was necessary for a guest at the Akakura Western Lodge to inform the hotel of his time of arrival, either by a letter sent prior to his arrival by train, or by telephone once he had arrived, and a weasel would be sent to meet him.

"But I'm staying at the inn," Cooper said, a little frustrated. "What does it say about the inn?"

"Ah," the student said again. "Ah." He turned the page, looking for additional information. He muttered to himself and shook his head unhappily. The Akakura Inn had the same arrangement as the Akakura Western Lodge, he explained; however, there was one unfortunate difference, in that the Akakura Inn had no telephone. Therefore the only way to insure transportation was to write to them in advance. However, the student said encouragingly, the Akakura Inn always sent its weasel down to meet the four o'clock train from Tokyo to pick up mail for the guests. If Cooper did not contact them before then, he could always catch that vehicle.

Cooper groaned inwardly. He simply could not wait that long. Undoubtedly Victor had already put somebody on his trail and Cooper had to take advantage of every minute. "Is it possible to walk up there?" he asked. "How far is it?"

"*Shiranai*," the student said, turning to the rest of the skiers, who had gathered around Cooper like students in a seminar room. There was much agitated discussion in Japanese and finally the student turned back to Cooper again. There was some difference of opinion about the distance, he said, but it was perhaps four miles and Cooper should have no trouble walking it since it was a clear day and there was no threat of storm. The trail was marked by poles bearing small red flags placed on the edge of the packed snow which had been compressed by the weight of the tracked vehicles and was therefore safe for walking.

Thanking the student, Cooper set off through the small village, following the winding lane through the drifts toward the open country. He passed a couple of houses where Japanese men were busy clearing their doors of the snow which had

207

fallen during the night and he smiled and spoke to them and they smiled and spoke back. At the edge of the village the line of poles began, flanking the cleated weasel tracks and forming a trail across the fresh layer of snow into the distant hills. As he walked, he decided that the lack of transportation was more of a blessing than a curse. He felt revived by the hike, and the view of the valley which lay to his left was magnificent: the widely spaced farmhouses buried to the eaves in snow, chimneys pluming smoke into the sky, the groves of fir trees with the snow heavy on the branches. He was reminded of a trip to the White Mountains he had taken with Nan shortly after they were married, days of laughter and snug, warm, intimate nights. There was something purifying about country like this; he found it impossible to be grim or depressed about anything.

For the first hour the trail was fairly open, then it began to climb through the trees and he was forced to slow his pace as he struggled up a steep ridge. He stopped on the crest for a breather and watched a party of skiers in bright sweaters sweeping down a hill far to his left, kicking up a powdery wake of snow, a blur of color against a dazzling blue-white slope, leaving an echo of laughter behind them.

He continued his climb in silence, emerging from a clump of firs to find himself confronted with an unbroken view of the Nakayama Valley and the groves of leafless and deciduous trees far below, etched gray against snowy fields, and in the far distance the serrated and rugged granite folds of mountains which edged the Hakama Crater. Passing a final row of trees, he caught his first glimpse of the inn nestled against the foot of a slope, the snow banked against it. It was hardly what he had expected; not a traditional Japanese inn at all, it was more in the architectural style of a Swiss chalet.

He stamped the snow off his shoes before he entered the lobby, a room with a steeply pitched, open-beamed ceiling and a massive stone fireplace with sofas grouped around it.

He registered at the desk and accepted the apology of the clerk, who took it as a personal responsibility that Cooper had been forced to walk from the station. Cooper was impatient to get to his room but he realized his stay here would be much pleasanter if he allowed the clerk to ease his conscience, so he listened to the aspirate manifestations of remorse and then denied it had been any inconvenience at all. He had really enjoyed the hike and was none the worse for it, but he could use a hot bath. The clerk pounded a bell to summon a boy and Cooper followed him up the narrow staircase to the second floor, allowing him to carry the attaché case only when he realized this would be easier than trying to talk him out of it. He fumbled in his pocket for a tip which the bellboy declined and then Willa opened the door to Cooper's knock, embracing him, laughing, delighted to see him. Taking off his coat, he looked around the room, noticing a pile of papers on the bed where Willa had been working.

"Where's Myoko?" he said.

She took his hand and led him to the window. He saw Myoko with a group of Japanese children on a slope to the side of the hotel. She was throwing snowballs, laughing. "She's really in her element here," Willa said with a smile. "A real snow girl." She embraced him again, impulsively. "I was worried about you," she said.

"There wasn't any trouble," he said. "Have you been working?"

"Trying to work," she said, beginning to clear the papers off the bed. "But I have to admit I don't really give a damn about Japanese veterans. Now, tell me what happened."

He sat down on the edge of the bed, suddenly tired from the long walk. He told her everything that had happened, including the interview with Lu Hsiao-p'ing and the precipitate theft of the Q document. "I don't know how long we're going to have up here," he concluded, "but I know for sure it's not going to be an extended holiday. Have you seen Mrs. Klaus?"

"No," Willa said. "I walked over to the lodge with Myoko to buy some things and I checked to make sure Mrs. Klaus is there. But that's as far as I went."

"Good," he said, stretching out on the bed, abandoning all thoughts of the hot bath for the time being. "I'll go up there this evening, but right now I think I'll take a nap."

"Go to sleep," she said, kissing him. "Is there something I can get for you?"

"I came up without anything," he said. "If you can find a razor and a toothbrush I'd appreciate it."

He was asleep by the time she opened the door to leave.

2

They had dinner in their room and he enjoyed it immensely, laughing as Myoko described her experiences in the school and the number of times she had almost slipped and asked, "Which one?" when somebody asked about her father. Cooper was reluctant to leave but there was too much to be done. He kissed her good night and asked Willa to stay with her. He did not want Myoko left alone for a moment.

"I'm sure she'll be all right," Willa said, "if you need me to come along."

"No, I want to make the initial contact by myself," he said, putting on his overcoat. "And you might be thinking about someplace to store that attaché case."

"All right." She kissed him warmly. "Come back as soon as you can."

"I will."

The path between the inn and the lodge was plainly marked and in the light of a full moon he had no trouble finding his way. The Akakura Western Lodge was a large establishment, a hundred rooms or better, glossy and obviously expensive. It had something of the unfriendly air of a Tokyo hotel about it. The desk clerk was haughty and unco-operative and it was only with extreme persistence that Cooper was able to pry any information concerning Mrs. Klaus out of him. Mrs. Klaus had a suite of rooms on the first floor, past the arcade. No, there was no telephone in her quarters. Mrs. Klaus did not like to be interrupted in her work.

Cooper went down the arcade corridor lined with shops designed to appeal to the Western tourist with plenty of money and little taste. There were windows full of beautifully lacquered and exquisitely assembled boxes and multi-trayed cabinets which had no practical use whatsoever. He passed a lounge bar where skiers were gathered around in an alcoholic community sing and finally arrived at Mrs. Klaus's suite. He knocked on the door.

"Who is it?"

"It's Dr. Cooper, Mrs. Klaus," he said. "I wrote you from Tokyo."

She was not what he had expected her to be. From her letter, from the persuasive sadness of her writing, he had pictured her as subdued, introverted, and she was not. She was a tall, attractive woman in her early forties, her hair long and black, her features angular; she was dressed in brightly colored slacks and loops of silver jewelry clinked about her wrists when she moved her hands. All of her movements were swift, precise, designed not only to attract attention but to project an aura of competence as well. This was a woman who knew what she was about.

She had been working on sketches of the lobby and they were propped up on the couch and leaning against the wall; swatches of material were spread over the furniture and pinned to the door, as if it was imperative that everything she intended to use be in plain view so she could absorb it all at a glance. Lighting a cigarette, she picked up one of the swatches, a gay red print full of busy little figures, studying it as if she had no time to waste in conversation. "You're the one who's working on some sort of project about my father, no?" she said with a trace of a French accent.

"Yes," Cooper said.

She snipped off a piece of the material and held it to one of the sketches. "Soon after the war a man named Hollenstein came to see me," she said.

"I'm familiar with his work," Cooper said.

"Then you know what he did to my father. All because I was naïve. I answered whatever questions he asked me."

"I don't have any axes to grind," Cooper said. "May I sit down?"

"If you wish. I have been thinking about your letter and I don't know that there is anything else I can tell you. He was a very kind man, a very religious man. I never discussed politics with him. He was my father and I was his daughter and we loved each other. That is really all there is to be said. And about the manuscripts he left me—they are quite worthless. When my husband died in Geneva, I was penniless, so I tried to sell them. A dealer in antiquities offered me five francs for them and he was being generous. He wanted them to use as decorations in lampshades."

"I should still like to see them," Cooper said.

She glanced at him sharply and ground out her half-smoked cigarette, lighting another one immediately. "I know you will understand this. I have a suspicious mind. Before we talk any more I want to know exactly what your project is."

"Of course. It isn't very complex. The Nazi government uncovered a series of manuscripts which purported to be letters concerning the execution of the Apostle Paul for murder and an exposé of a political rebellion which failed, an insurrection which Jesus Christ was supposed to have led. The Nazis were enthusiastic about these documents because, if they could be proven authentic, it would have been a simple matter to discredit Christianity and replace it with a nationalistic religion. Your father was spared in order to go to work on the project, probably the translation and annotation."

"And he did this?"

"I think he began to," Cooper said. "I have letters from Nazi officials to him, commending his work."

"So you think he willingly co-operated with the Nazis toward the destruction of Christianity?" she said without rancor. "And yet you deny you wish to do him harm." She sat down now, and in the light of a table lamp, her eyes were sober, grave; there was a grim irony to her mouth. "First, let me tell you why he co-operated with men he hated, with an ideology he detested. He did it for me, for my welfare, yes, but more than that. Because of this." She struck her flat stomach with an open hand. "Because I was female and could bear him a grandson, if he could only keep me alive long enough for me to be fruitful. He was a Jew, orthodox, patriarchal, a very narrow man, a Jew in the old sense of the word. He traced his rabbinical ancestry back a thousand years. And then came the war and he fought and encouraged his people to fight and to die rather than bend in the slightest way and degrade themselves. Could the Germans make my father yield? Never. I saw him beaten so that his shirt would not stop the blood. It soaked through his shirt and his vest and his suit coat and even his overcoat as well. And he would not betray his people or his religion. And then, perhaps by accident or maybe his God did it to him—who knows these things?—all of the males in his family died, were killed, extinguished. My brother died, my uncles, all my cousins, everybody, until only he and I were left."

. . . *They are all taken from us,* the letter to Silverstein said. *They exterminate us. They grind our seed on the rock until there is no generation to follow us.*

She paused to light another cigarette. Her hand was trembling. She put the lighter on the table and replaced the hand in her lap. "I was a sickly adolescent. In the Warsaw ghetto I would not have lasted another six months. And if I died, then the family, the proud family, would die as well. So my father went to work for the German government. We moved to Berlin and we had a warm apartment and I had doctors and my father even had enough influence to send me to Switzerland for my health."

213

"The Germans let you leave the country?"

"They had no need of me," she said wryly, fully in control of herself now. "My father was being most co-operative. He accepted a new name and became a Nazi. And there was no thought of his trying to escape. If he had left the country the Jews, his former friends, would have killed him. They would have killed me too perhaps except that I married a good Jew shortly after I arrived in Switzerland. And I signed a statement denouncing my father. That helped also. My father had gone to so much trouble to get me out of the country, I would have done anything to stay alive." She sighed. "All of that was over a long, long time ago. So why make it live again?"

"The documents can do a great deal of harm."

"So?"

"So I think your father knew these documents were false," Cooper said quietly. "I think he had proof of it. That's the only way I can explain what happened. If the Germans had executed him because his work was finished, they would have published the results immediately. But they didn't. I think your father was a very brave man, Mrs. Klaus. He discovered a basic flaw in those papers, perhaps another document which proved them to be an early forgery. Then he arranged for that proof to be protected, put beyond the reach of the Nazis, and once it was done he informed them of the fact. They sent him to Auschwitz immediately and abandoned the project."

"And you think the manuscripts I have might be that proof?"

"Yes," Cooper said. "There's a copy of one of his letters to you preserved with the collection, a letter saying he was sending you a key."

"I don't remember that letter," she said.

"The information in it might not have been meant for you," Cooper said. "It might have been his way of com-

214

municating with the man who would eventually come into possession of the documents, a way of letting him know where the answer could be found."

"The answer is not in the manuscripts he sent me," she said firmly. "They have been examined by experts. There is nothing there."

"May I see them?" he asked. "It's possible the men who examined them before didn't know what they were looking for."

She shrugged. "All right," she said. "They are in one of my trunks. It will take a while to find them. Will you come back in the morning?"

"Of course," he said. When he reached the door an afterthought occurred to him. "By the way, is your son here with you?"

"My son?" she said, startled.

"Your father mentioned a grandson in his correspondence."

"Oh, that," she said with a humorless smile. "He wanted a grandson so I could not disappoint him. There was no child. I could not conceive, except on paper. The child was fiction. It had no life except in the letters I wrote to my father. So you see, all of this was quite in vain, everything he did. If there is a God, He must be quite sardonic." She pursed her lips as if there was something else she wished to add, then she shrugged. "In the morning, then?"

"In the morning."

3

Two days after Christmas, Willa gave up. The article was no further along than it had been on her arrival. She put in a call to her agent in New York from the lodge, waiting around until it could be completed, keeping Myoko in the recreation room and dreading the moment when she would have to explain her delinquency to a man who secretly believed she was on the alcoholic skids anyway. Moss Hardwick was a wiry little man who had built his reputation on calling a spade a spade, sometimes with devastating effect. This quality had drawn her to him in the first place; now it terrified her.

She tried a game of ping-pong with Myoko but it didn't work. She was in no mood for defeat and the girl trounced her soundly. Willa smiled lamely and retreated to the lobby, risking the frost of the desk clerk by asking if her call had come through yet—it had not, she would be paged when it did—drifting over to the conversational area in front of the fireplace to join the rest of the culls from the vigorous sport of skiing. There were two Japanese toddlers on the braided rug near the hearth (too young for the slope and the slalom); a Japanese boy, his right arm in a cast, sat on a divan, keeping company with a Japanese girl whose right ankle wore a similar badge of honor (the wounded); a fat and ancient gentleman in a gray kimono sat next to a middle-aged woman who was nursing an infant (too old, too weak, too infirm); and as Willa settled in a chair on the periphery of the group the adults all gave her a fleeting glance as if to determine what handicap of age or physical condition kept her from the snowy slopes.

She settled down with a French-language copy of *Réalités* and tried to occupy herself with translating the French in an article about Algerian artists who did something or other with the clay red and sold the completed something or others to the somebody or others who visited the southern villages in the winter. She kept an eye on the entrance to the bar across the lobby, but she could see no activity whatsoever through the archway, no comfortable puttering around with glasses and bottles on the part of a friendly bartender who might be cajoled into mixing her just one drink before the opening hour of noon. It was a foolish rule anyway, dictated by economics, governed by standardized behavior which made a drink at 12:01 P.M. more socially acceptable than a drink at 11:59 A.M.

Wandering back to the recreation room, she watched Myoko defeating a boy her age who was obviously off the ski slopes only because he was so choked up with a cold that he wheezed every time he took a breath. He was hard put even to keep up with a flashing ping-pong ball, much less to hit it with his paddle. *God*, Willa thought, *why should I feel so desperate most of the time?* It wasn't logical. Myoko was the one to feel desperation. No control over her life, absolutely none, her future dependent on so many variables, on the tug of war between Victor and Cooper, on the fortunes of her mother and the shifting pattern of Japanese law, and yet here she was, laughing, her face glowing with the exertion, vital, alive. Maybe it was because she was eleven years old, incapable of projection, unable to exist in anything except a present moment which happened to be enjoyable.

And take me, Willa thought, *I'm always on the edge, always just about to be desperate or just about to be afraid, always so unsettled, so nervous, so ready to be occupied and taken over.* It frustrated her. She had all the ingredients necessary to happiness and she was unable to mix them in the proper proportions. She could not live in this instant; she was too weighted down with the accumulation of past failures, retreats, and capitulations, and too aware of the pitfalls that awaited her in the immediate future (the telephone call to Moss; the grinding mill of Japanese jurisprudence which would chew her up counterclockwise and spit her out in one of two directions, jail or home).

At noon, as she was about to send Myoko to the dining room and make a detour to the bar, Cooper came in, giving Myoko a hug and asking the two of them to lunch. Myoko dominated the conversation during the meal, babbling happily about the ping-pong games and her ski lessons and the people she had met. Willa was relieved to find that whatever antipathy she had felt for the girl had now disappeared. The school had done wonders with her, she realized. Evidently

Myoko had an ear for language; her English was a hundred per cent better and the army expletives had been winnowed out of her speech.

Myoko bolted her lunch and asked to be excused to go back to the recreation room and it was only when she was gone that Willa could see what a real effort Cooper had been making. He was quite depressed. He had eaten practically nothing.

"How's it going?" Willa said.

"I just finished looking through them."

"And?"

"Nothing," he said, bewildered. "Absolutely nothing. She has a small suitcase full of papyrus fragments and it's all junk, tag ends of rolls, scraps, none of it with the slightest relationship to the documents."

"Then why should Baum-Brenner send them to her?" Willa asked. "I mean, what's the point in going to all that trouble for something totally worthless?"

"I don't know," Cooper said. "There's only one piece in the bag with enough legible writing on it for me to be sure what it is, and apparently it's third century A.D., an inventory of grain stores in a village south of Rome. Another scrap has a few Greek words on it but the rest of the inscription is blurred and faded, as if the whole thing had been soaked in water. Other fragments have Latin words on them, again almost illegible, in varying states of blankness. One scrap has nothing but a row of fairly parallel squiggles on it, with the one on the left extremely vivid and the one on the right barely discernible. There's not even any consistency to the types of papyrus used. I tell you, it's a scrap heap."

"So what do you do now?"

"I don't know," Cooper said. "Mrs. Klaus has agreed to let me take the fragments when I leave here. I need a reference library to do the right kind of job on them. I don't think I'm going to find anything but I have to exhaust every possibility before I take the final action."

"The final action," she said quietly. "And what will that be?"

"If I can't find a way to disprove the Baum-Brenner papers, then I'll destroy the Q document."

"Destroy it?" she said, startled. "Mind telling me why?"

"I'm not sure in my own mind," he said. "I've always prided myself on being a cold, objective, impersonal man when it comes to my work. When I've published anything, it's represented a conservative point of view, all very defensible. I know this doesn't seem like an answer, but there's such a thing as being too rational, too impressed with the demonstrable things of the world. Do you see what I'm getting at?"

"No," she said, "I don't."

"I try to tell myself that if the Baum-Brenner papers can't be disproved, then they should be published. I try to tell myself that as far as most people are concerned it won't make a bit of difference. The people who have faith are going to continue to believe and the people without faith won't be affected one way or the other. But I know it isn't true. The world isn't like that. If Dr. Lu is successful and the collection goes to Red China they'll kill Christianity once and for all. It's pretty easy to kill a religion if you can demote a god to the status of a mortal. It doesn't make any difference if you can prove he was a fine mortal and a good man, just so long as you can prove he's not a god."

"And you think these papers do that?"

"Yes."

"Then you don't think they can be disproved."

"No, I don't think they can."

"It seems to me you're contradicting yourself," she said, agitated now. "You're going to extremes. You know this is true, so you're going to destroy it."

"I don't think these papers are authentic," he said.

"Come off it," she said. "You said it yourself, you can't find anything wrong with them."

"I don't have any demonstrable proof that these papers are bogus but I know they are. And I think that in one time, in one place, Baum-Brenner was able to prove it. All logic points to that. The whole thing is too airtight, too perfect. He died because he was able to disprove it. Maybe that proof has been destroyed somewhere along the line, but it existed."

"You *think* it, you *feel* it," she said, disgusted. "It's an intellectual whim and you know it. You're rejecting this because you don't want to believe it, that's all it amounts to."

He nodded soberly. "Maybe you're right," he said. "I lost my faith somewhere along the line. Maybe I'll never get it back, maybe I'm beyond it, but I don't want to believe these documents are true."

Oh, hell, she thought, incredulous, a little sick to her stomach. What was the point of sitting here and arguing with him when nothing she could say would make any difference one way or the other? If he was going to destroy the Q document he would destroy it and that would be the end of it, and in either case her big chance was going to go down the drain. Christ or no Christ, what difference did it make? She was still going to have to get through the rest of this afternoon and all the afternoons to come and a big religious dispute or the lack of it would have no effect on the pattern of her endless hours, waiting to be filled. *Take care of me,* she wanted to say, *gather me in and fill me up and give me something to do and then tell me I do it well.*

She said nothing. He checked his watch. "I have to get back," he said. "Are you and Myoko going to be here the rest of the afternoon?"

"Yes."

"I'll see you later," he said.

After she had finished her coffee she went to see about Myoko and found her in the lobby, curled up on a divan in front of the fireplace, buried in a book. Willa did not disturb her. Instead she stood in front of the window, looking out at the weasel crawling down the slope, its cleated tracks digging into the snow as it clattered down toward Taguchi to pick up passengers from the afternoon train. She wanted to go back to the inn and lie down for a while; she suddenly felt the overwhelming desire to sleep but she couldn't leave until the call came through. It occurred to her that she could cancel the call and send a cable instead, pleading illness perhaps, but she could not allow herself the luxury of that final cowardice.

She stayed in the lobby the better part of an hour, until she saw the weasel returning from the village, and then she decided to permit herself just one drink. She was going to need a little therapeutic strengthening before she talked to Moss.

She ordered a double scotch and just had time to finish it before the bellhop found her. The call was ready. She took it in one of the telephone rooms off the lobby, her heart pounding wildly, her hand sweating against the receiver.

The conversation was even worse than she had feared it would be, complicated by a bad connection.

"Did I get you out of bed, Moss?"

"I can't hear you, Willa. Are you there? Can you speak a little louder?"

"Yes," she shouted into the telephone. "Can you hear me any better now?"

"A little. Did you get my cable?"

"No."

"I sent a cable yesterday. You haven't moved, have you? Are you still living at the same place?"

"I haven't moved. But I've been in Akakura for the past few days."

"Akakura? What in the hell is Akakura?"

Little by little, communication was established, their posi-

221

tions fixed, figuratively and literally. He had sent the cable because the magazine was on his back and Warren was a real bastard when it came to pushing. Warren was mad because he hadn't had any word from Willa and Moss had assured him the manuscript was on the way.

"The article isn't in the mail, Moss," she said. "I just can't get into it, that's all." There was a pause. The line crackled. "Did you hear me, Moss?"

"I heard you."

"Well then, say something clever. At fifteen hundred yen a minute, I can't afford any silences. Get me off the hook this time. Tell him I have the Asiatic dysentery, an old war wound acting up, something like that. All right?"

"Take another week," he said. "I can stall him that long."

"I don't want another week," she said. "I can't do the story. Just tell him, okay?"

"No," Moss said. "You leave Warren in a hole, he'll use you to get himself out. You know how he is." Yes, she knew all right, she had seen one of Warren's memos once, a memo decimating a writer who, pressured by deadlines and an urgent need for money, had manufactured a couple of high-level quotes and a bunch of statistics to complete an article and had been caught at it. This private memo, devastatingly funny, written with the barbed wit Warren was noted for, had been mimeographed and circulated around New York. Crucifixion with a smile. As far as she knew, that writer had never been published since. "Look, Willa," Moss said. "Just give it a try. You're a lousy judge of your own work. Finish it up and send it to me and we'll see what happens."

"All right," she said.

She wouldn't do it, of course. She was dry and the piece simply wouldn't come, but there was no way she could convince Moss of that on the telephone. He didn't understand her. He thought writing came out of some psychic faucet— "turn it on and give me about five thousand words, baby"—

and maybe in the old days she had been able to do it, but no more. These days, she had to drag the words out of her mind, one at a time. She sat in the telephone room a full five minutes after she had put the telephone down and then she went to the desk to pay for the call. Y12,960. It seemed impossible she had been on the phone nine minutes.

She decided to have one more drink before she took Myoko back to the inn. She was still in the bar an hour later when Cooper came down the hall from Mrs. Klaus's room, carrying the suitcase. He sat down beside her at the bar and ordered a martini. "Did you get your call through?" he asked.

She nodded. "The telephone is a very efficient instrument. In the old days I might have been blissfully ignorant of catastrophe for a whole week or two, but now I can have my calamity instantaneously. I could have sworn he'd offer to cover for me."

"And he didn't?"

"No, he didn't. I have a week to put up or shut up."

"Maybe you can finish the article at Kyoto," he suggested. "I think it might be a good idea to get out of here."

"Victor hasn't found us yet," she said. "Maybe he drew a blank."

"There's no sense taking chances. Besides, there's a Catholic library in Kyoto that's bound to have the references I need." He finished his drink. "It's getting dark. We'd better get Myoko and head back for the inn."

Willa nodded. She drained the last drop of scotch from the glass. "We can pick her up on the way," she said. "She's in the lobby."

"No," Cooper said. "I just came through there."

"Then she's probably back in the recreation room taking advantage of that flu-ridden kid at the ping-pong table."

"You get her then," Cooper said. "I'll meet you at the side door. I want to get a timetable for the trains out of Taguchi."

She was feeling better now. Cooper's calm sanity had a restorative effect on her. Whether Warren sliced her into pungent little paragraphs or not made no difference in the long run. She would make him eat his words before she was through. Her confidence came flooding back.

She walked back to the recreation room and found it deserted except for the wheezing little Japanese boy, who was plinking darts into a circular target on the wall. He tried to be helpful, she had to give him that, but between his laryngitis and his poor English he had a hard time of it. He didn't know where Myoko was. She had been here earlier but he wasn't sure when she had left or where she had gone.

Cooper was not particularly alarmed when Willa told him. Looking through the window of the lobby, he could still see sunlight on the higher slopes of the mountains. "She may have found somebody here to lend her a pair of skis," Cooper said, "or she may have decided to go back to the inn. You never can tell what a girl that age is going to do." He told Willa to check the ski lifts here and he would make a quick trip back to the inn to see if she was there. If he wasn't back inside an hour, Willa was to assume he had found Myoko and come back to the inn by herself.

He walked briskly down the path toward the inn. Across the wide valley the snowy ridges glowed salmon-colored in the light of the setting sun and below him the valley floor was already plunged into twilight. The lights had begun to come on in the distant farmhouses. The air was cold and brittle, and in the frozen quiet the crunch of his shoes against the snow was amplified a hundred times.

When he reached the inn he toured the lobby. Failing to find Myoko among the skiers gathered around the fireplace, he asked the desk clerk if he had seen her. No, the desk clerk said, he had not seen her. But he hadn't been able to keep a close eye on the lobby because a new party of skiers had arrived on the late train and he had been very busy trying to get everything ready for them.

Cooper thanked the clerk and went upstairs, a little irritated that Willa had not kept a closer watch on the girl and saved him all this unnecessary searching. A child of eleven had poor judgment. It was possible Myoko had met another girl and gone to her room, or perhaps she was still out on the ski slopes somewhere, reluctant to come in before the last light had faded from the hills. He opened the door to his room and clicked on the overhead light.

He felt a little sick. Nothing had been left intact. The furniture had been systematically demolished, cushions sliced open, disemboweled, the gray stuffing strewn on the floor. The tatami mats had been ripped loose. The emptied luggage was strewn around. A man with a knife had been here, soundlessly slashing his way across the room. Cooper opened the door to Myoko's bedroom. Her clothing had been thrown across the floor. Her suitcase was upside down on the gutted mattress of the bed.

Methodically, Cooper closed both doors and then went downstairs to the desk. "Do you still have the attaché case I left with you?" he asked the clerk.

"Yes, sir," the clerk said. "Do you wish it?"

Cooper did not answer. He went out of the lobby on the run, trotting all the way back to the lodge. The last glint of sunlight was gone from the peaks now. There was a faint afterglow in the western sky and the stars had begun to pop through the deepening blackness, glittering and coldly remote. Despite his exertion, he was chilled to the bone by the time he reached the lodge, not only from the dropping temperature but from the realization that he had been too confident, misinterpreting quiet for security and isolation for protection.

Willa was waiting at the lobby entrance when he arrived. Her face was ashen, and she clutched his arm as if she would fall, leading him across the lobby without a word toward the reinforced quiet of the telephone room. The lobby was full of people gathered around the fireplace area where a pair of geishas were dancing to the discordant music of samisens, drums, and a mournful wooden flute.

Cooper closed the door of the telephone room against the noise. He forced himself to remain calm now. Nothing would be gained by anger at her for what she should have done. If he was to help Myoko at all it would have to be done calmly.

"What happened?" he said.

She sat down in a chair, her hands shaking as she took out a cigarette and lighted it, closing her eyes against the sudden sting of smoke. "Two Japanese men came up this afternoon, on the weasel," she said. "The driver thought they were registered here. They came into Taguchi on the train from Tokyo." She paused, puffing on the cigarette. "The driver didn't see them for the next hour. Then he was servicing his weasel, putting oil in the damn thing or something like that, when the men came to the garage, down the slope from the lodge. They had a girl with them."

"Myoko?"

She nodded. "They told the driver the girl was desperately sick and that they were doctors and that they had to get her on the five-thirty express to Tokyo." She paused again, sucking on the cigarette, grimacing as if she could not find the right words with which to express herself. The driver wasn't a very bright man, she went on, and he had one of those rote-type mentalities so characteristic of the Japanese, a mind that adhered closely to what he had been told to do by his employers. He was not supposed to take the weasel out unless the assistant manager of the lodge called him and told him to.

The men told him they had official approval and he tried to call the assistant manager to confirm it but his telephone connection to the lodge had gone out—only later would he discover the wire had been cut—and lacking specific instructions to cover an emergency like this, he had yielded to the insistent orders of the two men. The girl looked sick. She was

226

only semiconscious, her eyes were glassy, and she could not stand by herself. Too, the men offered him ten thousand yen to make the trip. He found it impossible to turn down the extra money. He drove them to Taguchi, where he waited while the station agent flashed an emergency signal to flag the train which ordinarily made only a single stop at Karuizawa. The men took the girl aboard.

"Five-thirty," Cooper said. He looked at his watch. It was now thirteen minutes to seven and somewhere in the mountains the train roared down the grade toward the Kwanto Plain and Tokyo, carrying a drugged girl and two of Victor's men. Slowly Cooper moved to the table and picked up the telephone. He told the operator he wanted to call Tokyo and gave her Victor's number. It took twenty minutes to get the call through. Victor's voice, when it came on the line, sounded tinny and far away.

"I was hoping to hear from you, my dear boy," Victor said. "I was just thinking of you this afternoon and wondering why you felt compelled to mistreat my trust in you, to abuse our relationship, so to speak, especially at this time of year when the spirit of peace on earth and good will toward men should be prevailing. But I want you to know that I have the spirit of forgiveness in my heart, dear boy, and I am quite ready, should you show the proper feeling, to let bygones be bygones."

"You have the girl, don't you?" Cooper said.

"Let us say she is now under my control," Victor said. There was a momentary pause on the line. "I understand how you feel," Victor continued sympathetically. "I can read your sentiments because I am attuned to them and I know what a sense of loss you are suffering now, at this moment. But you must remember, my dear boy, that the girl is my property after all and that you transgressed when you didn't return her to me. I am quite blameless in this."

"All right," Cooper said. "What's your proposition?"

"Proposition, my dear boy?" Victor said. "Proposition? That's such an ugly word, it has hostile connotations, and in any event it is inapplicable here. Because you must remember, my dear boy, the document which you took belongs to me just as the girl belongs to me, so I am really not open to bargaining. No, if I were willing to make some arrangement, some modification in the girl's future, it would be because I value your friendship considerably more highly than you do mine. I'm really not the heinous creature people make me out to be. You should know that better than anybody else, my dear boy. So I would suggest that you bring the Q document back to Tokyo with you and then perhaps we can sit down together as reasonable men and discuss what can be done. And to give you a more definite schedule, so there will be no misunderstanding, I shall expect you tomorrow evening at seven-thirty."

"I'll be there," Cooper said.

"One other thing," Victor added, "although I don't know how interested you will be, considering the current state of your emotions, but a most interesting situation has developed here. The Vatican is sending a representative after all. Evidently the Curia is not as unapproachable as I thought it would be. We should have a tremendously exciting time. In any event, I shall look forward to your arrival."

As Cooper put the telephone down Willa began to cry, burying her face in her hands. "God, God, God," she said, her words muffled. "I'm so sorry."

Cooper put his arms around her. "It's not your fault," he said. "Everything's going to be all right." Words, thin comfort, and he was not deceived by saying them. There was no way to rationalize what had happened. It was quite apparent to him now that he would be confronted by a choice and that either way would result in loss and tragedy.

Ten

1

AT THE moment there was little point in deception and, even if there had been, he could not afford the time to carry it through. The only important thing now was to protect the Q document, knowing that as long as he retained possession of it he would have a bargaining position for the girl's return.

The long train ride back to Tokyo was miserable. The heating system had gone out in the coach shortly after the train left Taguchi and an apologetic English-speaking train guard had offered the occupants an alternative. They could either sit here in the cold darkness or they could stand in the already crowded coach ahead of them where the heat and lights were still working. Cooper and Willa chose to stay where they were and as the rest of the passengers filed through the passage to the coach ahead Cooper felt reasonably sure Victor had not assigned an extra man to remain at Taguchi and follow them when they caught the train. Besides Cooper and Willa, the only people who stayed behind in the darkened coach were a pair of Japanese newlyweds who had become sufficiently Westernized to appreciate the opportunities offered by the circumstances, and a middle-aged woman who sat near the front of the coach with a crying baby.

The train guard supervised the transfer of passengers and then disappeared into the pullman section, returning with an armful of blankets which he passed out to the people who had chosen to stay, and within a few minutes there was a congregation of train officials and employees at the front of the car, flashing lights at the ceiling and holding an agitated discussion about what should be done.

Cooper tucked the blanket around Willa's legs. "It's a hell of a thing," she said quietly. "When they finally get around to writing my biography and come to what should have been a slambang end, they'll have to say I died an unspectacular death. 'She froze to death on the Shin-etsu line.' "

"Why are you so hard on yourself?" Cooper said.

"Because I don't believe in plogglies," she said.

"In what?"

"Plogglies. You mean you've never heard of a ploggly?"

"No."

"They're very important creatures," she said. "Very handy. Indispensable, you might say. I went on a reading kick once when I was drunk and I got hold of this book about plogglies. They're invisible creatures you're supposed to use as excuses for the things that happen to you and the things you do wrong. For instance, it was a ploggly that made me go get a drink and leave Myoko alone. Another ploggly kept me from writing the article. But there are good plogglies too. One of them arranged for me to go to Korea and another dictated the articles to me and another one fixed things for me to win the Pulitzer prize. Why they do these things I don't know, but it's very nice to have a supply of plogglies around to take responsibility for every occasion. But unfortunately, much as I would like to, I have never been able to believe in plogglies." She lighted a cigarette and in that brief instant, as he saw her face in the flare of the match, he knew what a pretense this wry humor was. She was pale, frightened, confused. For all her experience, she was one of the most naïve women he had ever met, just as Myoko, for all her naïveté, was one of the most worldly.

Willa smoked her cigarette in silence for a few minutes, watching the train boys with blue arm bands unfolding a ladder in the middle of the aisle and supporting a man who wore a red arm band as he ascended the ladder and tried to keep his balance against the swaying motion of the train while he unscrewed a plate in the ceiling above his head. "I didn't betray you," Willa said in a small voice. "I took money from Victor, but I didn't betray you."

This brought Cooper up short. "You took money from Victor?"

"He's an insecure little man despite his bulk," she said. "He paid me to call him every day or so and tell him that you were being a good boy, that you had no intention of destroying the documents when you found out what they were."

"He's known all along?"

"He knew before he gave you the first document to translate. I think he was afraid to spring it on you all at once, that Christ was a fraud. He wanted you to find out for yourself."

"I underestimated him," Cooper said. "But why tell me all this now?"

"I don't know," she said. "Maybe because I love you, whatever the hell that means. And maybe because I don't want you to trust me." He started to interrupt but she put her hand on his arm. "Please, darling, let me finish. If they turn the lights on, I won't be able to say it and I have to. I'd like to be different but I'm not. I'm a hungry bitch, maybe because I was whelped one and never had the inclination to be otherwise. Everything in my life has gone sour—marriage, career, everything. When I get back to Tokyo, I'm liable to be deported or thrown into jail because I changed some dollars into yen illegally and got caught at it and I have nowhere to go because I've loused things up in New York. And now I love you and I want to marry you, but I can't even do that because you can't trust me and I can't trust myself. I sold you out a little when I agreed to watch you and if I get a chance at the Q document I'll sell you out big. I'll bootleg a translation or sell it outright or make a deal with the devil if I have to. Because all my life I've always told myself whenever I started something new, 'This is going to be it, the final success.' And it never is. Everything's sour and I can't blame the plogglies." She leaned back against the seat now. From the darkness, the child fretted noisily, a querulous, rasping sound. "So whatever you decide to do with the documents, count me out. I'm fond of Myoko, I don't want to see her get hurt, but I'd sell Christ himself down the river if it meant the really big one, the one I never had."

"I see," he said.

"And now let's drop the whole subject."

"Willa . . ."

"Please."

"All right," he said.

She finished her cigarette and then carefully put it on the floor, extricating her foot from the blanket to grind out the glowing coal. Taking off her shoes, she curled up on the seat, her feet beneath her. She closed her eyes. He couldn't tell whether or not she was really sleeping, but he did not try to talk to her. He watched the man on the ladder as he removed the plate and groped among tangled wires and conduits while the flashlights poured an unsteady light into the hole. Apparently the men were not equipped to make the repairs, because after a brief burst of earnest discussion they folded up the ladder and left the coach.

The baby in the forward section quieted almost immediately and Cooper became aware of a far more subtle noise from the newlyweds to the rear of the coach. Love. The desperate need of one human being for another, in this case a physical passion which either could not or would not be postponed, the secret urgency expressed and released on the uncomfortable seat of a darkened railway coach.

He thought of Nan, in whom the emotional conduits had somehow been short-circuited and sex was not a part of love but connected with some obscure and deeper need which he could not fathom. He looked at the woman sleeping to his right, all but hidden in the enveloping folds of blanket pulled up about her face. He had become aware of her needs and had the desire to respond to them. Spasmodically, he felt a sharp physical desire for her. He felt comfortable with her, sorry for her, amused by her. But could these interweaving emotions, this interlocking chain of responses, be summed up as "love"?

He did not feel the same thing for Willa that he had for Nan but he was older now, late thirties instead of early twenties, and no man ever steps into the same river twice. The river changes, the man changes, from moment to moment. Nothing is ever the same. The sweet and raucous turbulence of his early days with Nan could never be repeated or recaptured—they were only imperfectly remembered after all this time—and he could not really say he wanted to go back. He had never fallen into the error of idealizing his youth. The only thing he regretted losing was that blind confidence of twenty, the unvanquishable belief in the rightness and goodness of things and in his own ability to make the world into anything he wanted it to be.

The forward door opened again and the rectangle of light spilled into the aisle from the passage. The furtive sighs and smothered groans ceased immediately, love frozen in its consummation. The train guard entered the car, flashing his light on the overhead panel once again, studying it while he scratched his head. Then, nodding to himself as if to reassure himself that nothing could be done, he clicked off his flashlight and retreated, closing the door behind him. The sound from the rear of the coach did not resume.

But the entrance of the train guard had awakened the child and now it began to cry again. Cooper reached down to touch the cool surface of the attaché case on the floor, wedged beneath the seat. He would have to come to a decision, rationally, objectively, dispassionately, making his choice and not surrendering by default. He could not see Myoko sacrificed, made into an animal to serve the animal in man. In the south of Japan there were farmers who raised beef cattle by keeping a newborn calf immobile in a darkened stall so that it remained quiet and its muscles never exercised the function for which they had been created. It was hand-fed, gorged with food, and in all their free hours the members of the farm family came to it in turn, massaging the flesh, night and day, breaking it down so that the meat of loin and shoulder and flank was marbled with fat, so tender it seemed to fall apart on the plate and dissolved on the palate. When the calf became cow, when it was heavy enough, it was slaughtered. And the Japanese were experts at *bonsai*, the art of taking a small tree and so artfully stunting it, twisting it into aesthetically pleasing shapes, that it grew old and matured without ever realizing the pattern instilled by nature into the seed.

And under the practiced tutelage of skilled erotics, what might Myoko become in ten more years? Would it be possible to stifle the resiliency, the humor, all of the normal components of this girl, to make of her a creature designed for a single function? He had no doubt it could and would be done. The consequences of a choice made in that direction were predictably certain.

On the other hand, the damage which would be done by returning the Q document to Victor would be equally as sure. That shaky, erratic, childish scrawl purported to be the hand of Christ, the subtle blasphemy of those phrases in the light of the other documents, would destroy him. The rantings of a political madman with a messianic complex, the fervent appeals of a warrior to the oppressed to form a divinely sanctioned army, the chant of the shaman preparing the ignorant for battle against overwhelming odds.

One country shall rise against another and great earthquakes shall shake the world and pestilence will come and famine as well. The men of this world shall see untold horrors and the sky shall be marked with signs. And before all this is finished, you shall be persecuted, bound before authorities and scourged and beaten. But say nothing, neither think now about what you will say then, for I will enable your tongue to speak and give you such words then that no one will be able to dispute or contradict what you say. And some of you will be betrayed by those you trust, your wives and your mothers and your children, and they will try to destroy you because you follow me. But you cannot be destroyed. Endure and you shall follow me to glory. . . .

The beatitudes, consummate bliss, blessedness, but only for the adamant warrior.

Blessed are they who die in my name, for they shall see God revealed. Blessed are they who are reviled and persecuted for my sake, for they shall see God revealed. Blessed are the poor, for they will be rewarded in many ways. Blessed are the meek who oppose me not . . .

The subtle shift in emphasis, virtue reversed, the Messiah coming to urge men to fight, to die for him, the kingdom of earth, not heaven. The end was certain. To release these documents would crucify Christ again.

His thinking went around in circles. He could make no decision, not here, not now. He pulled the blanket up around him against the gathering chill of the car and tried to stretch out, but the seats were not designed for a man of his size and he was too stiffly uncomfortable to sleep.

The train reached Shinjuku Station at five o'clock and he nudged Willa awake. She blinked sleepily, startled, as if for a moment she had no idea where she was.

"Where are we?" she said drowsily. "Tokyo already?"

"Shinjuku," he said. "We're getting off here."

"We're not going into Tokyo?" she said.

"No, we have the advantage if Victor doesn't know where we are. And I want to see O'Connor."

She nodded and began to fold the blankets as Cooper retrieved the luggage from the overhead racks. When the train pulled to a stop Cooper led the way onto the platform and then waited near a steel pillar until the train moved out again, making absolutely sure they were not being followed before he led the way down the stairs into the street. There was not a sign of dawn in the eastern sky and the night was bitterly cold. He shivered slightly as he walked down Shinjuku Street with Willa at his side. With the approach of morning, the flamboyant picture palaces near the station were dark and only a few of the Christmas decorations strung along the street were still lighted. The decorations were top hats and dice, champagne bottles and toys and ornamented Christmas trees and the omnipresent balloon-shaped variations of Santa Claus and his oriental reindeer.

They checked in at a small Western-style hotel and the maid brought tea and hot towels, retiring discreetly after much bowing. The tea revived Cooper somewhat and he was positively elated when he discovered a connecting bathroom with a shower. He stood beneath the stinging spray of hot water for the better part of a half hour, feeling the tension drain out of him. When he came out of the bathroom he was a little surprised to find Willa sitting at the window, smoking a cigarette and staring down into the street.

"I thought you'd be asleep," he said.

"I had enough sleep on the train. When I was in Korea, I cultivated the habit of making myself believe that whatever amount of sleep I got was enough and now I can't shake it. The water's still hot if you want some more tea."

"I need something to keep me awake," he said, "but first

I'd better get dressed." He turned toward the chair where he had left his suit.

"That's going to be something of a feat," she said, smiling, "considering the fact that I sent your suit out to be cleaned and pressed."

"At this hour?"

"We members of the Tokyo Guild of Cleaners and Pressers never sleep," she said. "At your service twenty-four hours a day. No job too big, no job too little. Large enough to serve you, small enough to know you. And as my father used to say before he went out for his day of petty larceny on a respectable level, 'A man can't be his confident best in a wrinkled suit.' So you might as well relax. It's too early to go anyplace anyway."

He smiled despite himself and sat down on the edge of the bed, taking the cup of tea which she poured for him. "A hotel in Shinjuku," he said musingly. "If anybody had told me, a year ago today, that I'd be sitting in a Japanese hotel in my shorts having tea with a woman at five o'clock in the morning . . ."

"Six," she corrected. "Where do you think you'll be at this time next year?"

"I can probably guess that," he said. "I can't tell you the exact house or the exact room maybe, but all the houses near the Cummerland campus look pretty much the same. And the odds are I'll be asleep at this time of morning."

"You have an advantage," she said. "Now, as for me, I could be anywhere. I could be having breakfast on the terrace of an expensive apartment overlooking the East River or boozing it up, having one for the road in a skid-row bar in Rome. It all depends on how well I nurture my little flame of talent between now and then."

"You don't have to leave it to chance," he began. "Last night—"

"Last night was one of my occasional lapses into honesty,"

237

she said lightly, cutting him off. "I don't like honesty. It isn't good for a woman. It's like a harsh light. It doesn't bring out my best features. And if I remember rightly, you agreed not to push it."

"I'm not pushing anything," he said. "I've been doing a lot of thinking. I want you to marry me."

She looked at him abruptly, quizzically, her smile fading. "Why?"

"Because, wherever I am next year, I'd like you to be with me," he said. "Because I love you."

"And you love Myoko too?"

"That has nothing to do with this."

"Darling," she said, "you are one of the sweetest men I've ever met and I've had my share of fantasies about you. I've seen us in all sorts of impossible situations . . ."

"But?"

"Yes," she said. "There's a 'but,' a whole flock of them. I'm a realistic woman and I have a sharp eye for catches." She stood up now and, moving to the mirror on the wall, began to inspect her hair. "I can see myself on your campus, darling, I know exactly how it would be. I booze it up and I have a reputation for a sharp tongue and a pointed sarcasm. Caustic, that's what Moss calls me." She pulled her hair back from her face, gathering it at the nape of her neck, worrying the strands that continued to slip out of her nervous fingers. "I'd try not to, but I'd end up tumbling those hallowed walls of yours, ivy and all. I'd either shred a few faculty wives or be shredded by them. It wouldn't work. Put it all together and it spells disaster. You can't take me back there any more than you can take Myoko."

"There's no guarantee," he said, "and you're right, you wouldn't fit into the stereotyped role of a professor's wife. But as long as we're being realistic, you should know that you could get away with anything you wanted to do. You won the Pulitzer prize. A lot of people have won it, of course, and

238

since you did it, you think nothing of it. But Cummerland is a small college and the people around there still think a Pulitzer prize is a real achievement. As far as your being caustic is concerned, you won't lack for sparring partners. And as far as drinking is concerned, you'll find plenty of people on the faculty, both men and women, who'll be delighted to have a precedent for taking their bottles out from under the table. All in all, I think you'd bring new life to the old place."

She laughed and her hands stopped torturing her hair. "God," she said, "you make it sound attractive."

"It could be. I know this isn't romantic, but we need each other. I'm a pretty sober man most of the time and it's easy for me to get sidetracked into abstractions and the remote past until I sometimes forget I'm flesh and blood. But around you I don't have the chance to forget it. And you—you enjoy thinking the worst of yourself because you can't live up to an impossible ideal. That's what I think anyway. If you marry me, maybe I can re-educate you along more realistic lines."

"You're a very persuasive man," she said, coming over to sit beside him on the bed.

"Then you'll marry me?"

"No," she said quietly. "You make marriage sound like a campus lark, but I know better. I don't believe in plogglies and I don't believe in never-never land. I'm me here, I'd be me there. So let's just leave things as they are. All right?"

"For the time being."

She kissed him, a long, quiet kiss. "Do you want to make love to me?" she said.

"Yes. Very much. But there isn't time for it, not now."

"All right," she smiled. "Just asking. You want to work?"

"Yes," he said. "I have to go over the fragments again before I see O'Connor."

"Then I'll leave you in peace. I'll go down on the street and see what kind of breakfast I can put together at this ungodly hour."

239

While she was gone, Cooper spread the papyrus fragments on the floor, in the vain hope that the pieces which made no sense singly might fall into a collective pattern, but they did not. He repacked them and then sat smoking his pipe and looking down into the street as the sky turned slate gray in the east and the sun came up behind a heavy overcast. The riddle of the fragments perplexed him. He could see in them no hint of design, no spark of reason.

When Willa returned with fishcakes and wine and rolls of rice in seaweed, he allowed himself to be caught up in her enthusiasm for the unorthodox. He laughed at her story of a colonel in Korea who, under the influence of alcohol, somehow got his directions reversed in unfamiliar terrain and led half a division fifteen miles in the wrong direction, barely avoiding a full-scale battle with a British division he mistook for the enemy. In turn, he pulled out his favorite campus stories, the ones that revolved around confused students and equally addled professors, and he was quite pleased when she found them amusing. But even while they talked a part of his mind continued to work on the problem at hand, forecasting the day and making out a mental schedule. He wondered if there had ever been a time in his life when this was not the case, when he had allowed his mind to let go completely, accepting whatever this moment offered without planning for the next. He thought not.

He had been conditioned to accept life as a basically grim business which had to be managed and manipulated and planned, not so much to achieve the good as to avoid the bad. He could well remember his father fidgeting in the study, those long fingers fiddling impatiently with the silver chain across his black vest, a practiced smile on his face in deference to one of the elders who had made an attempt at humor. Cooper's father had smiled easily, quickly, but this expression was a concession to the false standards of the world, as if he was saying, "I realize you must joke and I will go along with you as long as you recognize that levity must be brief because there is so much serious work to be done in the world."

Remembering his father, Cooper's feelings were mixed. In reality, his father had been quite unreasonable, but at the moment Cooper envied that single-mindedness which simplified all things into antipodes: good, evil, black, white, God, Satan, heaven, hell. In the context of his life, in the pattern of his movement from manse to church to the homes of his parishioners, there was never the slightest deviation from the moral position he had set for himself. Nor was there ever a need for him to question it. He chose good over evil, white over black, God over Satan, and, hopefully, heaven over hell. What would he do in a situation like this? Cooper wondered. And yet, even as he asked the question, Cooper knew what his father's choice would be. He would destroy the Q document without the slightest hesitation.

It was eight o'clock before the suit was returned. Cooper put it on, knotting his tie in front of the mirror while Willa watched.

"What's your schedule for today?" she asked.

"I'm not sure."

"Is there anything I can do to help?"

He nodded as he put on his overcoat. "I'll appreciate it if you'll stay close to the hotel, especially this evening. I may want the Q document in a hurry and it would take too long for me to come out here after it."

She gave him a dubious look. "You intend to leave the Q document here with me?"

"Yes."

She shook her head slowly. "No," she said. "I meant what I said last night. Take it with you."

"I don't have time to worry about a place to keep it."

"You're a bad liar," she said firmly, "and I appreciate the gesture. But you take it with you. I mean it. It may not be here when you need it."

"Then the decision will be taken out of my hands, won't

it?" He kissed her briefly. "I love you, Willa. I'm leaving the document here."

She did not look at him for a long moment. Then she shrugged. Something seemed to relax within her. "All right," she said. "I'll wait for your call. Good luck."

He kissed her again and then went downstairs to catch a taxi to St. Justin.

2

"Meaningless. They have no significance at all as far as I can see," Father O'Connor said, sliding the last fragment into the center of his desk. "Perhaps in his last days Baum-Brenner became irrational. Perhaps he thought he saw something in these scraps which didn't actually exist."

"I don't believe that," Cooper said, picking up the pieces of papyrus one by one and returning them to the suitcase. "There was never the slightest hint of irrationality in his letters."

"Nevertheless, it could have happened. A man who is spiritually sick doesn't think as other people do. It's not psychosis, he just doesn't see things realistically." He turned to the teakettle on the electric hot plate. The water was close to boiling. "I know what this is because I have gone through it. I caught your infection, I think. Or maybe it came from the documents, I don't know."

"Have you recovered from it?"

"Not completely, no," the priest said, pouring the boiling water over the teabags in a pair of cups. "I'm able to believe only because I have been able to divorce my faith from the intellectual process. Whenever I put my faith to a test, I always fail somehow. The results are never what I want them to be. I borrowed a pistol when I went to see Victor Hawkins. But I found I couldn't use it once I got there. The idea of force was so suddenly alien to me, so repugnant."

"It wouldn't have done any good," Cooper said. "You

couldn't have scared him. And even if you had killed him, the sale of the documents would only have been delayed."

"Perhaps that was it," Father O'Connor said vaguely, as if he had not been listening. "I didn't really believe my faith was strong enough to persuade him, so I had to carry a weapon." He sighed. "And my attempt at a final resolution merely put the Church in the position of being blackmailed."

"You can't blame yourself for what Victor does," Cooper said. "The idea of the competition would have occurred to him anyway. He's been in this business a long time. Who's coming from the Vatican?"

"Dr. H. B. Vacelli, from the Vatican Library."

"He's a good man."

"You know his work?"

Cooper nodded. "I met him a long time ago, at a meeting in Boston."

"He's flying in this afternoon and I'm taking him to see the manuscripts, all except the Q document. I understand you have that."

"Did Victor call you about it?"

"He wanted me to intercede with you, to convince you that you were making a foolish mistake. That's what he said, but I rather think he hoped I would slip and give him some idea where you were."

"And did you?" Cooper asked flatly.

"No." The priest grimaced at the teabags steeping in the cups and removed them gingerly, depositing them on a saucer. "It's a poor grade of tea but it's all we have on hand at present." He passed one of the cups to Cooper. "What will happen if you don't return the Q document to Hawkins?"

"He has Myoko," Cooper said. "He took her from Akakura."

"I see." Father O'Connor sipped from the cup and the steam fogged his glasses. "Then I take it he intends to make a trade with you."

243

"I think so," Cooper said.

"And suppose you decided not to trade. Suppose you decided to destroy the document. What would Hawkins do?"

"There's a house in Hong Kong that specializes in young girls," Cooper said. "Victor would send her there."

Father O'Connor nodded unhappily and Cooper knew what he was thinking. He was striking a balance in his mind, weighing impossible alternatives. "I've been doing a lot of reading in the past week," he said after a long pause. "The *Wichtige Enthüllengen über die wirkliche Todesart Jesu.* Are you familiar with it?"

"I've heard of it," Cooper said. "I've never read it."

"*Important Disclosures Concerning the Manner of Jesus' Death*," Father O'Connor said. He removed his glasses to wipe the fog from the lenses with a handkerchief, squinting slightly. "It was supposed to have come from an ancient manuscript found in a cave at Alexandria, the work of a contemporary of Jesus who saw him taken down from the cross and revived by the Essenes, who used him as a political tool. It was a crude piece of work. But when it was published in the 1840s there were riots in the streets between the people who believed it and the people who wanted to suppress it." He replaced his glasses on the bridge of his nose, blinking as Cooper came into focus again. "The broken heads and the bloodshed weren't the worst part. The book went through five editions, maybe more. A great many people took it seriously. There is no way to estimate the number of souls lost to God through its influence."

"You don't have to be indirect with me," Cooper said.

"I don't know any other way. It's a painful situation. But I would ask you to consider leaving the girl's problem to the authorities."

"And destroy the Q document."

"Yes."

"What authorities do you suggest I leave her problem to?"

244

Cooper demanded. "The girl has no religion and no church is going to stand up for her. She was sold by her own mother and the police don't give a damn about her one way or the other. She's being used as a pawn, I know that, but she's still a human being and I'm responsible for her."

"A terrible dilemma," Father O'Connor said, shaking his head. "On one hand, it's a choice between a scrap of paper and the innocence of a child. In another way, it's something quite different, a choice between the souls of thousands and the body of one."

"And you could make that choice quite easily, I suppose?"

"I don't know that I could make it at all," Father O'Connor said. "I'm a poor priest and the answers to dilemmas are somehow beyond me. I love children and if I sacrificed even one of them I would be haunted by it for the rest of my life. But I love Christ too and I know that, without him, there is no life at all. I don't know what I would do and I can't advise you. I should be able to but I can't."

"Nobody can," Cooper said. "This is one decision I have to make by myself." He stood up now. "I have to be going. I have some research to do."

Father O'Connor nodded, a heavy resignation on his face. He led the way to the door. "God help you," he said quietly, as a prayer. "God help you."

3

When Cooper arrived at Victor's place he was ushered into the office by Itsugi, who then disappeared, leaving him alone. Removing his overcoat, Cooper folded it and put it on the bench, sitting down in the chair next to the desk to begin what he knew would be a considerable wait. The pressures of a planned delay, anxieties generated by concern for a girl who was at this very moment somewhere in this building and the knowledge that he could do nothing about it, yes, that was what Victor intended. *Well, he's going to be disappointed,* Cooper thought. *It won't work, not on me.*

He filled his pipe and slouched down in the chair, trying to put his mind into constructive channels, thinking about the papyrus fragments again. Perhaps he had made a mistake in assuming that all of these scraps were equally important. It was entirely possible that only one significant piece was hidden in that confusion of fragments. This was something he had not considered before but it made sense. It would have been easier for Baum-Brenner to get a whole assortment of scraps out of the country without the careful scrutiny a single one would have received.

Abruptly, his speculation ended. He was sure he had heard something, a metallic click, the muted closing of a door latch in another part of the building perhaps. He looked around the room, listening, but if there had been a sound it was not repeated. He heard nothing more. The room was perfectly quiet, soundless, so insulated against the slightest intrusion of noise that the silence was oppressive. He was aware of the rhythmic inhalation and exhalation of his own breath. He tapped his pipe against the rim of a bronze ashtray, emptying the bowl, but the sound of wood striking metal was dull, unresonant, absorbed by the spongelike quiet.

He looked at his watch. Seven forty-five. He had now been here fifteen minutes. Standing up, he walked around the room, taking time to inspect the fat-bellied bronze buddha, green with age, sitting on a teak pedestal near the door, and the painting on black velvet which occupied the wall across from Victor's desk—"That painting was done by one of my girls, dear boy, a love token." One of my girls, a singling out of an individual, implication of a group, and for the first time Cooper became fully aware of the second floor and what was going on there at this moment perhaps, over his head, scarcely four feet from him—"We're trying something new, dear boy, a Saturnalia . . . we're going to hold a

Black Mass, something that hasn't been done in this area, at least not to my knowledge."

He moved on to the carved screen that separated the lavatory from the rest of the office. The carving was incredibly detailed, with one scene superimposed on another and that upon a third, cryptomeria trees and Samurai warriors with winged metal helmets in the foreground and behind them the walls of a castle with an open gate. Through the gate a Japanese nobleman was visible, standing in front of another wall with an open door through which Cooper could see the tiny but perfectly formed figures of women in kimonos. Certainly the details of that final layer, wood yielding to the flick of a knife no wider than a hair, must have been done under magnification, the eyes of the carver squinting, his hand braced, with only the tips of the fingers moving to manipulate the cutting edge.

A work of art created by a carver centuries dead by now, urned ashes in a subterranean niche, topped by a stone slab, ashes of son next to father and grandfather, generations in a narrow crypt. A disillusioned carver, Cooper thought, or perhaps one who saw the world for what it was when he created this allegory in wood, the Samurai, invincible, about to storm a castle with only a single man standing in their way. The man was not armed, the gates were open, and on all the faces, warriors, nobleman, and women alike, were the same impassive expressions of resignation, as if all accepted what was happening as a predestined sequence of events, that it was fitting the strong should take the weak and the weak should not resist.

"I'll cash her in, of course, much as I would a stock that has gone sour . . . there is a house in Hong Kong . . ."

Eight o'clock now. He returned to the chair and sat down again, filling his pipe, occupying himself with the ritual, dipping the charred bowl into the tobacco pouch, tamping down the loose shreds, striking a match. He was drowsy now, irritated that Victor should persist in so foolish a course of action.

At eight-thirty, precisely one hour to the minute from Cooper's arrival, the door opened and Victor swept in. His smile had an apologetic overtone and he looked rushed and harried. "My dear boy," he said to Cooper, "I am simply abject at having had to keep you waiting like this but you have no idea how much pressure is generated on me by the approach of New Year's Eve. You would be amazed if I told you how many people, having come here only once in the past year—only once, mind you—expect preferential treatment for the one big gala of the year. I am having to lower my standards to put on a dozen extra girls I know absolutely nothing about, strangers, simply on faith and the recommendations of people who have no taste in such matters."

His shoulders shrugged massively. He pinched the bridge of his thick nose, the harassed artist, the creator resisting the irresistible pressure of time. "Excuse me for boring you with my problems, but I want you to know the delay was strictly unintentional." He nodded toward Itsugi, who had followed him in. "We are ready for dinner."

"I won't be here that long," Cooper said. "What we have to discuss won't take more than five minutes."

"You might be right, dear boy," Victor said, "but I have learned from experience that nothing is ever accomplished when one is tense. It will be a light supper. Nothing heavy."

There was no use arguing with him, Cooper realized. "That's up to you," he said.

"Fine. I'm pleased to see that something of our old friendship still remains, a spark of concession, so to speak. I must admit, dear boy, I was emotionally upset when you left so precipitously the other evening, but then it never occurred to me that we were not entirely in accord or I wouldn't have been so careless, putting the temptation in your path. So perhaps to some extent the whole thing was my fault. *Mea*

248

culpa." He fingered a gold button on his red velvet vest. "Why did you pick Akakura as a refuge?"

"It's remote," Cooper said.

"Yes, it is that, I must admit. And it's a stunningly beautiful place, so perhaps your trip wasn't a complete waste."

When Itsugi wheeled the dinner cart into the room Victor excused himself and disappeared to wash his hands, returning to sit down at the table. He attacked with great relish the food that was set before him. During the meal he said little, his massive jaws chewing, his cheeks quivering, his lips smacking as he washed down the food with a large glass of mineral water. It was only when the meal was finished and Itsugi had wheeled the serving cart out of the room that Victor consented to discuss the matter at hand, approaching the subject indirectly.

"You really should try one of these strawberries," he suggested, popping one into his mouth from the bowl which had been left on an end table. "They are exquisite."

"No, thanks," Cooper said.

"I can understand," Victor said, his jaws reducing the strawberry to pulp in a single motion. "I am never hungry myself after a long trip. Dr. Vacelli and I were discussing that this very afternoon. He's a most delightful fellow, by the way. He absolutely radiates erudition."

"Did you show him the collection?"

"Partially, my dear boy. He really had so little time, a glance here, a snatch of translation there, but after all, he had Father O'Connor with him and he had your translations and the scientific reports. It doesn't really matter. He can't afford to let these papers go to the Red Chinese and he knows it. He will have to bid whether he wants to or not."

"Bid?" Cooper said.

"We're having an auction tomorrow," Victor said with mounting excitement. "I had considered having Dr. Lu and Dr. Vacelli submit written bids and so forth, but that would be much too slow a process. And it excites me, dear boy, to consider the prospects of a face-to-face confrontation, East against West, atheist against Christian, with so very much resting on the outcome, a whole way of life, so to speak. I've rented space at Booth's in Yurakucho—not the main auction hall, it's much too roomy for something of this sort, but one of the smaller anterooms. They have proper facilities for displaying the documents and they guarantee us complete privacy."

"You're a little premature, aren't you? You're not even sure they're willing to bid."

"Gambling has always been one of my pleasures," Victor said, smiling. "And in this particular case, I should say that all the odds are in my favor."

"I'm tired," Cooper said. "I didn't sleep on the train and I have a headache. So if you don't mind, let's get this over with."

"The scholar's mind," Victor said. "Always probing straight to the heart of a matter, the central essence. I'm not belittling that characteristic, dear boy, not at all. I envy it because I am so easily diverted down attractive and unimportant bypaths." His pudgy hand described a vague arc. "You are a straight line and I a curved line. That, I think, is the difference between us." The fingers settled on the last strawberry in the bowl. He put it into his mouth with a gesture of determination, as if everything extraneous had now been cleared out of the way and the serious discussion could proceed. "All right, a course of action." He wiped each of his fingers separately with his handkerchief, slowly, carefully, as if he were polishing expensive silver.

"First, of course, dear boy, you will have to return the Q document to me tonight. That is the capstone of the collection and there would be no sale without it. Secondly, you will make yourself available at eight o'clock in the morning to discuss the documents with Dr. Vacelli and Dr. Lu. You will also make a written certification of the collection, completely unqualified. This will be absolutely indispensable to

Dr. Lu's bid, but I'm sure you can see that for yourself, dear boy. If you certify them as genuine, it will be very difficult for Dr. Vacelli to prove otherwise. Therefore, he will be placed in an increasingly difficult situation. He will be compelled to compete." He inspected his fingers critically, turning the manicured nails to the light, searching for any remaining trace of stain from the strawberries. "I think that covers it pretty well," he said. "It's a little complicated, I'm afraid, but I think you understand me, dear boy."

"I understand you," Cooper said, "but I won't help you."

"Oh?" Victor said, unperturbed.

"I won't help you blackmail the Church," Cooper said. "And I won't jeopardize my chance to go back to the States."

"I can see your point of view, and I can sympathize with it," Victor said. "It would be extremely awkward for you, of course, politically speaking." He stood up now, stretching slightly as if sitting too long had made him uncomfortable. "But we really should consider the girl in this discussion. She is an integral part of this situation."

"Myoko?"

"Yes."

Cooper took the time to fill his pipe, wishing he had slept and that his mind was clearer. He had to move cautiously, with no show of emotion or involvement. There could be no bargaining for something he did not want. He puffed at the pipe until the coal was glowing. "I'm sorry for the girl and I'd like to help her," he said. "I'm perfectly willing to return the Q document in exchange for her release. But that's as far as I will go."

"Much as I dislike saying it, that simply won't do," Victor said.

"That's all you'll get. You can take it or leave it."

"And you could see her sold to Hong Kong?"

"She isn't my problem after all," Cooper said.

"My dear boy," Victor said indulgently, "I really can't believe that. And you really shouldn't expect me to. You took a considerable risk concealing her in your room. You spent a large amount of your money to put her in that school and buy her clothes and equipment."

"You knew that?" Cooper was startled. "Why didn't you take her?"

"I didn't want her," Victor said. "And it gave you pleasure to take care of her, dear boy, you needed that responsibility, so to speak, having lost a beloved child of your own. I first knew that on the evening you interceded in Myoko's behalf. You had a void which needed to be filled."

"You planned the whole thing," Cooper said.

"Let us say I planted the seed. I had the old man assist in her escape. It was the old man who suggested to her the possibility that you might offer her shelter."

"All of this just to develop a weapon against me."

"Not a weapon, a defense. In case I needed it. And I must confess, I am disappointed to be put in the position of having to employ it. I resent having to be devious. But I suppose it has worked out quite well, all in all."

"If you followed us to Taguchi, why did you wait so long to take her?"

"My man who was watching the school was negligent," Victor said. "But then it was a bitterly cold night and he was looking for you to pick up the girl for her holiday recess. All in all, I can't say that I blame him too much. It didn't take long, however, to pick up the track. Even in this cosmopolitan city, an American lady traveling with a Japanese child is not a usual occurrence."

"You didn't need to go to all this trouble," Cooper said. "You could have stopped me on the way back from Taguchi and had both the document and the girl."

"My dear boy," Victor said tolerantly, in the same tone of voice a patient teacher might use with a pupil slow to learn, "your co-operation is every bit as important to me as the Q document."

"You won't have it," Cooper said. "I don't believe you any

252

more than you believe me. I don't think you'll risk losing the Q document."

"I don't think there is a risk." Victor was unruffled. "I think you're bluffing now. You are an extremely moral man and yet you are willing to return the Q document if I release the girl. Therefore I can only conclude that your desire to shelter the girl is stronger than your desire to protect your religion. That is the important matter, after all. The only thing we are discussing now is how much you are willing to sacrifice in order to save the girl. And since you are a moral man, conditioned by chivalry and a strong sense of profound personal loss, I think you would die, if necessary, rather than see her sentenced to the kind of life she would suffer in Hong Kong."

"Then you guessed wrong," Cooper said. "An even trade, that's all I'm offering."

"You do insist on suffering, don't you?" Victor said unhappily. "It is all so unnecessary. After all, I am not asking you to lie, dear boy, I am only asking you to profess something which you know to be true beyond the shadow of a doubt. That truth is unpleasant, to be sure, but it is still the truth, and you have always been a man devoted to it. You compromise nothing by doing it. You retain your integrity—and other scholars will vindicate you against whatever attacks the uneducated might choose to make upon you—and you spare an unhappy little girl a lot of needless unpleasantness." He kept his eyes on Cooper, pursing his lips speculatively as he waited for an answer. He sighed heavily and placed his hand on the telephone. "Now, shall I call and arrange her transportation to Hong Kong?"

Cooper said nothing for a long moment, then he shook his head. "No," he said quietly, defeated. "We'll do it your way."

"Of course, my dear boy." Victor removed his hand from the telephone and lowered himself into the chair behind his desk. "Now, the practical details. Miss Cummings is still with you, is she not?"

"Yes."

"And she has the Q document, I presume?"

"Yes."

"Very good," Victor said. "How long will it take her to get here?"

"I won't make the exchange here, not in this building."

Victor frowned. "My dear boy, you are in no position to—" He stopped abruptly, shrugged. "All right," he said. "Where do you suggest?"

"My hotel in Shimbashi. In an hour and a half."

"That's satisfactory," Victor said. "I'll see you there."

4

Cooper called the Shinjuku hotel from a booth on the street and was reassured when Willa answered at the first ring. He told her what had happened and asked her to meet him at the hotel in Shimbashi as soon as she could make it.

"I'll catch a taxi," she said.

"You'll probably make better time on the electric line," he said. "I have to see you before we meet Victor."

"All right. I'm ready to move."

He put the telephone down and did nothing for a long moment, leaning on the low shelf in the booth, suffering from the inertia of fatigue. One thing at a time, that was the only way he was going to be able to get through tonight and tomorrow. One thing at a time. He lifted the receiver again and called his hotel, alerting them that he was back in town. He wanted his room heated before he got there. The desk clerk was impersonal. The orders were received and acknowledged.

Cooper walked down the crowded Ginza to a small novelty shop which maintained a checking service for the convenience of tourists and there he redeemed the bag containing the papyrus fragments. He walked back to the hotel with a sense of defeat, not only for himself but for Martin Baum-Brenner as well.

In his room, the charcoal had been lighted in the hibachi; everything was clean, neat, just as he had left it. He spread the fragments out once again, fighting the desire to rest awhile. He went through them one by one and found nothing. Picking up the largest piece of papyrus, he held it under the light from the lamp. It was peculiarly shaped, an irregular triangle with serrated edges where the brittle strands of papyrus had separated from a larger sheet.

The shape perplexed him. It was tantalizingly familiar, yet he could not remember where he had seen it before. The content, too, seemed familiar, an agricultural inventory, a listing of grain dispersed and consumed by Roman families now long dead and forgotten. He took an envelope from his writing table. Slipping the fragment into it, he put it in his pocket. Perhaps he would have a chance to ask Vacelli's opinion. He went back to the other fragments and was still puzzling over them when Willa arrived. He embraced her briefly and then checked his watch.

"They'll be here in a few minutes," he said, "and we have a lot of ground to cover. I won't be able to talk to you after they get here and it may be some time before we're able to have any privacy together."

"What do you want me to do?"

"First, take Myoko to St. Justin's, to Father O'Connor." His mind functioned better now that he was dealing with specific things which needed doing. "I'm sure he can find a place for her until her vacation's over, then we'll send her back to the School of the Americas."

"Is Victor going to leave her alone?"

"He'll keep his word," Cooper said. "After you take her to St. Justin's, you go to the police, this lieutenant, what's his name?"

"Taiga."

"Yes. Taiga. You go to him and agree to testify against the

255

man who sold you the yen and against the man who bought it. In return, you want a signed statement from the police or a responsible government official, clearing you of any complicity. You did it through ignorance. You will probably have to sign a statement promising to leave the country. This will save them the expense and trouble of deporting you. But get them to agree to give you sixty days' leeway."

"Do you think they will?"

"Yes, I think they will," Cooper said. "I'd like to think they'd turn you down out of principle. And I'd like to believe in ideal law and love and that justice triumphs in the end, all by itself, but I don't have time to fool myself. I have to be practical. All I want now is for you and Myoko to be safe, to have a chance."

"And what about you?" she asked quietly. "What kind of chance are you giving yourself?"

"I don't know what you mean."

"You could foul up the auction if you wanted to, couldn't you?"

"Maybe," Cooper said. "I don't know."

"I could always take Myoko up north," she said quickly, extemporizing. "We were foolish last time. We took too much for granted and left ourselves exposed. But if we were careful we could get away with it."

"You'd do that for me?"

"Hell," she said, "I know what it is to be eaten up by guilt and compromise. You want to flush Victor down the drain, then go ahead and try."

For one illogical moment he was tempted by the grand gesture, but immediately he thought better of it. "No," he said. "It wouldn't work. There isn't any place in Japan where Myoko could go that Victor wouldn't find her sooner or later. And if you left Tokyo now you'd end up in a Japanese jail. I don't want that."

They heard footsteps in the hall and in a moment the knock sounded on the door. Cooper opened it and bent down to embrace Myoko, who ran into his arms, weeping, while Victor stood in the hall, a sympathetic expression on his face.

"Did he hurt you?" Cooper asked Myoko. "Did he hurt you in any way?"

"No," Myoko said, her crying subsiding as she buried her face in the hollow of his shoulder.

"You're safe now," Cooper said. "You're safe and everything's going to be all right." He stood up, releasing the child to Willa, turning toward Victor.

"And now, if you please," Victor said, "I would like to see the document. Not that I don't trust you implicitly, but I have discovered it never does any harm to be absolutely certain."

Cooper handed him the attaché case and Victor relayed it to Itsugi, who opened it on the floor and removed the Q document, partially unrolling it while Victor peered down at it. "It seems to be in order," he said. "None the worse for its journey." He nodded to Itsugi. "You may put it back."

"I'm sending Myoko out to St. Justin's," Cooper said to Victor. "I take it you have no objections."

"None, dear boy."

Cooper took Myoko in his arms one last time. She had stopped crying now. "I love you," he said. "Be a good girl and do what Miss Cummings tells you to."

Myoko nodded and kissed him. He stood up and turned to Willa. "The auction should be over by twelve-thirty, one at the latest. I'll come out to St. Justin's."

She kissed him. Her face was very white. "Good luck, darling," she said.

Victor waited until the girl and the woman had gone down the stairs and then he heaved a lugubrious sigh, as if the time for sentiment had passed. "And now, dear boy," he said to Cooper, "if you will accompany me, we can get the certification dictated and signed. My car is downstairs."

Cooper said nothing. He followed Victor down the stairs toward the waiting car, with Itsugi bringing up the rear.

Eleven

1

By two-thirty in the morning the classifying papers had been completed and Cooper had signed a certification of the documents. Victor dismissed the young male stenographer and then turned to Cooper. "If you'll pardon my saying so, dear boy, you look quite terrible," he said solicitously. "If I were you, I'd avail myself of this opportunity to get a little sleep. We have perfectly luxurious accommodations here if you care to take advantage of them."

"No," Cooper said. "I'll go back to the hotel."

"Then I'll have my car brought around."

"Don't bother. I want to walk."

"I don't blame you," Victor said sympathetically. "It is a time for reflection, since we are so very close to one of those moments of crisis and reflection which are so rare in life. One age is coming to an end and another is beginning, so to speak, milestones in the progress of humanity, and still I have two all-night parties going and at this time of morning they always need reviving. May I see you to the door, dear boy?"

Once Cooper was on the street, enveloped by the bitter

cold of the wind blowing down from the mountains, he changed his mind about walking and caught a hundred-yen cab back to his hotel. The room was chilled and drafty, and the outside shutters banged and rattled in the gusts. He re-kindled the coals in the hibachi and, wrapping a blanket around him, sat down to look into the book he had bought that afternoon. He had gone to a Communist bookstore in the small hope of finding something by Dr. Lu Hsiao-p'ing and had been surprised to find that Dr. Lu was an extremely popular historian in the bloc of Communist countries sympathetic to the Red Chinese point of view. His work was represented by a wide shelf of books in English, French, and Japanese translations, brightly colored, well printed, thick and inexpensive volumes with such titles as *The Inevitability of Chinese Marxism* and *The History of Cults in China.*

Cooper had contented himself with buying the latter in an English version, remembering from something he had read that all Christian denominations were referred to as "cults" in the terminology of the People's Republic, and now he used the sleepless hours of the early morning to open it and thumb through it. In the back of his mind there existed a vague hope that Victor might have been guilty of oversim-plification when he equated the Chinese and Vatican scholars with the powers that supported them. It was possible Victor was wrong, that Lu and Vacelli might be more suspicious of the Baum-Brenner collection than they were of each other. But as Cooper forced his way through the heavy prose of Lu's book this hope became more and more remote until he was forced to abandon it altogether.

Lu Hsiao-p'ing's *History of Cults* was limited exclusively to various branches of the Christian faith in China, beginning with the ideological battle between Pope Alexander VII and the Emperor K'ang Hsi in 1715, occasioned by the Pope's attack on Confucianism, a skirmish which ended with the expulsion of the Jesuits from China two years later. There was some discussion of the Protestant Christianity introduced into China after the T'ai-p'ing revolution in 1850, but for the most part the book was a polemic attack on Roman Catholicism, an attempt to lay many of the social ills of the old China at the doorstep of the priests.

Lu Hsiao-p'ing was especially fervent against the Vatican. As of 1958 and the Pope's encyclical letter advising priests to withhold sacraments from any persons who co-operated with the Communists, the Chinese Catholic Church had divorced itself from the authority of the Pope and most of the European priests had been forced from the country. Control of the Church was left in the hands of Chinese priests who had accepted the official Communist pronouncements regarding separation from the Vatican. Lu Hsiao-p'ing's position in this fight was unmistakably clear. Not only had he figured prominently in the formation of the government policy which had brought about the separation, but he favored the abolition of the Christian church in China altogether.

There was no hope of agreement between Lu Hsiao-p'ing and Vacelli; they were as completely unalike as two scholars could be, not only in their religious philosophies but in their approach to history as well. Lu Hsiao-p'ing was a man with a ponderous, slow-moving, exhaustive mind which concerned itself with details, however minor and niggling they appeared to be, and his history was solid and overwhelming in the bulk of its minutiae. Vacelli, on the other hand, had a swift and agile mind and he dealt more with the large sweep of history than with its details. Lu saw man pulling himself from the protozoic slime to make a slow and agonizing journey toward the perfection of an atheistic Marxist state he would create for himself. Vacelli saw man eventually triumphant under the aegis of a divine providence which made him more than a rational animal responsible for his own destiny.

Cooper read until four, quitting only because of the headache and blurred vision which always came when he had gone too long without sleep. Taking three aspirins, he set his alarm clock for six-thirty, lying down on his bed mat to close his eyes, coming awake no more than an instant later, it seemed, with the alarm jangling in his ears. It was six-thirty. Even with two and a half hours' sleep, he felt better. His headache had subsided, his vision was perfectly clear. When he had shaved and dressed he went down to the Ginza for coffee and then set out at a brisk pace through the cold morning air for the auction house in Yurakucho.

As he entered the room at Booth's, he realized what an unerring instinct Victor had for selecting the perfect setting, the proper atmosphere. The auction room was comparatively small, dominated by a conference table in its center with display cases containing the documents set against the walnut-paneled walls. The high-ceilinged room exuded an air of unimpeachable respectability; it was more like a museum anteroom than a place of business. Above the display cases hung faded medieval tapestries of knights in battle. It was a fitting decoration, Cooper decided, entirely appropriate.

The principals had already arrived. Dr. Lu stood above the display case containing the Q document, which had been unrolled to its full length and pressed beneath protective sheets of glass. He was wearing the same rumpled uniform he had worn on the night when Cooper first met him but he seemed disquieted now, ill at ease in these surroundings. He did not turn as Cooper entered; he continued to peer down into the case, his face screwed up against the smoke of his cigarette.

Dr. Vacelli sat at the far end of the table, making notes in a small black book, and Victor was laying out the copies of the classification papers on the table. He smiled over at Cooper, a thin, strained, absent smile, while he placed a silver tray with a water pitcher and four glasses in the center of the table. "Good morning, Dr. Cooper," he said. "Have you met Dr. Vacelli here?"

Vacelli stood up as Cooper approached. He extended his hand, making a slight, stiff, European bow. He was a physically small man in middle age, wiry, with alert eyes and a formal manner which made him seem brusque. "I am delighted to see you again, Dr. Cooper," he said in precise, clipped English.

"It's been a long time, Dr. Vacelli."

"Have you met Dr. Lu Hsiao-p'ing?"

"Yes, I've had the pleasure," Cooper said, turning to shake hands with the Chinese.

Dr. Lu nodded perfunctorily.

"Since we're all here," Victor said, "I would suggest that we get under way."

"I understand that you have allowed time for discussion, Mr. Hawkins?" Vacelli said.

"That's correct. As much time as you wish."

"Very well. There are a number of points which I would like to have clarified."

Cooper sat at Vacelli's right, facing Victor across the table, and then Dr. Lu seated himself, lighting another cigarette from the smoldering fragment of the first. Unfolding a paper filled with rows of Chinese calligraphy, he laid it flat on the table and smoothed the creases out of it with his spatulate fingers. "I wish to make a statement before we proceed," he said. Without looking to Victor for either approval or comment, he began to read from the paper, translating it into English in a nasal, emotionless voice.

At first Cooper could see no point to it and then he realized that it was, in effect, a disclaimer on the part of the People's Republic of China. As a matter of principle, the Red Chinese refused to recognize the right of any individual or group to lay claim to a property which rightfully belonged to the People's Republic, meaning, Cooper supposed, the documents in the Baum-Brenner collection. It was entirely possible, Cooper realized, that this ambiguous statement meant that the Red Chinese were going to refuse to bid on property which they considered rightfully theirs anyway. Cooper glanced at Victor to see if he had caught this subtle implication. Victor had. His face had an underlying pallor which made his smile tentative, incongruous. Once Dr. Lu had finished reading his statement, he folded the paper into quarters and returned it to his pocket.

Vacelli studied him quizzically. "Am I to understand then that you are here as an official representative of your government, Dr. Lu?"

"That is correct."

"And that your government claims ownership of these documents?"

"Yes."

"On what grounds?"

Dr. Lu flipped his thumb against his cigarette. The ashes sheared off and fell into the ashtray on the table in front of him. "The priest who had them in his possession was on trial by the people of China," he said. "His library was under a confiscatory order to be used as evidence in that trial. When he fled the jurisdiction of the people's court he took these documents with him. As far as my government is concerned, they are still property of the state."

"I see. On what charge was Father Stafford being tried?"

"He was an agent for a foreign and subversive power," Dr. Lu said as a matter of non-arguable fact. "He spread false rumors and discord against the government. He indulged in espionage against the state for the Catholic Central Bureau."

"Nonsense," Vacelli said, irritated.

"The charges were proved," Dr. Lu said with no change of expression. "He was found guilty in absentia."

"I won't argue with you," Vacelli said. "But since you have clarified your position, then I shall clarify mine as well. I am not here as an official representative of either the Roman Catholic Church or the Vatican. So if your statement was made to warn me against an action your government might take subsequent to this meeting, then I accept it, but as an individual only. No one other than myself is responsible for my actions. Do I make myself clear?"

Dr. Lu responded with a vague flutter of his hand as if to imply that whatever Vacelli said made little difference one way or the other. Move and countermove, Cooper thought. Dr. Lu had opened up the possibility of an attack on the Vatican should Vacelli be successful here; now Vacelli had cut off that possibility.

Vacelli consulted his notes, then looked up at Cooper. "I have spent some time going over the background of these documents and there are certain things which are not clear to me. For instance, exactly what kind of study did Dr. Ikeda and his staff make of the documents?"

"They only made tests on the physical papyrus," Cooper said. "They made no attempt to assess the validity of the content."

"Dr. Ikeda was paid for his work?"

"The fee went directly to the university," Victor said, interrupting. "It was an insignificant amount."

"I see." Vacelli picked up the photostatic copy of Ikeda's report. "Now, let us consider the radiocarbon dating. How many tests were run on each document?"

"One."

"Only one? Isn't it customary to run several for the purposes of comparison?"

"There was insufficient trim from any of the documents to permit more than one."

Vacelli shrugged slightly. "Since we lack a series of tests, I would say that the results we have here are little better than an educated guess." He consulted his notes again. "And I would have to say the same for any attempts to date the documents through paleography. It's an inexact science at best. Excluding any consideration of content, strictly on a paleo-

264

graphic basis, your estimate could be off a hundred years or so in either direction, couldn't it?"

"On that basis, it's possible," Cooper said.

"I take it that the ultraviolet tests eliminated the possibility of palimpsests?"

"Yes."

"Were any chemical tests made to determine the composition of the various inks?"

"No," Cooper said. "That was impossible without destroying a part of the texts."

"Infrared studies were made?"

Cooper nodded. "As far as I can determine, the original writing on these documents has not been tampered with."

"Did you participate in any of these tests, Dr. Cooper?"

"No."

"They were ordered by Mr. Hawkins?"

"Yes."

Vacelli gave Victor a dubious glance as if to imply that anything instigated by him was automatically suspect. "Very well, then. Let us proceed to another point, the sale of the documents. I am led to believe that the transaction was made, not by Father Stafford himself, but by two Chinese who represented themselves as his parishioners. Is that correct?"

"Yes," Cooper said.

"Do you have their names?"

"No, I don't."

"If you will permit me," Victor interrupted, "I think I can clear up this definitely minor point. I did not make the arrangements in Hong Kong personally but I had a trusted representative act in my behalf. The Chinese couple approached my representative with a specimen portion of the manuscript collection, a sampling, so to speak. Through my influence, slight though it may be, I was able to aid the unfortunate priest in his desire to reach Hong Kong and I accepted the manuscript collection in lieu of any payment for my services. There was no reason to record the names of the Chinese couple so I did not. But I am sure that information can be determined if it is important."

"What is the name of your representative in Hong Kong?"

"Mr. Philip Beemer."

"Is he a barrister?"

"A solicitor."

"Where can I contact him?"

"I am not absolutely sure. He is a very peripatetic gentleman, constantly on the move."

"I see. But your efforts were successful then. Father Stafford was brought out of Red China?"

"Yes. The unfortunate man died shortly thereafter. From a fever, I believe."

"And was buried in Hong Kong?"

"Presumably."

"But you have no specific information as to the name of the doctor who treated him in that final illness or the exact cause of his death or the place of his burial."

"Unfortunately, sir, I do not."

"Perhaps I have some information which will interest you," Vacelli said curtly, opening his notebook and riffling through the pages until he found what he was looking for. "Before I left Rome I had time for a certain minimal research. Yes, here it is." He began to read. "Father Lewis Stafford, stationed at Sacred Heart in Chengchow since 1923. Nationality: English. No living relatives. He was born in Harbin in 1895 and educated in the Harbin Seminary." His eyes raised from the page. "He served as a parish priest in the poorest section of Chengchow, in a poverty so unalleviated that his parishioners could not support themselves, much less him. It was not uncommon for him to find a starving child abandoned on the steps of the church when he arose in the morning. He always found a way to feed them. He was known as 'the coolie priest' and whenever he received gifts from friends in Europe he sold them in order to help his people. He was a well-loved, dedicated man who ate only enough to keep himself alive and distributed everything else to the poor. But if he was wise in the ways of God, he was not well educated by any modern standards. Harbin Seminary was an inferior school. His grasp of classical languages was not good. He knew only enough Latin to attend to his religious duties. He was not a scholar."

"I beg your pardon," Victor said curiously. "This is all very interesting, Dr. Vacelli, but I fail to see what it has to do with the matter at hand."

"Permit me to finish, please. He was a good man, but I am sure of this: if he had by some accident come across one of these documents he would not have known what it was. He could not have bought a collection like this, he had no money. Nobody would have given it to him. And yet you would have me believe that a notorious collection such as the Baum-Brenner papers fell into his hands, that without being able to read a word of German to translate the letters he knew what the documents were, and that when he found himself threatened with arrest and the papers in danger of confiscation, he fled, an old, sick man, traveling hundreds of miles to Hong Kong, and that there he lapsed into a convenient fever which made it imperative for a nameless Chinese couple to barter this collection, and that he conveniently died before he could explain how he came into possession of these documents."

"Are you accusing the People's Republic of manufacturing the documents?" Dr. Lu asked.

"Your government is not above it," Vacelli replied, agitated. "I can believe that your government could either create these documents or present a set of bogus ancient documents to the world under false circumstances designed to generate belief. You've resorted to every other form of persecution to destroy the Church, to kill God in your people. Why not this?"

"I assure you, Dr. Vacelli," Victor said hastily, his thick

hands laced together on the table in front of him in an attitude of supplication, "as improbable as it may seem, as many gaps as we are unable to fill in the progression, these are the authentic Baum-Brenner papers. The collection itself is prima facie evidence of that."

"It will take more than your word to convince me of that," Vacelli said. He turned to Cooper. "But for purposes of discussion, suppose I am willing to believe that this collection was made by Baum-Brenner. Nothing is proved by that, not unless you can tell me where he got the manuscripts. Can you do that?"

"No," Cooper said candidly. "I can't."

Again Victor interrupted. "I'm sure you are aware, my dear fellow," he said to Vacelli, "that the known papyrus fragments in the world number in the hundreds of thousands. It's only my opinon—and I don't offer my opinion as an expert, I would not presume to do that—but it's entirely possible the Nazis collected these items for Baum-Brenner from a number of different sources."

"If these were fragments, I might agree," Vacelli said. "But these are full scrolls and of such importance that to believe they would be hidden in some dusty vault for two thousand years, unrecorded, waiting for the Nazis to discover them, is an impossibility."

"Nevertheless," Victor insisted, "the documents *do* exist after all. And certainly other finds of large magnitude have been made under equally improbable circumstances. If my memory serves me correctly, it was a ragged Arab shepherd who discovered the Dead Sea Scrolls while chasing his dog."

"Quite so," Vacelli said. "But the Dead Sea Scrolls were found in specific caves full of artifacts and archaeological context. It is customary to examine the cave from which scrolls are taken before making a judgment. And here we have no cave, nothing." He picked up the classification papers and studied them briefly. "These represent your work, Dr. Cooper?"

"Yes," Cooper said.

"Done of your own free will, without duress?"

Victor looked up, startled, alarmed.

"Without duress," Cooper said.

"You examined the German correspondence found with the documents. You are convinced then that this is the Baum-Brenner collection."

"Yes," Cooper said, "I am."

Vacelli nodded. He pivoted slightly in his chair until he was facing Cooper and then, consulting his notebook, began a point-by-point inquiry into the Lucretius Septimus letter and the Pauline sequence, his probing sharp and incessant, almost vindictive in tone, as if the anger kindled in him by Lu Hsiao-p'ing was now vented on Cooper. He followed the line of Cooper's own doubts, expressed in Cooper's conversations with Father O'Connor, augmenting them with his own misgivings. Cooper was not sure what Vacelli intended to do, whether he was trying to negate any hope Dr. Lu might have of validating these documents in the eyes of the world, or whether his polemic remarks stemmed from his own personal sense of outrage.

The questioning covered the Luke letter, the Neo-Hebraic and the Aramaic documents and lasted better than two hours. Cooper's headache returned. During the interrogation Dr. Lu said nothing at all. He sat relaxed in his chair, smoking one cigarette after another, his eyes vacant as if his mind were elsewhere. Victor, on the other hand, followed every word with increasing nervousness. The white silk handkerchief had come out of his pocket to begin a fluttering circuit of the drooping folds of flesh around his neck, terminating in the broad plane of forehead.

When Vacelli had finished his questioning he pushed back slightly from the table, adjusting the knife-sharp creases in his black trousers before he crossed his legs, studying a page in his notebook again as if he had satisfied himself as to the spurious nature of these documents and now had no interest in them whatsoever.

Cooper's eyes caught on a detail in one of the tapestries, a tumultuous scene of battle in which wave after wave of armored men were sweeping up a hill toward a smaller army protecting the crest. And on the brow of the hill, surveying the legions brought against him, there stood a man who, from the golden aspect of his armor and the richness of the battle flags which surrounded him, was obviously royal, a king perhaps, or a prince. His whole attitude was one of invulnerable disdain. From the dignity of his stance, the confidence on his face, one could assume that he was not troubled by the formidable display of strength against him and the obvious desperateness of his position. His right arm was raised; in his mailed hand there was a sword. He was at the moment of command. But behind him, in the woven fabric of stylized trees and brush, an enemy on horseback was charging him unseen, lance lowered, and in another moment the royal commander would be impaled and the grand eloquence of this moment of courage would be shattered.

Victor looked to Dr. Lu. "Do you wish to make any inquiries, sir?" Dr. Lu shook his head slowly. "Then we will proceed with the auction," Victor continued brightly, trying to preserve his aura of unshakable optimism. "These documents will be sold as a collection and all bids will be made in American dollars. Payment can be made either in American currency or pounds sterling at the option of the buyer, but payment must be effected before the documents can be removed. Now, do I hear five hundred thousand dollars as an opening bid?"

Cooper looked from the Italian to the Chinese. Vacelli had closed his notebook now and was studying the water pitcher on the table with an apparent unconcern for what was taking place in this room. Lu Hsiao-p'ing sat stolidly in his chair, impassive, his hands on his knees.

"Five hundred thousand," Victor said again. "Do I hear five hundred thousand?"

There was still no response.

"Come now, gentlemen," he said coaxingly, with a painful smile, "I simply cannot believe that you are hesitant about a collection which is easily the most valuable literary find in history, not to mention the inestimable ramifications of the material contained therein. Five hundred thousand dollars, gentlemen, an infinitesimal sum, considering everything. Do I hear five hundred thousand dollars?"

Lu Hsiao-p'ing moved slightly in his chair. He mumbled something but the words were lost in the sound of the chair scraping against the floor. Victor turned to him expectantly. "I beg your pardon, Dr. Lu?"

Dr. Lu scratched his left temple, the fingernail ruffling the short thatch of iron-gray hair. "One three," he said distinctly.

"One three?"

"I bid one million, three hundred thousand dollars," Dr. Lu said.

Vacelli turned in his chair, the small book sliding out of his hands to hit the floor, unnoticed. The room was alive now, the current had been turned on. There was a vibrant glow to Victor's face; he was shocked, galvanized.

Lu Hsiao-p'ing's strategy was perfectly clear, his intent was unmistakable. Despite the dubious history of the collection, he had examined the documents and was satisfied as to their authenticity. It was possible his would be the only bid and, if that were the case, the figure had to be high enough to attract widespread attention in the world press. It was quite obvious that Lu Hsiao-p'ing was acting under instructions according to a prearranged plan, and in that single astronomical bid was revealed the ultimate use to which these documents would be put. Propaganda, pure and simple. Vacelli's strategy had failed. The ice was broken.

"I have one million three," Victor said. "Do I hear one four?"

Slowly, after a considered pause, with desperate reluctance, Vacelli nodded.

"One four. I have one four. Do I hear one five?"

Lu Hsiao-p'ing raised his thumb slightly.

"Thank you, I have one five. Now, one six, do I hear one six?"

"One six," Vacelli said.

"One seven."

Victor's eyebrows raised quizzically. He turned to Vacelli, silently urging, waiting.

"Two million dollars," Vacelli said firmly.

"Two one," Lu Hsiao-p'ing said immediately, unintimidated.

"Two two."

"Two three."

"Two four."

At two million five hundred thousand the bidding slowed, jumping not by hundreds now but by fifties, climbing with almost imperceptible nods of the head on Vacelli's part and impatient hand signals from Dr. Lu. The level rose to two million six and two million seven and the delight diffused through Victor's face. He had been perfectly right, Cooper realized, this was no longer a contest between individuals. It was a conflict of antipodes, the impossible realized, the identification of Vacelli with good and Lu Hsiao-p'ing with evil complete.

At two million seven, Dr. Lu hesitated a moment and then raised it to two million nine hundred thousand, two hundred thousand dollars in a single bid, and now Vacelli faltered. Cooper could sense the dilemma which confronted him in that quiet pause, the authorized limit now reached, the question in Vacelli's mind, could he go higher, counting on the money to be raised to back his verbal contract? Was the physical possession of these manuscripts worth more than the financial drain it would entail? Vacelli poured himself a glass of water, drank it slowly, returned the glass to the table. "Two million nine hundred and fifty thousand dollars," he said. There was finality in his voice. This was his last bid, the outer limit passed, and Cooper knew he would go no further. Victor knew it too. Without a word he glanced toward Lu Hsiao-p'ing.

"Three million," Dr. Lu said, quietly, instantly.

Victor's polite turning to Vacelli now for response was a formality only. The bidding was done. Vacelli did not move. He was frozen in his seat. "Do I hear three one? Do I hear three one?" Vacelli said nothing. Victor tapped his pencil on the table with a slight clicking sound. "Sold to Dr. Lu Hsiao-p'ing. Three million dollars." And on Victor's face there now appeared an expression of wild and terrible relief, of frantic joy. "Congratulations," he said. "My heartiest congratulations, my dear fellow."

Lu Hsiao-p'ing shrugged slightly. Vacelli stood up, very pale. "I will tell you this," he said to the Chinese, so angry he could contain it no longer. "When you release these documents you had better be prepared for a fight which may engulf not only you and your scholarship but your country as well. We are very zealous of our Christ. We will not see him defamed."

Lu Hsiao-p'ing remained silent, unaffected, his hands repeating the ritualistic movements of lighting another cigarette. Vacelli turned abruptly and walked away from the table to the display case containing the Q document. Cooper followed him as Victor edged his chair closer to Dr. Lu to settle the final details.

Vacelli looked at Cooper with no malice as he approached. His anger had flared and cooled; he was left with a residue of irritated resignation. "So the battle begins," he said quietly. "Not right away, of course, but only after he has had time to build his wall of minutiae between man and God. And then perhaps, in a year or so, we will be permitted to examine that wall and attack it and find the weaknesses and blast away a brick here and a part of a brick there to let the light shine through."

"I lived with these documents a long time," Cooper said. "I was sure, in the beginning, that Baum-Brenner knew they were false and left behind some kind of key to disprove them."

"But now you don't think he did?"

"No."

"And you believe these papers represent the truth?"

"I believe them to be authentic."

Vacelli sighed. "An illusion often seems real and reality often seems illusory. Man has reached the point where he has the skill and the technique to deceive his fellows and even himself. But even if he fools himself he does not change the reality. I became a student of history because I was determined to discover what is real in the story of mankind and what is important. And I found it is not man's kingdoms or his nations or his political institutions. All of these die eventually as man himself does. And it is not his cleverness or his social perceptions—even a monkey is clever and an ant has a highly developed social sense—and the difference is only a matter of degree." He looked toward Victor and Lu Hsiao-p'ing at the table but he really did not see them. "The only important thing in man is his immortal soul and his relationship with God. That is the only thing that differentiates him from the animal, the only thing important." He looked down at the Q document. "And I do not believe my Christ wrote that. I cannot believe that my saints, mortal though they were, conspired to make a god of a political madman. I believe time is the servant of truth. If he had been a fraud, he would have been exposed as such a millennium ago."

Cooper looked down at the Q document, studying the agitated strokes of ink on the papyrus, and quite suddenly, unprepared for what he saw, he knew the truth, the whole thing, as if it had existed in his mind for many weeks, needing only this last visual impression to give it final form. "You're right, of course," he said. "Completely right." He turned back to the table. "I think your negotiation is premature, Victor," he said, his mouth dry. "The Baum-Brenner collection is incomplete."

Victor pivoted toward him, startled, suspicious. "Incomplete?"

"Yes." He looked toward Vacelli. "If you will have a seat, Dr. Vacelli . . ."

"My dear boy," Victor said with subdued antagonism. "If you will remember, we had an agreement . . ."

"An agreement that I should confirm the truth," Cooper said. "What I believe to be the truth anyway, nothing less, nothing more."

Vacelli sat down now, openly curious.

"In what way is the collection incomplete?" Dr. Lu said flatly.

"I'll answer the questions as I go along," Cooper said, "but you'll have to let me think things through as I go. I wasn't even aware of what had happened until just now. During the discussion of these documents, the questioning, we touched on the collection of letters which Baum-Brenner left behind, correspondence which seemed irrelevant because it dealt only with the background of these papers and didn't touch on content at all. Baum-Brenner also left a number of papyrus fragments with his daughter, but after I spent some time studying them I came to the conclusion that they too were irrelevant and inconsequential, a piece of an agricultural inventory from the third century, nonsensical lines and patterns, some pieces smeared into complete illegibility.

"I couldn't see any real importance to these things, but

Baum-Brenner insisted that both the correspondence and the fragments were pertinent—he even numbered the letters so we could make sure none were missing. So if he attached such importance to these things we can't dismiss them. We have to try to determine why and how these things are pertinent." He paused, feeling better now that he had begun to talk, sorting through the confusion of his impressions, clarifying as he went along.

"The letters he left behind are meant, I think, to be a record of his suffering. They reveal the extent of the Nazi terrorism in his life, the complete obliteration of his family with the sole exception of a daughter, Anna, and they seem to offer, in an indirect way, a defense of his actions. It is as if Baum-Brenner purposely left these letters behind to explain himself to posterity, to say to the grandson he hoped to have, 'I collaborated with the Nazis only to give you a chance to be born, to continue the house of Baum which otherwise would have ended with my death.' I think we can accept this explanation at face value. This was the motivation for what he did.

"The other part of the correspondence deals with the relationship between Dr. Hans Kerrl and Baum-Brenner and it gives us some idea of what Baum-Brenner is doing for the Nazi government. He appraises a series of documents removed from a monastery in Poland as worthless. We presume that this was his regular function and that the Nazis overlooked the fact that he was a Jew and a leader of Jewish resistance, making an Aryan out of him and changing his personal history just to assure his continued co-operation as an assessor of ancient documents. He is given special privileges; Kerrl makes an appointment for Baum-Brenner's daughter with his personal physician in Berlin. Later, Baum-Brenner's daughter is allowed to leave the country.

"So we carry our presumption further. Since Baum-Brenner gets special treatment, we assume that he is not only a translator and an assessor but a very important one. We presume that somebody discovered the documents we have in this room and that Baum-Brenner was assigned to annotate them and make an official translation. This translation would be used to stamp out Christianity in the Third Reich and allow the substitution of Adolf Hitler for Jesus Christ. The Germans had no desire to abolish God; Hitler was a strong believer in divine providence and enough of a psychologist to want to capitalize on the strong religious feeling in his country.

"To sum it up, Baum goes to work for the Nazis as an appraiser, uncovers these documents perhaps and realizes their importance, is given special privileges, has his name changed to Brenner, and co-operates fully with the Nazis.

"This change of identity tells us something else. It shows that the attack against Christianity was to be made only within the Third Reich itself. The German government controlled what the German people could read and see and hear, therefore they could make an Aryan out of Baum and call him Brenner and the people inside Germany wouldn't make any objection. But the world outside their control would recognize the fraud immediately and whatever work Baum-Brenner was doing would be suspect. So we can assume the Germans never intended to make an assault on world Christianity. No, what Baum-Brenner was doing was meant for local consumption only.

"The project was vitally important to the Germans and it attracted the attention of the higher echelon. Goebbels himself was interested in the project as he was an intelligent man, not a mad visionary like Hitler or a fanatic astrologist like Himmler. This was an immensely practical project with every chance of success.

"All of this seems to be logical, seems to be true, and I say *seems* because it was not. There are some basic flaws in this reasoning, a number of which can't be overlooked or minimized. First, Martin Baum was a Jew and not just a Jew but the epitome of Jewishness, a leader in the Warsaw resistance, a rabbi. And the Nazi persecution of the Jews was more than political. It was a wild, frenetic combination of hatred, suspicion, and fear which was whipped up to the point of insanity and made of the Jews a contamination which was to be stamped out at all cost. The whole point of the Nazi persecution was neither the confiscation of Jewish property nor the limiting of Jewish rights but the complete extinction of the Jewish people.

"So Martin Baum-Brenner was the most illogical choice for this project the Nazis could have made. His very Jewishness was a threat to the project itself, because the hatred of Jews was not limited to non-Christians in the Third Reich. Suppose the fact leaked out that a Jew had done the work on a project which killed Christianity. It would have caused a resistance to belief which could have been avoided quite simply by having a Christian scholar do the work. So we have to ask ourselves, was the use of Baum-Brenner a necessary risk?

"Perhaps there was a lack of Christian scholars. That would explain it. Was there no Christian in the Third Reich who would undertake the translation of Aramaic, Neo-Hebraic, Greek, and Latin documents? Perhaps the German Christians refused to co-operate with the Nazis. That would make sense all right, but unfortunately it isn't true. There were only a handful of Christian dissenters in Germany. The majority of ministers and priests did as they were told. Most of the Christian scholars remained silent and inoffensive or co-operated fully with the new regime. I'm not blaming them. We're all human and we do what we feel we must. Nevertheless, Kerrl or Goebbels could have made a choice from two dozen or more scholars in Germany who could have translated these documents with every bit as much skill as Baum-Brenner and with the additional and very practical advantage of being non-Jewish.

"We have to conclude, therefore, that Baum-Brenner was used by the Nazis for something which no one else could do. He was indispensable. We can assume he was spared for more than the work of a translator or appraiser."

Cooper poured himself a glass of water from the pitcher on the table. There was not a stir of motion in the room. Cooper drank the water.

"Now," he said, continuing, "if these assumptions are true, what possible need did the Nazis have for this rabbi? We can find partial clues to the answer in the letters, little hints Baum-Brenner left behind to lead us to the truth. He complains about the temperature and humidity in his quarters. He complains about the ink and leaves us a copy of the printer's bill—an exorbitant amount. Curious. Ink is relatively cheap in any culture. Even the most wasteful writer needs only a few ounces to write a full book.

"Baum-Brenner spent enough to buy gallons of ink or, as an alternate explanation, perhaps he spent this large amount of money for a very special kind of ink. Why? Was he an eccentric who could work only if he had precisely the right physical conditions and materials? Hardly. He was a rabbi who had endured privations of a terrible kind and he was a practical man.

"Let's leave this a moment and consider the papyrus fragments he sent to his daughter. Are they nonsense? Do they represent the vagaries of a mind losing touch with reality? No. He was completely lucid when he told his daughter what they represented, a key, an explanation to what he was doing. By themselves, these fragments mean nothing. Without the documents in this room, they're worthless. But in the context of our investigation they're remarkably significant. They show beyond the shadow of a doubt that Martin Baum-Brenner did not translate Aramaic and Neo-Hebraic and Greek and Latin documents into German, but that he did the exact opposite." He paused slightly. "In other words, all of the documents in this room are forgeries, all came from the same hand, all are the work of Baum-Brenner."

"I simply cannot tolerate this," Victor said, interrupting, rising to his feet. "This is nothing more than conjectural fantasy, and I must warn you, we will not be taken in."

"Let him continue," Vacelli said firmly, with quiet authority.

Victor sank down into his chair again. Cooper continued, slowly, trying to leave nothing out. "This is hard to accept," he said. "I know that, but it is the only explanation which fits all the facts. Consider first the time element. Baum-Brenner began work on the project in 1943 and was sent to the *Vernichtungslager* at Auschwitz in 1944. He spent approximately fifteen months on the project. My translation of the documents took less than two and I had to work through the Neo-Hebraic phrase by phrase or I could have done it in less than a month. And the Nazis certainly would not have permitted such a long delay in a basically simple translation of such importance. But, knowing the problems inherent in a forgery of this magnitude, we can only wonder how he was able to accomplish it in the time he did."

As he continued, building up the structure piece by piece, he could almost feel what Baum-Brenner must have felt in those days of hell in the Warsaw ghetto, vitiated by deprivation, emaciated, disillusioned by the mysterious ways of a God who would permit His people to be so wantonly destroyed, a God who would inflict such extreme torture on His most faithful servant, Martin Baum. The torment is more than corporal, it is spiritual, psychological, the agony of watching a family which has endured centuries of persecution coming to an end.

"At a finite point—a specific day, hour, minute, second—the capacity for suffering reaches a limit and Martin Baum can take no more. In that moment he makes a decision. The continuity must be preserved, his daughter and his hope must survive at any cost. But how? What can a bankrupt man trade for survival? To the Nazis, his life is a worthless commodity and will be forfeit anyway, and even a public recanting of his faith will do no good. His faith is secondary; it will be automatically extinguished when the last Jew dies. Martin Baum suffers and he thinks, using his imagination to create an idea which will have far more value to the Nazis than the life of a single, sickly girl. An ingenious idea it is, and with his years of training and research it is exclusively his, a negating series of documents to crush belief in Christ and permit the deification of Adolf Hitler. Only he, Martin Baum, is equipped to do it.

"It is an outlandish, impossible, bold, and daring plan; it is discussed, dissected in the Ministry of Church Affairs, passed upward to Kerrl, who arranges to interview the old man in a cold office decorated with the symbolic trappings of the new faith, the swastika, the iron face of a god with a mustache. Ideas are exchanged, the project probed, the bargain made, subject to correction if it does not turn out. The Nazis have nothing to lose. They will supply Baum-Brenner with what he needs and if he succeeds they will permit him and his daughter to live. If not, the gas chambers of Auschwitz will erase the mistake and what happens here will be nothing more than a temporary delay on the road to extinction.

"The transfer to Berlin is made, the new apartment, the fresh identity, and Baum-Brenner is supplied with papyrus rolls from a Polish monastery. He makes a preliminary evaluation: present content worthless. And now the multiple phases of his work begin simultaneously, the creation of a subject matter to be forged and the means of forging it and a language to put it in. There are no extant examples of Neo-Hebraic to guide him; he must create it. He must find a way to accomplish what most scholars consider impossible, a way to bleach the ancient ink off the papyri to leave not only a surface unblemished to the naked eye, but one which will not

281

be exposed as a fraud by ultraviolet photography. He picks the scroll in best condition, sets it aside. This will become the Q document. On this he will write the words of Christ. He takes a second roll, too short for the proposed Paul or Luke, in excellent condition, and decides this will become the letter from Lucretius Septimus to his commanding officer, Tigellinius.

"The work begins and some scraps of papyrus bleach in the sun and bake and others are left immersed in water and diluted acids. He tries some of the ancient methods, saturating the scraps with milk and applying flour under pressure to absorb the ink. He uses a variety of solvents in his attempts to obliterate a variety of different inks. On some fragments, the ink hardens and becomes permanently indelible; on others, soaking in shallow pans, a vague cloud arises from the written words, hovering over them in the clear liquid as the residue left by pen on paper begins to weaken and soak loose and float free. How many experiments must there be to free these shreds of the stubborn past, how many times the papyrus goes to pieces under the strength of the solution designed to bleach it.

"And while he checks these fragments in their baths, a self-taught chemist now among his other functions, he begins to sift from his mind those subtle points of history which, when connected by imagination, will form the directive narrative line he wishes them to take. And through all this he worries about his daughter and mourns his people and complains to Kerrl about the temperature and humidity in his rooms, not for himself, survivor of the cold, wet misery of the Warsaw sewers, but for the papyri which, like delicate flowers, demand a precise balance of heat and moisture. The papyrus leads him to despair, becoming brittle enough to break in dry heat and soggily unworkable if he overcorrects.

"He must be facile with his pen, duplicating the ancient scripts with enough authenticity to fool the experts who will examine his work and compare it with known examples from the period which he attempts to counterfeit. The Lucretius Septimus letter comes first, the easiest to do with examples of scribed documents to guide him. Painstakingly he incorporates just enough facts (Suetonius, the rebellion in Britannia) for the document to be confirmed and trusted, the proof of the part becoming the truth of the whole. A delicate art, this, creating the artifacts of a past which never was. Next come the Arimathea letter and the Q document, the old man's reprimand, the pathetic, terrible rantings of a mad warrior Messiah. Is there a parallel here? Does Baum-Brenner consciously or subconsciously draw in these words the portrait of another mad Messiah, Hitler himself? Possible. Probable.

"And through all this he makes continuing experiments with various inks and pens which will counterfeit the look of age, not only to the naked eye but to the infrared cameras as well. Perhaps he has his suppliers duplicate the ancient formulas for ink (there are many of these, all accessible) against the possibility of chemical analysis. After the Q document, he writes Luke, and now the pressure increases from higher up. Perhaps Baum-Brenner's stamina is beginning to give way. Perhaps his daughter coughs too much, racking, hollow coughs which shiver along paternal nerves, and he fears for her safety in a shattered, cold city. He persuades the authorities to let his daughter go to Switzerland.

"Accelerated schedule now. A brilliant piece of inspired luck. No need to bleach another scroll for Paul, he decides; use the blank ends of a number of scrolls, the *eschatokollion*, and paste them together. He approaches the terminal phase of his painstaking work, and how many months it must take to counterfeit the erratic script of the fiery Paul. Or perhaps it came naturally, easily, to an old man who was beginning to feel a madness of his own.

"Finished. The work is finished and sent up to be checked by a member of the Ministry of Church Affairs who can be trusted and who will detect error, deliberate or accidental, if it exists. But there is no error. The forgery is perfect. And now he receives word of the birth of his grandson. With the next generation assured, Martin Baum-Brenner thanks his God and now, in a moment, a peaceful triumphant moment, destroys the fabrication he has built so laboriously over the long months.

"He pulls the piece of thread and the intricate fabric unravels. For Martin Baum-Brenner is an honorable man and will do nothing to jeopardize the faith of others, and now he goes to Kerrl and tells him so. There is a record of this entire process, of what has happened here, in the bits and pieces of papyrus on which he practiced until his technique was perfect, shreds containing nothing except the parallel lines of ink as he tested various pens, fragments imperfectly blanched, pieces which would not take the improperly blended ink and so allowed it to run and smear. The whole process has been recorded in the evidence of its failures."

Cooper paused. "What happened after Baum-Brenner told Kerrl what he had done," he said finally, "we can only guess. It's quite certain neither Kerrl nor Goebbels could take a chance on using the documents, not with potential disaster awaiting them, should the scheme be exposed. And in a way it's a sad commentary on people in general that the Nazis didn't really need those documents after all. The majority of the church people in Germany were quite willing to make the substitution of Hitler for Christ without batting an eye. Too, by the time Baum-Brenner finished his work, the Third Reich was approaching its final hours." He sipped from the water glass again, his mouth dry. "As to how the documents reached Red China and came into the possession of Father Stafford, we will probably never know. Perhaps they were stolen by Japanese officials in Berlin on the presumption they had commercial value. More likely some German official sold them. It really isn't important." He shook his head slowly, wonderingly. "In one way, these documents are worthless. But in another, a more important way, they represent the legacy of a truly great man."

Victor blinked. He had a curious expectancy on his face, but whatever rage he felt, whatever despair at seeing a potential fortune tottering on the brink, were held firmly in control. Cooper had to give him credit for that. "That is all very interesting, dear boy," he said in a matter-of-fact voice, as if he had been tolerant long enough but now had to set things straight. "It is ingenious, I must say that for it. It is positively ingenious, but I also must say that I, for one, do not believe it. Without proof, it can be nothing more than a remote possibility."

"He left proof," Cooper said. He removed the envelope from his pocket and took out the serrated triangle. "Baum-Brenner was an astute man," he said. "He went to great pains to leave behind an indisputable proof. This is a piece of the grain inventory, third-century Roman, which Baum-Brenner mentioned in one of his letters to Kerrl. It is one of the fragments he sent to his daughter."

He walked over to the display case containing the Q document and Vacelli helped him remove the segmented glass from the first section. "A record of his process would be incomplete if all he left behind was a collection of isolated fragments," Cooper said. "So he carefully removed distinctively shaped pieces from each of these documents and it was these pieces he used for experimentation. By putting these pieces back into the sheets from which they were taken, we can see the whole pattern of his forgery and have some idea what these rolls contained originally, just as this piece proves the Q document was written on a scroll which formerly contained an agricultural inventory."

He placed the serrated triangle into the irregular hole in the Q document. It was an exact fit.

Twelve

HE STOOD at the rain-smeared window of Willa's room, looking down onto the circular pattern of umbrellas moving along the narrow sidewalks. A fish truck edged its way through the traffic toward the wider stream of the Ginza, and across the way Cooper could see a banner going up between two buildings, a strip of cloth decorated with bright red calligraphy, an advance notice perhaps of some neighborhood festival. It came to him as something of a startling realization that whatever it was he would not be here to see it and that his absence from this neighborhood, this city, this country would not make a particle of difference one way or the other. The press of people was too great here. Looking down at them, he felt as if they were competing for the space to move and the air to breathe and a place to live, and by tonight his room would be rented again and the tatami floor where he had slept for so many months would be expunged of any trace of him and there would be no gap in the pedestrian tide to mark his departure.

"What are you thinking about?" Willa said behind him.

"I was just feeling mortal," he said. "Tokyo is a good place for feeling mortal."

She came to stand by him, her arm touching his. "Are you sorry to be leaving?"

"No," he said. "Not really. But I feel it should make a difference that I'm going."

"It does," she said. "Maybe in no way that seems significant to you, but it does." She looked out at the rain. "Do you think they'll clear your flight in weather like this?"

He nodded. "I checked with the air line. It's a low storm." He turned to her now. Everything had been said and yet he felt that there was so much more to be discussed and resolved and settled, now that time was running out. "It would work out, you know," he said quietly. "I don't like leaving you behind."

"Maybe it would work but I doubt it," she said. "We used each other to escape into for a while, but now we don't need to escape any more."

"It was more than that," he said.

"Was," she said. "Past tense." She smiled now, trying to lighten the conversation. "Besides, you won't be leaving me behind by very long. I have been given exactly thirty days to rid this cherry-blossom land of my presence."

"Then why wait?"

"I don't know. Unfinished business, maybe."

"Unfinished business?"

"It's all very vague in my mind," she said. "Maybe I'll go up to Akakura again and see Mrs. Klaus. I think she'd like to know what kind of man her father really was. And maybe I'll write the story, I don't know. But I feel, in a way, as if I have to earn the right to go home. Do you know what I mean?"

"No," he said. "Not exactly."

"Let me put it this way then. I have to stay until I find out what I am and make up my mind as to what I want out of life. I can't leave until I know where I'm going. Is that any clearer?"

"Yes," he said. "I can understand that."

Over the drumming of the rain he heard the thin and impatient bleating of the horn and he looked down to see Father O'Connor's Fiat sitting at the curb. Cooper put his arms around Willa and gave her a long, quiet kiss.

"Send me a cable when you get to New York," she said. "I'll be worried about you."

"I will. And I want to hear from you."

"As soon as I know, I'll write you."

"Good-by, Willa."

"Good-by, darling."

When he reached the sidewalk the doorman scurried ahead of him, keeping the umbrella over Cooper while he opened the door to the little car. He put the single suitcase on the rear seat and then acknowledged Cooper's tip before he hurried back into the hotel.

Cooper stood in the rain, looking up at Willa's window. He could not see her but he knew she was watching. He waved once and then he climbed into the car, bracing himself as Father O'Connor released the clutch and the Fiat shot off down the street.

"I intended to get here sooner," Father O'Connor said, peering through the clear swath cut by the blade against the rain on the windshield. "I thought you might like to go out to the School of the Americas on the way. But the rain slowed me down. We'll have to hurry to get to the airport on time as it is."

"It's all right," Cooper said. "I said good-by to Myoko last night."

"I see." He concentrated intently on the street ahead as if to minimize what he considered prying. "Do you intend to keep her in school there?"

"Yes."

"I discussed her future with Father Laurent. If it's too

288

much of a financial burden on you to keep her there, we can make arrangements to get her into St. Agnes school."

"She likes it where she is," Cooper said, "and I can afford it. I don't have any other responsibilities." Father O'Connor frowned slightly and said nothing. "Don't you approve of that?" Cooper added.

"Of course I approve," Father O'Connor said, a little fretfully. "But I had hoped you would be getting married again soon."

Cooper smiled. "You're never content, are you?"

"I'm a poor priest," Father O'Connor said, "but I know the way things should be and I try to help them in the proper direction. I always seem to end up frustrated, perhaps because there are never any clear-cut resolutions in life. Nothing is ever tidy. Things simply change and whatever meaning there is to life gets obscured somehow by the living of it."

He stepped on the brake to avoid crashing into the back of a bus and Cooper was startled to find that the little Fiat had stopped abreast of Victor's place. Through the screen of rain he saw a trio of American military officers sprinting between the front gate and the door of the building. *Business as usual,* Cooper thought. *Everything changes and everything remains the same.* He thought of Martin Baum-Brenner and wondered if, only for a moment perhaps, when the rabbi had the letter in his hand announcing the birth of his grandson and realized he had accomplished the impossible, if in that second he had felt the victory and from that victory had extracted the meaning of life.

The traffic surged ahead, the Fiat following, and Victor's place was left behind. *Rest in peace, Martin Baum,* Cooper said to himself. *Rest in peace.*